The Nancy Drew Mysteries

More 2 books in 1 in Armada

Carolyn Keene

Nancy Drew

The Secret of
Shadow Ranch

The Mystery
of the 99 Steps

Armada
An Imprint of HarperCollins*Publishers*

The Secret of Shadow Ranch and
The Mystery of the 99 Steps
were first published in the USA in 1965 and 1966
respectively by Grosset and Dunlap, Inc.
First published in Great Britain in 1971
by William Collins Sons & Co. Ltd.

First published together in this edition
in 1993 by Armada
Armada is an imprint of
HarperCollins Children's Books,
part of HarperCollins Publishers Ltd
77-85 Fulham Palace Road
Hammersmith, London W6 8JB

3 5 7 9 10 8 6 4 2

Printed and bound in Great Britain by
HarperCollins Book Manufacturing, Glasgow

The Secret of
Shadow Ranch

Carolyn Keene

CONTENTS

CONTENTS

·1·

A Curious Stranger

"HERE I am, girls!" exclaimed Nancy Drew as she hugged her two best friends. "All set for an exciting holiday at Shadow Ranch."

"I hope you had a good flight," said Bess Marvin. The pretty, slightly plump blonde was not smiling as usual. Nancy wondered why.

"Are we glad to see you!" remarked George Fayne, an attractive tomboyish girl with short dark hair. She glanced anxiously around the crowded waiting room in the Phoenix air terminal. "Let's go where we can talk."

Nancy looked at the cousins with keen blue eyes. "What's the matter? Is something wrong?"

Bess bit her lip, then burst out, "Oh, Nancy, we can't stay! We all have to go home tomorrow!"

"But why?" asked Nancy, astonished.

"Because there's a mystery at the ranch," George said bluntly, "and Uncle Ed thinks it's not safe for us to be here."

Bess put in, "But, Nancy, if you could convince Uncle Ed you can solve the case, maybe he'd let us stay. However, I'm not so sure I want to. It's—it's really pretty frightening."

"I can't wait to hear what the mystery is," Nancy said excitedly.

George insisted on collecting Nancy's suitcases at the baggage-claim section. "But save the mystery until I come back!" George said and hastened off. Bess led Nancy towards an attractive sandwich shop in the air terminal.

On the way, admiring glances were cast at the two girls. Titian-haired Nancy was a trim figure in her olive-green knitted suit with matching shoes. Beige accessories and a knitting bag completed her costume. Bess wore a pale-blue cotton dress which showed off her deep suntan to advantage.

While they walked, Bess explained that her uncle had decided at breakfast to send the girls home. At his insistence, George had made reservations for a flight the next day.

"We told him what a wonderful detective you are and begged him to let you try to solve the mystery. He said it was too dangerous for a girl. George phoned you, but you'd already left." Bess sighed. "It's a shame! We could have had a super holiday!"

The three girls had grown up together in River Heights, and had shared many exciting adventures.

Several weeks before, Bess and George's aunt and uncle, Edward and Elizabeth Rawley, owners of Shadow Ranch, had invited them to spend the summer in Arizona. The Rawleys had easily been persuaded to include Nancy in the invitation.

Nancy's father, Carson Drew, a famous lawyer, had given his consent to the trip, but had asked his daughter to delay her departure for a week in order to do some work for him.

Now the young sleuth was eager to hear about the mystery at Shadow Ranch. She and Bess strolled into the sandwich shop and made their way among the crowded tables to a small one in a corner.

As they seated themselves, a slender grey-haired man in a tan suit sat down at the next table. Nancy placed her knitting bag on the floor between his chair and her own.

"What are you making?" Bess asked, nodding towards the bag.

"A sweater for Ned," Nancy replied. "I hope to finish it for his birthday. Originally I bought the wool for myself, but he admired the colour, so I decided to surprise him and knit a sweater for him. Do you think he'll like the style?"

"He'll love it. Not to change the subject, but there are some handsome cowboys at the ranch," Bess remarked. As she told Nancy of the fun she and George had been having, Bess grew more cheerful.

Just then George joined them. Besides the brown linen handbag that matched her dress, she now carried a big vacuum flask.

"I had a porter put your bags in the car," she told Nancy, "and I brought this flask back. We have to fill it with water for the drive across the desert. We started with two flasks. Bess and I finished the water in the other one on the way here."

When the waitress came to take the girls' order, Nancy and George chose soft drinks, while Bess studied the menu.

"This mystery has me so upset," she declared, "that my appetite is gone." Then she added, "I'll have a double chocolate sundae with walnuts."

Nancy and George grinned. "Poor girl," said George, "she's wasting away."

Bess looked sheepish. "Never mind me," she said. "Start telling Nancy about the mystery."

George tugged her chair closer and bent forward. "About two months ago," she began, "Uncle Ed and Aunt Bet acquired Shadow Ranch in payment of a debt. They'd always wanted to be ranchers, so they moved there and began working the property. But for the past month there have been so many accidents that they've decided the ranch is being sabotaged."

"At first they weren't sure"—Bess took up the story— "but after last night, Uncle Ed said there was no doubt."

"What happened?" Nancy asked.

"The phantom horse appeared," replied George.

Nancy's eyes sparkled with interest. "A phantom! Tell me!"

Bess shivered. "It's the weirdest thing—all glowing white and filmy! We saw it running across what we call the big meadow."

George added, "Shorty Steele—he's one of the ranch hands—says it's supposed to be the ghost of the horse which belonged to Dirk Valentine, an old-time outlaw."

"There's a very romantic legend about him," Bess said. "He was the sweetheart of Frances Humber, daughter of the local sheriff, who was the original owner of Shadow Ranch. One night when Dirk Valentine came there to see Frances, the sheriff shot and killed him. As he lay dying, the desperado put a curse on the Humber property, vowing that his horse would haunt Shadow Ranch. And whenever it appeared, destruction would follow."

"That curse came true," George said grimly. "This morning Uncle Ed found one of his windmills had been pulled down."

Nancy looked thoughtful. "Did the phantom horse make any sound?"

"No," replied George, "but just before it appeared we heard a weird whistle. The ranchers say the outlaw always called his horse that way."

"The phantom horse must be a trick, of course," said Nancy. "It sounds as if someone is trying to scare your aunt and uncle off their property." As she spoke, Nancy became aware that the man at the next table was listening intently to the conversation.

"But why—" Bess broke off as she felt Nancy's foot nudge hers under the table. George caught Nancy's warning glance and also understood.

Just then the waitress brought their order and the girls chatted lightly of other subjects. When they finished and their bill had come, Nancy reached for her knitting bag and gave a cry of alarm.

"What's the matter?" Bess asked.

"My bag! I can't find it."

George exclaimed, "I'll bet that man who sat next to us took it! He's gone too!"

The three girls jumped up and looked around, but the man was not in sight. George hurried outside to see if she could find him.

Nancy, meanwhile, looked on the floor nearby. Under the far side of the man's table lay the knitting bag. Quickly Nancy retrieved it.

"See if anything's missing!" Bess advised. "Maybe your purse has gone!"

Nancy made a search, but as far as she could tell, the original contents were intact. However, their arrangement seemed to be different. Had the man been snooping—and if so, why?

Bess paid the bill and the girls walked to the door. They met George coming in. "Didn't see him anywhere," she said. "I suppose he drove off. The thief! He—" George stopped. "Nancy, you have your bag!"

Nancy grinned. "Thanks for your help, anyway."

"I still don't like Old Eavesdropper," George declared.

As the girls walked through the terminal, Nancy stopped at a row of telephone kiosks. "Wait a moment," she said. "I promised to call home and let Hannah know when I arrived here."

Bess volunteered to fill the vacuum flask while Nancy phoned. "Give my love to Hannah," she called back as she hurried off.

"Mine, too," said George as Nancy entered the phone box.

Mrs Hannah Gruen was the Drews' warm-hearted housekeeper who had looked after Nancy since her mother's death when she was three. She and Nancy held a deep affection for each other.

Soon Hannah's cheerful voice came over the phone. "Don't worry about anything here, Nancy," she said. "Just enjoy yourself."

By the time Nancy hung up, Bess had returned. "I didn't tell Hannah I might be straight home," Nancy reported.

"She's going to get a big surprise when we turn up tomorrow," George remarked gloomily.

Nancy smiled. "Not if I can persuade your uncle to change his mind."

As the girls stepped from the cool building the afternoon sun was dazzling. Waves of heat shimmered over the parked cars.

"What are you doing?" George called to the stranger

George led the way past several lines of cars, then turned into a row and walked towards an old estate car. As the girls drew closer, they exclaimed in surprise. A man was dropping something through the open window of the car! *He was the eavesdropper who had sat beside them!*

"What are you doing?" George called.

The stranger glanced up, startled, then darted away among the cars.

Nancy dashed to the estate car, with the girls close behind her. There was a piece of paper on the seat.

Nancy picked it up. "A note!"

In crudely pencilled letters it said: "*Keep away from Shadow Ranch.*"

"Come on!" Nancy exclaimed. "We must catch that man and find out what this means!"

·2·

Dangerous Surprises

THE girls sped off in the direction in which the man had fled. At the end of the row of cars, they paused to look right and left.

"There he is!" Nancy exclaimed. The man was hastening towards the terminal. He looked back, then broke into a run.

Nancy and George sprinted ahead and saw him dash into the building. The girls followed, dodging people and luggage trucks, but the fugitive had disappeared among the crowd.

"Where is he?" Bess panted as she caught up with them.

"Gone," George said tersely. "No use looking for him in here."

But Nancy had not given up. Their dash into the terminal had excited curious stares from passers-by and a news attendant.

"Did you ever see that man before?" she asked the assistant behind the newspaper counter. "The one we were chasing?"

"No," he said. "What happened? Did he steal something? Should I call the police?"

"No, thank you," said Nancy. "But I'd like to find out who he is."

She questioned some other people nearby, but none of them had ever seen the man before.

Nancy returned to the cousins. "I'm afraid that's that." As they left the building, Nancy realized that she was still holding the note and tucked it into her knitting bag.

"One thing we've learned," she said as they crossed the car park again, "whoever the man is, he's connected with the mystery at the ranch."

"But why should he want to keep us away from there?" Bess asked.

"Perhaps for the same reason someone wants to drive your aunt and uncle off the property," Nancy replied.

When they reached the car, Nancy volunteered to drive. George agreed and acted as her guide through the streets of Phoenix.

As they left the outskirts, the road stretched before them like an endless white ribbon with brown desert on either side as far as the eye could see. Here and there were dark clumps of sage and salt grass. Beyond, on the horizon, lay the hazy blue shapes of mountains.

"That's where we're headed, pardner," George said with a grin. "One hundred and fifty miles of the hottest, thirstiest ride you ever took!"

For a while cars passed the girls from both directions, then grew fewer and fewer.

Bess, who had been unusually silent, spoke up. "What I can't work out is why anybody would want to take Shadow Ranch from Uncle Ed. It's in very poor condition."

George agreed. "It almost seems as if Dirk Valentine's curse has worked." She told Nancy that shortly after the outlaw's death, Sheriff Humber's fortunes had begun to fail. He had been forced to sell the ranch, section by section. One large part was now state property, on which old Indian cliff dwellings still stood. Finally Humber had lost the property altogether.

The next owner had tried to build it up, but he too had suffered bad luck. Others had followed and with each the ranch had fallen into a worse state of disrepair. Ed Rawley had been obliged to sink a lot of money into the place, trying to get it into running condition.

Nancy had listened thoughtfully. "The property must have some hidden value," she said, "if somebody wants it so badly now."

For a while the girls rode without speaking. The wind had risen and the rush of it past the open windows, combined with the roar of the engine, made conversation difficult.

Suddenly Bess gave a sharp exclamation. "Nancy! We completely forgot to tell you about Alice!"

George slapped her forehead. "My goodness! What brains we are!"

"Alice who?" asked Nancy.

"Our cousin, Alice Regor. She's fourteen," replied Bess. "She's staying at Shadow Ranch, too."

"That is, she hopes she's staying," George amended. "If we go home, she'll have to leave too."

"I feel sorry for her," Bess said. "She has a special reason for being here—and she's hoping you can help her, Nancy."

"Me?" Nancy exclaimed. "How?"

"We've told her about you," Bess confessed, "and what a good detective you are."

Nancy laughed. "Now, Bess, you know you don't

have to butter me up. Just tell me—what is Alice's mystery?"

Bess smiled. "I knew you'd try to help."

George explained, "Alice's father is missing. He's been gone almost six months."

She said that Ross Regor had been president of a bank in a suburb of Chicago, where he had lived with his family. Someone reported having seen him enter the bank on the night it was robbed. Mr Regor had not been seen since.

"Some of the newspapers implied that he was in league with the gang," Bess said, "but naturally none of his family or friends believes that."

"From the way the burglar alarm was tampered with," George said, "the police were able to identify the gang easily. A few days later one of them was spotted in Phoenix, but eluded capture.

"Because of that, Alice thinks the gang is hiding out in this area and holding her father captive. Or, if he was released, he's wandering around here, a victim of amnesia."

Nancy was instantly sympathetic. "That's not much to go on, but I'll do my best."

During the past five minutes the wind had been increasing and Nancy was using considerable strength to keep the wheel steady. Suddenly a brown swirling cloud of sand arose ahead of them.

"Sandstorm!" she cried. "Close the windows!"

Her words were lost as the wind shrieked and a stinging flash of sand hit their faces. While Nancy fought to hold the car on the road, Bess leaned behind her and managed to wind up the window. George closed the one on her side.

Nancy applied the brakes and the girls sat silent, astounded by the suddenness of the storm. The wind screamed and the sand sifted through the cracks round the windows and doors. The car rocked but stayed upright.

"Wow!" said George. "This desert is full of surprises!"

"Dangerous ones," Bess added.

After an agonizing wait, the wind gradually died and the sand settled enough to permit the girls to see the red glow of the sun. Quickly they opened the doors and stepped outside.

"Ugh," said Bess, shaking her head. "I have sand in my hair!"

When they had brushed their clothes, Bess took one of the flasks from the back of the car. Quickly she poured water into paper cups for all of them.

Nancy drank hers thirstily. "Umm, good old water," she said with a sigh.

"It was wonderful the way you held the car on the road," said Bess, helping herself to a second cup.

"Right," said George. "If we'd gone into the soft sand, we'd have been stranded!"

Nancy looked over the empty desert and shook her head. "How awful it must have been for the pioneers!" she said. "Imagine riding out here for days in a bumpy wagon or walking in the burning sun."

"With every drop of water precious," Bess said.

"They ran out of it, too, sometimes," George said soberly. "Uncle Ed told us that bones of pioneers and abandoned wagons have been found in many places."

"It's a ghastly thought," Bess remarked, and there was silence for a while.

Finally Nancy said, "If I read the mileage right, we

have about an hour's drive yet." She poured some
water from the flask on to her clean handkerchief and
wiped her face and hands. George and Bess did the
same, then the girls combed their hair and put on fresh
lipstick.

Bess giggled. "I don't know why we bother. There's
no one out here to see us but prairie dogs and lizards!"

"Cheer up," said Nancy. "You'll soon be back
among all those handsome cowboys!"

George poured the remaining water from the flask
into a cup and offered it to the others. Nancy and Bess
declined, so George drank it herself.

The girls got into the car and Nancy turned the key
in the ignition. The engine started at once.

"You don't know how glad I am to hear that," she
confessed. "I was afraid sand might have clogged the
engine."

As the car rolled along, Nancy said, "I've been
thinking about the mystery of Shadow Ranch. Tell me
more of the windmill episode. If somebody tore it down,
there'd have been a tremendous racket. Didn't the
Rawleys hear it?"

"No," said George. "And the mill wasn't torn down.
Uncle Ed thinks, from tyre tracks and bumper dents,
that someone used the ranch truck, drove to the east
meadow without lights, and backed hard into the
windmill a few times. Over it went. That night there
was a howling storm, so of course no one heard the
noise."

Nancy frowned. "Aren't there any dogs on the ranch?
Surely they'd have barked."

Bess nodded her head. "The Rawleys have a fine
watchdog. There wasn't a peep out of him. Besides, the

east meadow is some distance from the ranch building."

"Then," said Nancy, "the whole thing must have been an inside job. The dog knows the person or persons who did this. Have you noticed anything suspicious about the ranch hands?"

Bess and George said all the men seemed very nice. "But then," George added, "I suppose they'd be careful to avoid suspicion. Well, Nancy, you can see you have a job ahead of you."

"If Uncle Ed will let us stay," Bess said. "Say, is it my imagination or is it getting hotter in this wagon?" She mopped her forehead with a handkerchief. "Better start on the second flask of water."

As Bess turned round to reach for it, Nancy glanced at the temperature gauge. "Oh no!" she exclaimed. "We're overheating!"

Grimly she slowed down and stopped. The girls climbed out.

Bess leaned into the car and released the lock of the bonnet. Nancy and George, using handkerchiefs on the hot metal, tried to lift it. At first the bonnet stuck, then suddenly flew up.

"Look out!" warned Nancy, unscrewing the radiator cap. She jumped back, pulling George with her as steam and boiling water spouted from the radiator.

"Are you all right?" Bess cried anxiously as she hurried towards them.

"I am. How about you, George?"

"I'm okay," said George, brushing the moisture from her face and short-cropped hair. "Just what I didn't need. A hot bath."

"Good thing we didn't drink that other flask of water," said Nancy. "We'll need it for the radiator."

"There must be a leak in it," George said, looking worried. "The water'll run right through."

"It can't be too bad," Nancy reasoned. "After all, we came a long way before trouble started."

"That's right," George conceded. "We sh u'd be able to make it to the ranch." She went to the back of the car and quickly returned with the flask.

She removed the top and handed the jug to Nancy. who tilted it over the radiator. *Not a drop came out!*

·3·

Warning Rattle

"WE'RE stranded!" Bess exclaimed in dismay.

George stared at the empty flask unbelievingly. "It can't be!" said George. "Shorty Steele promised to fill it with water."

"He must have forgotten," said Bess. She peered up and down the road, but there was no vehicle in sight.

Nancy tried to sound unworried as she spoke. "We might as well get into the car and wait for the water in the radiator to cool off—or maybe somebody will come along and help us." She replaced the radiator cap.

"If we're not at the ranch for supper, Uncle Ed or someone will drive out to look for us," Bess remarked hopefully.

Time dragged by as the girls waited. Nancy tested the water twice. It was still boiling hot. They might have to wait until evening and she was not keen about the idea of driving in the desert after dark.

"It's like an oven in this car," Bess complained.

"Hotter outside," George mumbled.

Suddenly the girls spotted a speck moving towards them on the dusty road. With relief the girls watched it take shape as a pick-up truck.

"It's from the ranch!" George yelled, and dashed outside.

Bess followed, and when the truck stopped, she cried out, "Dave Gregory! You're a lifesaver! I was about to die of thirst and sunstroke!"

With a grin the tall, rangy cowboy swung down from the truck. Quickly Bess introduced him to Nancy.

Dave's handsome face grew stern when Bess and George explained what had happened. He pushed his hat to the back of his head, hooked his thumbs in his belt, and said, "Just what I figured. Three little dudes stuck high and dry. Mr Rawley warned you to check your water supply before you went out in the desert!"

"But Shorty promised he'd take care of it," said George.

Dave's eyes narrowed for an instant, then he said casually, "Well, this is dangerous country—you check your *own* gear, if you know what's good for you."

"We're sorry you had to come out after us," Nancy apologized.

"Mr Rawley's orders," he said coolly, and strode to the truck.

In a minute Dave was back with a large can and a vacuum flask which he handed to the girls. While they drank gratefully, he poured water from the can into the radiator of the estate car. He put back the cap and slammed down the bonnet. The girls returned the flask and thanked him.

Dave gave a curt nod, walked to his truck, and swung aboard. By the time Nancy had the car started, the pick-up had turned around and gone roaring down the road ahead of them.

"What's eating him?" George burst out. "He was about as friendly to you, Nancy, as a prairie dog!"

Nancy smiled. "Never mind. I can see his point."

She wondered, however, what the trouble was. She had not even reached the ranch and already two people had been mysterious and unfriendly to her!

She followed the truck down the highway, and finally on to a road which wound through the barren foothills of the mountains. It was nearly sunset when the girls entered a rocky pass and came out high above a valley. At the far side loomed a huge mountain with a group of low buildings nestling at its foot.

Bess pointed to them. "There's the ranch, and that's Shadow Mountain."

"I see how they got their names," said Nancy. "The great peak throws its shadow over the whole valley."

Half an hour later, they drove through a weather-beaten wooden gate into the ranch yard. Nancy pulled up to the ranch house, a long, one-storey adobe building with a vine-covered veranda across the front.

To the north of the house were the corral and stable. Beyond these stretched a large meadow, bordered by a wire fence. In the opposite direction lay the bunkhouse, and south of this, some distance away, a smaller, enclosed meadow. In it cattle were grazing.

A stocky sunburned man and a slender dark-haired woman hurried out to greet the girls as they alighted. "Bess, George!" exclaimed Elizabeth Rawley. "We were so worried. And this must be Nancy! We're very glad to see you, dear." She gave her guest a hug and a smile, but the girl could see a strained look in her eyes.

Mr Rawley took Nancy's hand in his large one and said cordially, "I'm mighty glad to know you."

"And I'm glad to be here," Nancy replied. Her host gathered the suitcases and led the way towards the house.

Suddenly Nancy heard ferocious barking and turned to see a huge black dog bounding towards her. Behind him ran Dave Gregory.

"Chief!" he shouted. "Come back here!"

With a snarl the dog stopped short and began circling Nancy, snapping and barking. She did not move and the animal grew calmer. Then, as she spoke to him softly, he sniffed her hand. Moments later, Nancy was stroking his thick fur. He was a handsome black German shepherd dog, the largest Nancy had ever seen.

The others had been looking on in amazement. "Young lady," said Ed Rawley, "I like the way you stood your ground. How about it, Dave?"

"Pretty good for a tenderfoot," the cowboy admitted, then said, "Come along, Chief. Your job is chasing coyotes away from the chickens." Obediently the dog trotted away towards the far end of the yard.

"The dog's full name is Apache Chief," said Elizabeth Rawley as she led the girls on to the veranda.

Just then a slender girl with dark curly hair and big sad-looking eyes stepped from the house. Bess introduced her as their cousin Alice. She said hello to Nancy and shyly followed the others along the veranda to Bess and George's room, which Nancy was to share. Another door led into the main hallway of the house.

Mr Rawley followed with the luggage. When the travellers had had a shower and put on fresh dresses, they heard a loud clanging from outside.

"That's cook ringing for supper," Alice explained to Nancy.

The girls hurried off to the kitchen at the far end of the house. Outside the screen door hung an iron triangle, still swinging. The big room was crowded with men who stood round a long oval table with a red-check tablecloth on it.

Nancy was introduced to a tall, thin man with sun-bleached hair. "This is Walt Sanders, my foreman," said Mr Rawley, "and some of my men."

Sanders shook Nancy's hand. Shorty Steele, a husky middle-aged cowboy, did the same. Next a good-looking red-haired cowboy was introduced as Tex Britten and his dark-haired pal as Bud Moore. With a glance Bess informed Nancy that these two were the nice cowboys she had told her about.

"Grub's ready!" called a high, shrill voice. "Everybody sit down!" A small woman with frizzy grey hair and a white apron bustled from the stove to the table bearing a big platter of steaming meat.

"This is Mrs Thurmond, our cook," said the ranch owner's wife.

In the confusion of taking seats, George had a chance to ask Shorty about the water he had promised to put in the station wagon. The cowboy's suntanned face showed surprise. "No, ma'am, I never said I'd do that," he declared. "You musta mistook my meanin'." He repeated the denial several times.

Nancy overheard Shorty and thought he was overdoing it. She wondered if "the misunderstanding" might not have been part of a plan to scare the girls away from the ranch.

After serving a hearty meal of roast beef, beans, corn fritters and salad, Mrs Thurmond produced two large delicious apple pies. When the last bite had been eaten, Ed Rawley stood up and a hush fell on the chatter at the table.

"Okay, men," he said brusquely, "who has first watch?"

"Me and Dave," replied Shorty, and the two left the kitchen together.

Quietly the rest of the men rose to leave and Mrs Rawley led the girls through a door into a large living room. Like the kitchen, it ran from the front to the back of the house.

Among the comfortable furnishings were several slim, old-fashioned rocking chairs and a round centre table with a brass lamp on it. Bright-coloured Indian rugs lay on the floor. At one end of the room was a huge stone fireplace.

"Tradition says that all the rocks in it have come from Shadow Ranch," Alice told Nancy. She pointed out a smooth round one. "That's an Indian grinding stone."

At the opposite end of the room, beside a door leading to the veranda, was a deep window. In front of it on shelves stood rows of coloured antique bottles.

"This is a lovely place!" Nancy exclaimed.

"We're sorry you can't stay to enjoy it," said Mrs Rawley as her husband entered from the kitchen.

"Yes," he added, "but it's too dangerous. We're under attack. We can't figure out by whom or why. I only know that if the damage keeps on, we won't be able to stand the expense. We'll lose Shadow Ranch."

Mrs Rawley explained that the sheriff could not spare a man to be a full-time guard at the ranch, so her husband and the hands took turns standing watch.

"Perhaps you have enemies who want revenge on you," Nancy suggested. "Or maybe your property has hidden value."

The owner replied that he could think of nothing to support either theory. Nancy then described the man at the airport and told of what had happened.

"The note's in your knitting bag," Bess spoke up. "I'll get it!"

She hurried to the girls' room and returned with Nancy's knitting bag.

The young sleuth took out the note and crossed the room to give it to the rancher. Bess started to close the bag. Instead, she idly picked up the half-finished sweater. Underneath it lay a small object loosely wrapped in dirty brown paper.

"What's this, Nancy?" she asked. As she lifted it, the wrapping fell off. For a moment Bess stared at the thing in her hand, then gave a little cry and flung it from her.

Nancy hurried to pick up the object. "The rattle from a snake," she said, holding it up for the others to see.

"Ugh!" exclaimed Alice.

Nancy retrieved the wrapping paper. There was pencilled writing on it. " 'Second warning!' " she read aloud.

Nancy turned to the grim-faced ranch owner and his wife. "Now more than ever," she said earnestly, "I want to solve this mystery. Won't you let me stay and help you?"

The rancher looked at her pleading expression and smiled. "We could certainly use a detective. And I've got to hand it to you, Nancy—you sure can keep your head." He glanced at his wife. "What do you say, Bet?"

Elizabeth Rawley nodded soberly. "All right. The girls may stay, but they must promise to be very careful."

Eagerly they agreed and George hastened to the telephone in the hall to cancel the plane reservations which she had made. In the meantime, Mr Rawley said he thought the notes and the snake rattle should be taken to the sheriff the next morning. "I'll go, Mr Rawley," said Nancy. "Maybe I should meet him."

When George returned, Mrs Rawley was saying, "Nancy, I think you should call us Aunt Bet and Uncle Ed. After all, you'll be one of our family."

Nancy grinned. "I'd love that, Aunt Bet."

"I wish you were going to work on my mystery, too," Alice said wistfully.

Nancy took the young girl's hand. "Of course I will," she said kindly, and Alice's blue eyes lit up.

Nancy told the Rawleys that she would like to get started with her sleuthing immediately. "May I question your men about the phantom horse?"

"Yes, indeed," Ed Rawley agreed.

One after another the ranch hands were summoned, but none of them could add anything to the information Bess and George had given Nancy.

"All of these men are new here," Mr Rawley told her after they had gone. "But Walt Sanders, Tex, and Bud are from an outfit in the next county. Dave's from Montana. Shorty's a drifter."

After a little more talk, Bess stifled a yawn, then suggested that the girls go to bed. She led the way out of a side door and down a hall to their room. Alice went into the next one.

Before long Bess and George were asleep, but Nancy lay wide-eyed, wondering about Dave Gregory. Why was he so hostile to her? Could he be one of the saboteurs? And what about Shorty? Was he to be trusted? Finally Nancy fell asleep.

Just after midnight she awoke suddenly, startled by a noise on the veranda. She sensed someone pausing at the door to listen. Then stealthy footsteps moved on.

"Now what was that all about?" Nancy asked herself.

Quickly she got up, put on her dressing-gown and slippers, and cautiously opened the screen door.

No one was nearby, but at the far end of the veranda, she saw a dark figure slip into the kitchen.

"Why would anyone be going in there from outdoors at this time of night?" Nancy asked herself. "I'd better find out."

She wondered if she should waken the other girls but decided against this, and tiptoed along the veranda to the kitchen. She opened the door and stepped inside the darkened room.

The next instant an unearthly shriek split the air and someone seized her!

·4·

A Red Clue

NANCY jerked one arm free from her attacker and fumbled for a light switch. Her fingers found it and the ceiling light over the dining table went on.

Clinging to her was Mrs Thurmond, the cook! She wore an old-fashioned nightgown, and her head bristled with curlers. She let go of Nancy like a hot branding iron.

"You!" she exclaimed.

"Yes me," Nancy replied, suppressing a smile. "I'm as surprised as you are, Mrs Thurmond."

"What's the matter?" demanded Ed Rawley as he and his wife, wearing dressing-gowns and slippers, hurried in from the living room.

Then Bess and George ran in from the veranda, with Alice behind them. "Nancy! You all right?"

Soon Walt Sanders, in night clothes, rushed into the kitchen. A moment later Tex and Bud clumped in. Nancy wondered where Dave and Shorty were.

"Bud and I were on watch," said the red-haired cowboy, "and were checkin' the stable when we heard the ruckus. What's up?"

Mrs Thurmond told her story. She had been asleep in her room, a small extension off the kitchen, when she

had been awakened by someone coming into the
kitchen through the screen door.

"I sleep light," she explained. "First I was afraid to
move. I listened hard, but I didn't hear anything more,
so I decided to get up and take a look. Just as I stepped
out of my room, what do I see but the screen door
opening and a dark figure steps in! So I jumped him
and hollered."

Nancy smiled. "And I was 'him'." Then she added,
"There *was* an intruder here, Mrs Thurmond, because
I saw him come in."

"He must have gone into the living room, then," said
Mrs Rawley. "There's no other way out."

Mrs Thurmond shook her head. "No, ma'am," she
said forcefully. "That door to the living room squeaks
and I didn't hear a sound."

George moved the door and the hinges made a noise.

"Then where did the intruder go?" Bess asked
shakily.

Nancy's keen eyes had spotted a trap door beside the
old-fashioned stove. "Perhaps down there."

"If he did," Ed Rawley said grimly, "he's caught.
That's the cellar and this is the only way out.
Dave," he ordered, looking beyond Nancy, "come with
me."

From behind her stepped the tall cowboy. He was
fully dressed and carrying a torch. She turned and saw
Shorty Steele standing just inside the screen door. He,
too, was in his working clothes. When had they arrived?
And why hadn't they gone to bed after coming off
patrol duty?

As Ed Rawley lifted up the trap door, Nancy said,
"I'd like to go, too, Uncle Ed."

The man hesitated, then said, "All right, but you stay well behind us."

The cowboy turned on his torch and Nancy followed the men down a flight of wooden stairs. She found herself in a shallow cellar which was empty except for a row of shelves against one wall.

At Nancy's request Dave held his light downwards so that she could look for footprints. But the earth floor was hard-packed and she could see no marks on it.

When the trio returned to the kitchen and reported no sign of the intruder, the cook shook her head. "He was a phantom," she declared, "just like that horse."

"Now, Mrs Thurmond," said Aunt Bet, "maybe you were so excited you didn't hear the intruder go through the living-room door."

The little woman looked indignant. "I have excellent hearing," she stated, "and that door *positively* did not squeak." Nancy found it hard to doubt Mrs Thurmond's word.

The young sleuth turned to Dave. "Did you just come from the bunkhouse?"

"No," Dave said quietly. "I was doing some extra investigating."

"Whatever that means," Nancy thought. She noted that Shorty had said nothing.

Mr Rawley did not question the men. A few minutes later everyone went back to bed except Tex and Bud.

Nancy woke at dawn and puzzled over the problem. Who was the intruder? What was he after? Where had he gone? Quietly she rose and dressed, then went to the kitchen to make herself a cup of tea.

Not wanting to heat the big kettle of water which stood on the old-fashioned range, she took a small pot from a hook on the wall and carried it to the sink. She turned one of the taps but no water came out. Surprised, Nancy tried the other, with the same result. "That's strange. I'll ask the girls about it."

She hurried to the bedroom and woke them. Bess and George said this had not happened before and George went to tell her aunt and uncle.

In a short time the hastily-dressed rancher appeared, completely puzzled. He led the way past the stable and the corral to a small wooden shed. Inside were an electric generator and pump.

After examining the machinery, Ed Rawley said one grim word, "Sabotage!" He showed the girls where some of the bearings were missing. "We'll need new ones before we can have any water."

"It's a shame!" George declared. "When do you think this mischief was done? And where were the guards?"

"What difference does it make?" her uncle said with a sigh. "The men can't be everywhere at once."

"What about Chief?" Nancy asked. "He didn't bark at the saboteur. Does this mean he knows him?"

Ed Rawley's jaw tightened. "I'd trust Sanders, Bud, and Dave with my life. They came highly recommended by friends of mine. As for the others, I accuse no man without proof."

"Nor would I," Nancy said quietly, and began looking for evidence. On the wooden floor were damp daubs of red earth. Outside the building was a wet patch of the same colour, but the prints were too confused to be distinguishable.

"Whoever damaged the pump may still have this kind of mud on his boots," Nancy thought.

The rancher's face was grey with worry. "This pump will have to be fixed as soon as possible. After the windmill in the east meadow was wrecked, I had to start using this pump, which only supplied the house, to water my cattle. There's another mill in the big meadow, but its supply is not enough for them. We're lucky to have one other source of spring water."

The three girls volunteered to carry water to the kitchen. They went to get buckets from Mrs Thurmond, who was pale and tight-lipped. She handed them kettles and large pots. Bess led the way round the house to the spring house, a windowless adobe structure built on to the back wall of the kitchen.

George opened the heavy wooden door and the girls stepped down on to an earthen floor. It was cool and so dim they could barely see the small stream of water coming from a pipe in the centre.

While waiting her turn to fill her kettle, Nancy went outside to look round. Between the ranch house and the foot of Shadow Mountain she noticed that a thickly wooded strip of land ran down to abut the big meadow.

"That's where the phantom horse is supposed to appear," Nancy reflected.

Just then Bess came from the spring house. "Your turn, Nancy," she called.

The young sleuth hurried inside and placed her kettle under the stream of water. While waiting for it to fill she noticed a stone vat against the kitchen wall. It was about three feet square with a hinged wooden lid. "That's where the old-timers stored milk products and eggs," she thought.

When Nancy reached the kitchen with her full kettle, Mrs Thurmond was serving breakfast. As the girls sat down, Dave and Shorty came in. Nancy glanced at their boots. There was damp red mud on both pairs!

As soon as the men had finished eating, Dave stood up. "I'm going to Tumbleweed to get pump bearings," he said to Nancy. "Mr Rawley said you wanted to do an errand in town. You can ride along with me."

Nancy was glad the sheriff had not been mentioned. She said, "I'll go, thank you, and I'll bring George."

Dave scowled. "I'll be in the pick-up," he replied abruptly and walked out.

Nancy hurried to her room to get the warning notes and the rattle. The pick-up was parked in the yard, and as soon as Nancy and George had climbed into the cab, Dave started it.

Without saying a word, he drove out of the ranch gate and turned on to a track which stretched down the valley. The girls appeared to be relaxed, but they could not rid their minds of a distrust of Dave.

Once he caught Nancy looking at his shoes. "Yes, Miss Detective," he said, "that's mud from outside the pump house. I was up before dawn this morning, and thought I heard a noise there. I didn't find anyone, though. Must have scared off the pump-wrecker, but he came back later."

George asked why Dave was up so early, but he did not answer or speak again until they reached a small town of old-fashioned wooden buildings. The cowboy parked the pick-up on the main street.

"I'll meet you here in half an hour," he said as he swung out of the truck. Nancy and George saw him go into a hardware shop several doors away. In front of the girls was a building with a sign: SHERIFF.

As the girls entered the small office a grey-haired man swivelled round in his chair and rose to greet them. "I reckon you're Miss Drew," he said in a pleasant drawl. "I'm Sheriff Curtis." His eyes twinkled. "Ed Rawley told me you're aimin' to help him find what's causin' the trouble at the ranch."

George spoke up. "And she will, if she can."

"I sure wish you luck."

After hearing Nancy's story and looking at the notes and rattle, he said, "I'll hang on to these as evidence and phone the state and Phoenix lawmen to keep an eye out for the hombre you saw at the airport. Keep me posted," he added gravely, "and be extra careful, girls."

Nancy thanked him and the callers left. They still had twenty minutes to spare. George said she wanted to purchase a cowboy kerchief in the general store, so Nancy strolled along looking in shop-windows. The town seemed almost deserted and many of the shops were not yet open.

Ahead, in the centre of the street, grew a large cottonwood tree with a wooden bench built round the trunk. Nancy walked to it and was about to sit in the shade, when her eye was caught by a tall stack of Indian baskets outside a shop marked: MARY DEER—GIFTS.

Nancy crossed over to look at them, then glanced through the window. Startled at what she saw, Nancy almost cried out. The shop was empty, except for a man with a black kerchief covering his face to the eyes. He was crouching in front of an open glass case, scooping jewellery into a paper bag!

Heart pounding, Nancy looked up and down the

street for help. But there was no one in sight. Boldly she stepped to the open door of the shop.

"Drop that bag!" she ordered.

With a startled gasp the man whirled, then charged straight at her.

· 5 ·

Desperado's Gift

THINKING quickly, Nancy jumped aside and toppled the tower of baskets into the thief's path. With a cry he stumbled among them and pitched forward, the bag of loot flying from his hand.

"Help!" shouted Nancy as she ran into the street and picked up the paper bag. "Sheriff!"

The man scrambled to his feet, and kicking the baskets aside, darted into a narrow passage between two shops.

At the same time, a young Indian girl and a man ran from the coffee shop next door.

"What happened?" cried the girl. "I'm Mary Deer." Quickly Nancy told her about the thief. "My shop—robbed!" she exclaimed.

"Almost robbed," said Nancy, smiling and handing over the brown paper bag. As the girl thanked her warmly, George, Dave, Sheriff Curtis, and a few merchants ran up. Nancy repeated her story rapidly and described the thief. "He wore a black kerchief over his nose and mouth, was in shirt sleeves, and had on dark trousers."

As the men dashed into the passage where he had vanished, Nancy turned to the Indian girl. She was wearing a vivid red beaded dress and had a glossy black braid over each shoulder. Nancy introduced herself and George.

Gratefully Mary Deer said, "You were wonderful to get this back for me, Nancy. I would like to give you a reward."

"That's not necessary. I'm glad I could help."

Mary Deer invited the girls into the shop, which was cool and smelled of leather goods. To one side stood a long glass case containing shelves of jewellery. One front panel was open and a shelf was empty.

"There's no lock on the case," Mary explained. "I guess I shouldn't have left the shop open, but I never expected customers so early." Then she added, "Where are you from? You don't sound like a Westerner."

Nancy explained that she was a visitor at Shadow Ranch.

The Indian girl smiled. "Then I have the perfect reward for you." She reached into the paper bag and took out a small gold object. It was a lady's old-fashioned watch on a fleur-de-lis pin.

"How beautiful!" Nancy exclaimed. "But I can't accept it. Surely you can sell the watch."

Mary Deer shook her head. "This is not for sale. I had it on display in my antique jewellery case. Since you are from Shadow Ranch, it shall be yours."

"But what has the ranch to do with it?" Nancy asked curiously.

The Indian girl explained that the watch had been a gift to Frances Humber from her outlaw sweetheart. "Here is his initial," she said, and pointed to a "V" and the date, June, 1880, inscribed on the back lid. Then she turned the watch over and showed Nancy a heart inscribed on the front. "That was Valentine's symbol," said Mary Deer. "Legend says he used it on personal belongings like his belt buckle and rings—even the brand on his horse was a heart."

"He sounds like a romantic man," remarked Nancy.

Mary agreed. "He left Frances a treasure," she went on, "but she never received it."

"A treasure?" Nancy said. "What was it?"

Mary shrugged. "Valentine's will merely stated that his personal fortune was to go to Frances and her heirs. The will did not tell where or what the treasure was. Some believe it was hidden on Shadow Ranch."

Nancy's heart leaped with excitement. Maybe this could explain the sabotage at the ranch! "Someone wants to force the Rawleys off the property in order to search for the treasure," she thought.

"Do many people know about this?" George asked.

"Nearly everybody round here has heard Valentine's story, except the part about the treasure being hidden on the ranch, which is something that only a few old-timers believed." Mary shook her head. "I doubt whether the present owners of Shadow Ranch have ever heard about it."

Carefully Nancy examined the gold watch. Perhaps there was a clue to the treasure in it! She pressed her nail against the edge and opened the lid, revealing the worn face of the watch.

"It still works," said Mary. "The back lid opens, too."

Nancy was disappointed to find that there was no picture or inscription inside either place.

"Where did you get the watch?" she asked.

"It was in a box of things I bought at an auction," the Indian girl replied. She explained that the items had

belonged to an old resident of Tumbleweed, Miss
Melody Phillips, who had been a girlhood friend of
Frances Humber. "Frances died in the East, and her
parents, who still lived on the ranch, gave these
mementos to Miss Melody. I know this history because
it was written on the cover of the box."

"Do you still have that?" Nancy asked eagerly.

The Indian girl shook her head regretfully. "I threw
the box and the other items away since they were
worthless. You must take the watch, Nancy," she added
earnestly. "Please."

Not wanting to hurt the girl's feelings, Nancy
consented. As she was thanking her, Dave strode into
the shop. He reported that the thief had not been
caught. "Sheriff says he'll keep an eye out for him,
Mary."

"That's good," the young shop owner said, then
showed Dave the watch. "I'm giving this to Nancy,"
she added, and repeated the history of the timepiece.

Dave seemed to be interested and examined the
watch closely. When he returned it, Mary pinned it
shyly to Nancy's blouse.

As the girls were leaving the shop with Dave, Nancy
noticed a small pastel drawing propped up on the
counter. "What a beautiful scene!" she remarked.

Mary said it was the work of an artist who lived on
Shadow Mountain. Struck by the lovely Western
landscape, Nancy bought the picture.

When the group walked outside, Nancy saw a tall
man in black jacket and pants seated on the bench
under the cottonwood tree. He wore a black ten-gallon
hat, and his light-brown eyes followed Nancy as
she passed him. It seemed to her that his gaze was

"Come and rope me, pardner!" *Bud challenged Bess*

fastened on the watch. Could he be the frustrated thief?

"He might have left his coat and hat somewhere," Nancy reasoned, "and put them on again after his escape. But why should he be interested in the watch, unless he's after the Humber treasure and hoped to find a clue in it?"

As Dave drove out of town, Nancy saw the tall stranger staring after them. "The name of the ranch is on the side of the truck," she thought uneasily. "If that man *is* after this watch, he'll know just where to find me!"

Halfway to the ranch, the girls pointed out Indian cliff dwellings high on the mountain slope. Nancy asked if this was the area once owned by the Humbers and Dave nodded.

"Good place to look for curios like pieces of pottery," George remarked.

"You girls stay away from there!" he advised sharply. When Nancy asked why, Dave explained that the stairs leading up from the valley floor were worn and broken. "Very dangerous," he said.

When they reached the ranch, Dave parked the truck at the stable. The girls heard laughter coming from the corral and saw Tex Britten perched on the fence. Bess was mounted on a brown horse and holding a coiled lariat.

"Watch me!" she called. "I'm learning to rope a steer."

Nancy and George walked over and saw Bud Moore put his hands on his head like horns and prance in front of Bess's horse. "Come on and rope me, pardner!" he said.

Bess frowned, bit her lip, and managed to get a noose twirling. Then *plop*—it dropped over the head of her own horse!

Tex gave a piercing whistle. George and Nancy burst into laughter while the "steer" helped blushing Bess to dismount.

"Never mind," said Nancy. "You didn't want to be a cowboy, anyway!"

As the boys called joking remarks about the next roping lesson, the girls walked off together. At the house Nancy told Bess, Aunt Bet, and Alice all that had happened in town. She showed them the watch and related its history.

"Shorty Steele is the one who told us the legend of the phantom horse," said Aunt Bet, "but he never mentioned the treasure. Maybe he doesn't know that part of the story."

"Or perhaps he kept it to himself," Nancy thought. Aloud she said, "Would it be all right if we hunt for the treasure?"

"By all means."

While the others were examining the old-fashioned watch, Nancy took the pastel picture from her bag and propped it on the living-room table.

Alice saw it and turned pale. "Nancy! Where did you get this?"

As Nancy explained, Alice picked up the painting. "My father did this—I'm sure of it!" She told them that Ross Regor was an amateur artist and always carried a small case of pastels with him. Whenever he had a few leisure minutes he devoted the time to sketching and Alice was positive she could recognize his work.

"We must find the artist," she said. "I just know he's my father!"

The others could not help feeling that Alice was clutching at straws. Nevertheless, Aunt Bet offered to take her young niece to town the next morning to question Mary Deer.

That night after supper Nancy slipped into a heavy jacket, took a torch, and went for a walk alone. She made her way past the stable, chicken coops and corral to the edge of the big meadow. As she stood thinking, the wind whistled down the valley and tossed the treetops. Chief came padding over from the stable and nuzzled her hand.

Nancy turned and looked back. There was a light shining through a crack in the spring-house wall! "Who'd be there now?" she wondered.

As she hurried to investigate, one foot stepped on a large twig. *Crack!* In a moment the light went out!

Her sleuthing instincts aroused, Nancy tiptoed to the door, pulled it open, and shone her light inside. Empty!

A shiver ran up Nancy's spine. It was impossible!

She walked away slowly, puzzling over the incident. Suddenly a long weird whistle sounded in the direction of the meadow. From among the bordering trees—as if in response to the whistle—galloped a white, filmy horse! The phantom!

·6·

Shorty's Shortcut

FOR a moment Nancy froze at the sight of the ghostly steed galloping across the meadow. Then she raced towards the fence, calling the alarm.

At the same time a yell came from the stable. "Phantom—phantom!" It was Shorty's voice. "Saddle up, everybody!"

There were answering shouts as the cowboys appeared on the run and dashed to the stable. The other girls rushed up to Nancy who was staring over the fence into the meadow. Chief joined the excited group. He began barking and made a beeline for the phantom horse, which had turned and seemed to be floating towards the far end of the meadow.

Soon the mounted ranchmen thundered out of the stable. Shorty took the lead. "Come on! This time we're gonna run that critter to earth!"

But the phantom horse was already far ahead of the pursuers. Only the dog was getting close. As the girls watched, the eerie figure reached the line of trees at the far end of the meadow. In the wink of an eye it vanished.

Bess drew a shuddering breath. "The ghost's gone! Right into thin air!"

"Nonsense," George said gruffly.

"How can anything disappear like that?" asked Alice.

"It's amazing," Nancy admitted. "We should have been able to see it glowing among the trees for a few moments." Suddenly she remembered the prophecy that destruction would follow any appearance of the phantom. "Come on!" she exclaimed. "The real trouble is somewhere else."

She and the other girls hurried back to the house. All seemed quiet there. A glance into the kitchen showed Aunt Bet trying to calm Mrs Thurmond. The girls hastened on to their rooms.

With an exclamation of dismay Nancy stopped in the doorway. The room she shared with the cousins was a shambles! Pillows were ripped, blankets lay on the floor. All the drawers had been dumped. Alice ran next door to her room and came back to say that it had not been touched.

"Someone wants us to leave Shadow Ranch, all right," George declared.

"More than that," Nancy said thoughtfully. "Someone may be looking for Frances Humber's watch."

"But only we girls and the Rawleys know Mary Deer gave it to Nancy," Alice objected.

"You're forgetting the man in town," Nancy said, "and Dave. Both were very much interested in it."

"Well, where *is* the watch?" asked Bess, looking fearful.

"I'm wearing it," said Nancy, "under my sweater." Before supper she had changed to a yellow blouse and skirt with a matching pullover.

While she and Bess and George began to clear up the mess, Alice hurried to the kitchen to tell her aunt and Mrs Thurmond what had happened. They hurried back to help. By the time the beds were made again and the pillows replaced with spare ones, the men had returned.

"The phantom got away," Ed Rawley said gloomily. "Chief was at his heels, but he hasn't come back and it worries me."

"I'm sorry," said Nancy. "I'm afraid we have other bad news for you." Quickly she reported what had happened.

"The purpose of the phantom is clear," she declared. "It's to frighten you and attract attention to the meadow while the real damage is being done somewhere else."

"If we could only catch the thing, it would surely give us a clue to who is doing all this," Ed Rawley said, and Nancy agreed.

The next morning at breakfast Dave reported that Chief still had not returned.

"The phantom got him, poor dog," Mrs Thurmond said dolefully. "Same as it will get us all."

As soon as the meal was over, Nancy said she was going out for a ride. She put on riding clothes and hastened to the stable where Tex saddled a handsome bay for her. Nancy was a skilful rider and she enjoyed the gallop in the meadow looking for clues to the phantom. But whatever marks it had left had been obscured by the pursuing horsemen.

At the far end of the field, Nancy rode into the copse of cottonwood trees where the strange creature had vanished. Here she found a path which led to the foot of the mountain and up the slope. Had the phantom gone that way?

Nancy reined her horse about and hurried to the ranch house, where she rounded up Bess and George. "Want to join me in a search party?"

"You bet," her friends chorused.

Shorty offered to lead them and within half an hour the four riders were following the path up the mountain.

It was a steep, high climb. All was silent, except for the creak of the saddles and the clop of the horses' hoofs on the stones. Finally the path levelled off and they came to a narrow stream, which they splashed across.

"This is just a small stream now," said Shorty. "But come one good cloudburst—and it'll turn into a roarin' flood so bad only a river horse could cross it. That's the kind you're ridin' now. They're big and don't get rattled—know how to swim with the current."

Near noon Nancy suddenly reined up. "Listen!" she said. Somewhere among the rocks overhead a dog was barking. Apache Chief?

Within a moment George glimpsed the roof of a cabin among the crags above. "Maybe Chief's up there!" she exclaimed.

Nancy observed that it looked as though the path they were on would lead to the cabin.

"I know a shortcut. Come with me," Shorty said quickly.

He rode ahead and led them to a side path. He explained to the girls that the other route became impassable farther up the mountain. After they had ridden for fifteen minutes Shorty stopped, pulled off his hat, and wiped his forehead with his bandanna.

"I gotta confess we strayed on to the wrong trail." He shrugged. "No use goin' back up. Gettin' too late. We better make tracks for the ranch."

Disappointed, Nancy and her friends followed him along a new trail which eventually rejoined the first path. They reached Shadow Ranch in mid-afternoon.

When they dismounted in front of the stable, Shorty said, "I'm mighty sorry we didn't find that dog."

Nancy replied, "So am I." She could not help suspecting that Shorty had pretended to be lost and deliberately kept them away from the cabin. She made up her mind to go back. The three girls discussed the possibility of his having double-crossed them.

"I'll bet he did!" George declared.

At the house they found Alice waiting for them, her face glowing. "Nancy," she cried out, "Mary Deer says the artist's name is Bursey and he lives in a cabin on Shadow Mountain!" The older girls exchanged meaningful looks.

"Alice," Nancy said happily, "I think I know where it is. We'll go there tomorrow. Maybe we'll find Chief, too."

That night Alice came to the girls' room. She was puzzled. If the artist *was* her father, why was Chief with him?

"I wish I could answer," said Nancy. "And, Alice dear, please don't get your hopes up too high. It may not be the cabin where the artist lives, although I have a hunch it's connected with the mystery of Shadow Ranch."

As Nancy spoke, she was turning the old-fashioned watch over in her hand. Absently she ran her finger along the front edge and suddenly felt a tiny obstruction. She pushed it and instantly a thin lid sprang forward.

"Why—it's a secret compartment!" she exclaimed.

On the top side of the lid was the small faded photograph of a handsome man with flowing dark hair.

"That must be Dirk Valentine!" Nancy cried, and showed it to the other girls. In the frame next to the picture of the man was a tiny corner from another picture.

"That one's been torn out," said Alice.

"It must have been a photo of Frances Humber," Bess observed.

Carefully Nancy removed the old picture. On the back in faded ink was the initial "V". In tiny script under it were the words: *"green bottle in—"*

"In *where*?" asked George.

"Perhaps the place is named on the back of the missing photograph," Nancy suggested.

"Let me see it," Bess requested.

Nancy handed her the watch. Bess looked it over carefully. Finally she sighed, replaced the picture, and put the timepiece on the dresser. "What can that odd message mean? If—"

At that moment the girls heard a dog whining. It came from somewhere in the darkness beyond the veranda.

Alice jumped up. "Listen!" she exclaimed. "Maybe that's Chief!"

·7·

Rockslide

THE girls dashed on to the veranda but could not see the big German shepherd dog.

"Here, Chief!" Nancy called.

From the dark yard came an answering whine, but the dog did not appear.

"Maybe he's hurt," said Bess as they walked towards the sound. Whines and barks filled the air as the searchers called again and again, but each time the sounds seemed farther away and definitely were coming from the big meadow. The girls reached the fence. Though they called repeatedly, there was only silence.

"Why wouldn't Chief come to us?" Alice asked.

The same question had been troubling Nancy, and the answer flashed into her mind. "Perhaps there wasn't any dog! Maybe someone imitated him to get us out of our room."

Bess gave a gasp of alarm. "Nancy! Your watch! I left it on the dresser!"

Hoping they would not be too late, the girls ran back to their room. All sighed in relief. The watch was still on the dresser!

"Thank goodness!" said Bess. "If it had disappeared I never would have forgiven myself."

George said, "We were gone long enough for someone to lift out Valentine's picture and look at the writing on it."

Nancy examined the picture carefully, but could detect no sign of its having been removed.

Alice spoke up. "What do you think those words on the back of the photograph mean, Nancy?"

The young detective thought they might be a clue to the treasure. "Valentine may have given the watch to Frances for a double purpose—as a gift and a way to tell her secretly where his treasure was hidden."

"You mean it's in a green bottle?" Bess asked incredulously.

Nancy shook her head. "More likely the bottle contains directions to it. Let's look over Aunt Bet's bottle collection."

She pinned the watch on to her blouse and hurried to the living room with the others. Nancy showed Mrs Rawley the clue in the secret compartment, and asked if any of the bottles in her collection had been found on the premises.

"Two," said the woman. "And one of them is green!"

The girls went to the window with her and she removed a dark-green, narrow-necked bottle from the top shelf.

"It was for liniment," she said, handing it to Nancy. "The old Western miners and ranchers used a lot of it. Collectors are always looking for those antique bottles. I found this one in an old shed behind the stable."

Nancy removed the stopper, turned the bottle over, and shook it, but nothing fell out. Nancy asked Alice to bring a knitting needle from her bag. When she returned, the girl detective probed into the bottle with the long needle.

"It's empty," was her verdict.

"We'll have to start searching the ranch for other bottles," said Bess.

That night Nancy went to sleep wondering if someone else might also be looking for the green bottle. The answer came after breakfast next morning as she crossed the living room. The green liniment bottle was gone from the window shelf!

Nancy searched the other shelves at once, but in vain. It was obvious that the dog whining had been a trick and someone had read the clue on the back of Valentine's picture!

Just then Dave passed the veranda door. Nancy called him in and asked what time he had taken guard duty the night before.

"Eight o'clock to midnight," he replied. "Why?"

"Just wondering. Did you hear a dog whine in the yard or see anyone?"

Dave had heard the dog but seen no one. When he had reached the yard, there had been no sign of the animal.

"Again, why?" The cowboy regarded Nancy quizzically.

"It was a trick to get us outside so someone could snoop in my room," Nancy replied. She looked him straight in the eye, and he met her gaze without flinching.

"I think you're right," he said, and added quietly, "Be careful, Nancy. You're on dangerous ground." He turned and walked away.

Was it a threat, or a well-meant warning? Nancy

could not make up her mind. Although Dave was gruff, Nancy liked his straightforward manner.

"I must tell Aunt Bet about this," the young sleuth thought.

The ranchwoman and her nieces were disturbed to hear about the missing bottle, but Mrs Rawley commented with a smile, "The thief must have hated himself for his trouble when he found out there was nothing in the bottle!"

"That's right," Bess agreed. "But he'll go on looking for green bottles and he just may find the right one before Nancy does."

Her detective friend grinned. "Let's not give him a chance!"

As the girls changed to riding togs, Aunt Bet told them of a ghost town on Shadow Mountain. "It's possible Mr Bursey lives there," she said. "You might go to it first, then circle round and on the way back visit the cabin where you think the dog is." She drew a map, then warned, "Be back by sundown. Mountain trails are treacherous after dark."

Nancy took her pocket compass and the girls picked up the lunch Mrs Thurmond had packed for them. Then they hurried to the stable.

Tex gave them the same horses they had ridden the day before, plus a large roan mare named Choo-Choo for Alice. But when the slender girl was astride, she began to giggle.

Tex, too, chuckled. "I don't think I can shorten those stirrups enough for you, Missy," he said. "We'd better put you on a smaller animal."

Bess volunteered to give Alice the horse she was about to mount and the switch was made.

"Choo-Choo's a perfectly good trail animal," Tex said. "Only thing is, she's no river horse."

"I'll remember," said Bess.

With Nancy in the lead, the riders cut across the big meadow at a gallop and started up the mountain trail. Nancy followed Aunt Bet's map, and after a long, hot climb, the girls sighted a group of weather-beaten wooden buildings clinging to the slope above.

As they rode into the streets of the ghost town they were struck by the silence and the bleached look of the sagging buildings. In front of a dilapidated hotel they dismounted and tied their horses to an old hitching rail. As they stepped on to the wooden sidewalk, Alice exclaimed sharply:

"Look!" In front of her lay a crushed blue crayon. "It's a pastel!"

Nancy dropped to her knees and examined the coloured powder. "This is fresh," she said with excitement. "It hasn't been scattered by the wind or mixed with dust."

Beyond the vivid splotch she saw smaller traces of blue and followed them swiftly to the end of the street. Below her, on the rocky mountain slope, she saw two men running.

In a moment they disappeared into a cluster of large boulders. Alice and the others dashed up behind Nancy just too late to see them. Though the girls watched, the men did not reappear.

"I just know one of them was my father," Alice moaned. "He must have dropped the crayon. Oh, Nancy, why do you suppose they ran away? Do you think he's a captive?"

"I don't know yet," Nancy replied. "But I mean to find out."

"Come on. Let's search the town," George urged. "We'll see if there's any sign of an artist living here. If he is, he'll come back."

Alice agreed, and the four separated in order to cover the ground more quickly. Nancy picked a tall house perched precariously halfway up the slope. She entered cautiously and found the ground-floor rooms bare. Gingerly she climbed the rickety stairs.

In the front room she found only a broken brass bedstead. Casually she looked out of the window. On the ground was the long shadow of a man with a big hat! Apparently he was standing round the corner of the building.

Nancy ran to another window and saw the shadow moving towards the rear. She hurried to the back of the building and looked out on to a steep rocky slope. Suddenly among the big boulders on the hillside she spotted a climbing figure in a black ten-gallon hat.

Nancy's heart pounded. Was he the man from Tumbleweed? Did he know she was in the building? If, as she suspected, he was part of the plot at Shadow Ranch, he may have come here to ambush the girls!

"Perhaps I can turn the tables and find out what he's up to," she said to herself. But Nancy realized that she might be cornered in the old building and knew she must get out.

Quickly she started down the shaky stairs. Suddenly there came a rumble, growing louder. For an instant Nancy thought it was thunder, and paused, then she realized the truth.

"A rockslide!" she cried out, but the words were lost in the roar as the entire building was jolted from its foundation!

·8·

Escaped Dog

NANCY lurched against the balustrade. Trying to catch her balance, she grabbed the rail. With a loud crash the whole framework broke and she plunged through to the floor below! Stunned, Nancy hardly noticed that the roar of the rockslide had subsided and the old building had come to a shuddering halt. After a while she became aware of voices calling.

"Nancy! Nancy, are you 'n there?" came Bess's frantic voice.

"I see her!" George's deeper tones were coming closer. As Nancy managed to sit up, she saw that the floor now slanted steeply downhill, and her friends were crawling up towards her.

"Oh, Nancy, are you all right?" Bess asked anxiously.

Nancy managed a shaky smile. "I think I'm just bruised. Now that I've caught my breath, I'll be fine."

George and Bess helped her to her knees.

"We'll have to crawl down," said George. "And the sooner the better. This building might start to slide again."

Nancy and her friends held their breath and gingerly crawled backwards down the slanting floor to the door. The sill was now almost waist-high. As they climbed out, Nancy saw that the building had slipped down to the road.

Alice, carrying a coil of rope, came hurrying up to them. "Oh, Nancy, thank goodness you're all right!" she exclaimed. She explained that George had sent her back to the horses for the rope in case they needed it.

Nancy looked uneasily up at the rocky slope behind the wrecked house. She squinted her eyes against the glare of the sun but could detect nothing moving.

"What do you think caused the rockslide?" George asked.

Nancy told the girls of having seen the man in the black hat. "Maybe he started a boulder rolling," she suggested.

"On purpose?" Bess asked, horrified.

"Perhaps," said Nancy. "I have a feeling it's the same man George and I saw in Tumbleweed. If he's after Valentine's treasure, this is one more move to scare us off the ranch."

George reminded her that no doubt there were other men in the county with large black hats.

"I know," Nancy admitted. She wondered whether the man had followed them there or had been disturbed by their coming.

The other girls said that so far they had found no signs of anyone living in the abandoned village. At Nancy's suggestion they started down the street and, without entering, looked into the few buildings that they had not already checked.

All the while Bess kept glancing over her shoulder to see if anyone was following them. When they reached the end of the street, she and George peered into a tumbledown blacksmith's shop.

Suddenly there was a rustling noise. Bess jumped back and squealed as something scurried past her.

"Really, Bess," George said in disgust, "you're hopeless. That was only a rat."

Bess blushed. "I can't help it. I keep expecting the man in black to jump out at us."

Nancy spoke up. "I think Bess has a point. We'd better get out of here. If the man is still around he just might cause another rockslide."

In a few minutes the girls had mounted their horses and were riding out of town.

"Are we going straight to the cabin now?" Alice asked anxiously. "Perhaps the men we saw were on their way to it."

"Yes," said Nancy. As soon as they were clear of the dilapidated buildings she reined in and studied the map Aunt Bet had given her. After consulting the compass, she led the girls around the back of Shadow Mountain on a narrow trail. Now and then they passed a tall, creamy yucca flower in bloom or startled a bird from a thicket of chaparral. But they saw no other living creatures.

Near noon the riders reached a level place where a cluster of high rocks cast shade over a shallow stream. Here they dismounted, watered their horses, and ate lunch. An hour later the girls were in the saddle again and presently rounded a rock outcrop. They found themselves looking up at a small cabin set among the rocks some distance from them. As the horses climbed towards it, their iron shoes rang against the rock and some of the loose stones clattered down the hill behind them. Suddenly a dog began to bark, then stopped.

"That sounded like Chief!" Bess exclaimed.

While still some distance from the cabin, the riders dismounted.

"Bess and Alice, will you stay with the horses?" Nancy requested. "George and I will take a look round."

The two girls walked stealthily up the hill and started to circle the cabin. They found that the rear wall was close to the side of the mountain and heavily overgrown with brush and small fern. There was an open window in the back wall, but a heavy sack was hanging across it so the girls could not see inside. They stood still for a moment and listened, but no sound came from within. Quietly they completed the circle and returned to the others.

"The door's open a little bit," Bess said softly. "Do you think anybody's inside?"

"There's only one way to find out," Nancy said with determination. "I'll go and knock."

As she started up the hill, the barking started again. The next instant, from behind the cabin, bounded a large black German shepherd dog.

"Chief!" the girls exclaimed.

The dog greeted them with frenzied barking and tail wagging. A short piece of rope hung from his collar. On his head was a swelling and broken skin.

"You poor old fellow!" said Nancy. She knelt beside the dog and calmed him, then carefully felt around the wound. "Someone knocked him out and has been holding him!" she said.

"But why?" asked Bess, keeping a wary eye on the cabin.

"Maybe because he got too close to the phantom horse," Nancy replied.

George looked puzzled. "What difference would that make? Chief can't talk."

"But maybe there's a clue on him—something to show how the trick was done," Nancy replied. The big dog stood patiently as Nancy examined him, but she found nothing unusual.

Bess volunteered to stay with the horses and the dog while the other girls went to the cabin. The trio walked up to it and Nancy knocked on the door. There was no answer. She knocked again, then pushed the door open cautiously.

The one-room cabin was empty, but plainly had been lived in. On the table stood two mugs and a coffee-pot.

Alice darted forward with a cry. Beside the cups lay an unfinished drawing and a pastel crayon.

"My father! He's been here!"

The mugs were half full of coffee. Nancy felt them. They were still warm.

"The artist and his companion have been here, all right," Nancy agreed. "And they left just a short time ago."

"Why would they do that?" George asked. "Unless they heard us coming and have some reason to hide."

"My father's being held prisoner," Alice said positively. She glanced at the older girls and read their thoughts. "You think he's connected with the phantom mystery because we found Chief here," she accused.

Nancy tried to assure her this was not the case. "Your father is innocent, but someone else occupying this cabin may be connected with the Shadow Ranch mystery."

Leaving the door slightly open as they had found it, the three hurried to report to Bess.

"The men may come back. Let's wait here and see," Nancy suggested.

The girls led their horses behind a pile of large boulders, out of sight of the cabin. Keeping Chief beside her, Nancy hid behind the screen of chaparral with the other girls and watched the cabin.

While they waited Nancy puzzled over the dog's appearance. He had run from behind the cabin, yet minutes before she and George had passed between it and the mountain without seeing or hearing the animal. It occurred to Nancy that he might have been tied up some distance away and broken loose.

But why had he been held? There seemed to be no lead to the phantom on him. "Perhaps it was only because his captor is not averse to stealing a good dog."

The afternoon wore on. It was hotter and increasingly cloudy. The men did not return.

Finally Nancy cast a worried look at the sky. "We must start back before it rains."

Alice begged to stay, but the other girls knew this was not wise. Nancy promised her they would come again.

With Chief at the heels of Nancy's horse, the girls started down the mountain, following a path which the River Heights visitors soon recognized as the trail they had been on the day before.

"So this path to the cabin is not impassable, after all," said George, "as Shorty had claimed."

Nancy remarked that the cowboy might have been mistaken, yet she admitted that his behaviour certainly made him a strong suspect in the mystery.

As the girls rode along, the sun vanished and a chill wind set in. Suddenly a few large drops of rain splattered into the dust. The next moment a downpour descended.

The horses snorted. A vivid flash of lightning split a

fir tree some distance up the mountain and the horses shied at the clap of thunder.

"Sit tight!" Nancy called over her shoulder, "and keep moving."

Moment by moment, the cloudburst worsened and the trail gradually became slippery mud. Far below in the valley they could see the sunlit meadow, untouched by the storm.

"I hope we make it," Bess said fearfully.

Suddenly Nancy had a chilling thought. They still had to negotiate the stream which they had crossed the previous day. And Bess's mount was not a river horse! She dare not urge her own mount faster, for the animal was picking his footing carefully. Yet, with each precious minute, she knew that the stream was rising.

When they reached its bank the four girls gazed in consternation at the rushing water.

"We can't cross that!" Bess wailed.

Nancy said the only alternative was to stay all night on the mountain. "And we're not equipped to do that. It's too risky. Come on, Bess. We can make it if we hurry!"

As she spoke, Chief whined and put his paw into her stirrup.

"He's begging for a ride," George said.

The dog leaped to a large rock beside the water and Nancy pulled up close to him. With her help Chief squeezed on to the front of the saddle and Nancy held him there.

"All right, boy," she whispered to him. "Here we go!"

She gathered the reins firmly and guided her horse into the water. The big animal did not fight the current, but swam along easily with it, heading gradually for the opposite bank. Before long, he found footing. As he clambered safely ashore, Chief jumped off and Nancy turned in the saddle to see how the others were faring.

One by one the big, dependable river horses made the crossing safely, but Bess, on Choo-Choo, was last. Would he behave? The animal entered the stream and walked until the water swirled around his shoulders. Then he stopped.

"If he doesn't swim he'll be swept away!" George exclaimed.

"Help!" called Bess. "He won't move!"

With the torrent rising fast, Nancy spurred her mount along the bank until she was some distance above Bess. Then she guided her horse into the turbulent water.

"Hold on, Bess! We're coming!"

Suddenly, a few yards upstream, part of the muddy bank collapsed, sending a huge surge of water sweeping over Nancy and her horse!

·9·

Tack Room Prisoner

KEEPING a firm grip on the reins, Nancy stuck tight to the saddle. In a few moments her mount steadied himself and began to swim towards Bess's horse. When they drew close, Nancy seized Choo-Choo's reins. While the frightened girl clung to the saddle, her horse was towed to shore.

"Oh, Nancy!" she exclaimed. "You were wonderful. You saved us!"

Nancy still looked worried. "We can't stay here," she said. "We're not out of trouble yet. I'm afraid the trail down is going to be slippery and wet."

George grimaced. "What's the hurry? We can't get any wetter than we are."

The girls looked at one another. Despite the situation, they could not repress giggles. All were drenched and mud-spattered, with water streaming from their hair.

"You're lucky Bud isn't here to see you," George teased Bess as Nancy led the way down the trail.

Bess shivered and made a face at her cousin. "I know I must be a sight," she said. "I can tell by looking at the rest of you."

The joking had served to relieve the tension and now the girls applied themselves to guiding their horses down the precarious trail. As they reached the bottom, the rain stopped, and the sun emerged hot and bright.

From there, the trip was easier. By the time they reached the big meadow, their clothes were almost dry.

Chief raced ahead to the stable, barking madly. Bess groaned. "Oh, he's making so much noise he'll bring out a reception committee and everybody'll see us!"

Nancy smiled at the remark, then warned the others to say nothing about the man in the black ten-gallon hat or the other two men to anyone except the Rawleys.

When the girls rode up to the corral, Dave and Tex and Bud were waiting there for them.

"Where did you find Chief?" asked Dave. He surveyed their bedraggled condition but made no comment.

Tex said, "Looks like you girls got caught in a little mountain sprinkle."

Bud grinned and said, "That was nothing. Wait till you all get caught in a real Western-style rain."

"No thanks," Bess retorted.

"We'll tell you all about the dog later," Nancy promised. The girls hastily dismounted and fled to the house.

After hot showers they dressed for supper. Nancy wore a powder-blue sweater and skirt, and brushed her titian hair until it gleamed. George wore a smart dark-green linen dress. She was ready long before Bess, who wore a yellow sweater and skirt and changed her hair-do three times.

"I want to look extra nice," Bess said, "to make up for the awful sight I looked this afternoon."

Before supper, the girls sat down in the living room with the Rawleys and told them of their afternoon's adventures. Nancy passed lightly over the stream-crossing incident, but Bess refused to let the matter drop. When everyone had gathered around the table, she bragged of Nancy's bravery. Nancy, always embarrassed by praise, changed the subject as soon as possible.

When the meal was over, Dave called Nancy aside on the veranda. "I owe you an apology," he said soberly. "That was a mighty fine thing you did this afternoon. I see now that you're not the tenderfoot nuisance I thought you were going to be."

Nancy smiled. "This is the first time since I arrived that you've been friendly. Are you always so gruff to newcomers?"

He flushed. "No, but I—" He hesitated. "Well, I had a special reason."

Before Nancy could ask him what it was, he said, "I have to go now. We'll talk again later."

Dave swung off the veranda and headed towards the corral. Nancy watched him disappear into the dusk, puzzled by his remarks. Was he guilty of something or not? She was aware that Ed Rawley trusted him. On the other hand, she had no proof that Dave had been telling the truth about the mud on his shoes.

She reminded herself that he knew about Frances Humber's watch and therefore had a reason to trick the girls out of their room and later take the old green bottle.

"Did Dave apologize in order to allay my suspicions of him?" she wondered.

As Nancy started towards the living room she met the other girls and Aunt Bet coming out.

"We're going to a drive-in movie," said Alice. "Want to come along?"

"I'd love to," Nancy replied, "but I think I'd better stay at home and keep watch." Bess and George offered to remain with her, but Nancy urged them to go on.

As Mrs Rawley and the girls walked towards the estate car, Nancy hurried to her bedroom. She changed into riding clothes, picked up a torch, and then headed for the stable. She had decided to saddle her mount and be ready to ride in case the phantom horse should appear. The young sleuth was determined to catch the ghost horse or examine its tracks before they were obscured by other pursuers.

As Nancy reached the stable, Dave came out leading a horse which he mounted at once. He carried a torch. "Just checking up," he said to her. "Snooping again?"

"Yes," Nancy replied. Quickly she changed the subject by asking whether anyone kept watch in the big meadow at night for the phantom.

"No," was the reply. "Shorty and I have the first patrol, while Tex keeps watch on the windmill and Bud stands guard at the east meadow. When it's their turn to ride patrol, Shorty and I will switch jobs with them."

He added, "The foreman is riding fence in the east meadow—we even have to do it at night now. That way the cattle will be guarded twenty-four hours a day."

Dave rode off and Nancy went through the stable into the tack room, a long frame building attached to it. She turned on her torch and saw rows of saddles hanging from the walls and bundles of blankets stacked on shelves.

After crossing the room, she lifted one of the saddles from the wall. Above it hung a bridle and bit which Nancy also took down, then she picked up a saddle

"I must get out of here!" Nancy thought desperately

blanket. Turning back, she was surprised to see that the door was closed.

Nancy hurried over, put her gear on the ground, and tried the door. It was locked! She remembered having seen a padlock hanging loose in the hasp outside. Had someone locked her in by mistake?

Nancy pounded on the door and shouted, but no one came. Suddenly she realized that under the guard system no one would be within hearing distance of her voice. Grimly Nancy wondered if Dave had locked her in. Had he guessed her plan and done it to foil her?

"I must get out of here!" Nancy thought desperately.

She played her torch round the long room and saw one window high in the wall. "I can squeeze through, if I can find a way to reach it."

At one end of the room Nancy placed a pile of blankets under the window. Then she stacked saddles on top until she was sure of reaching the window.

Nancy climbed the unsteady pile and tried to push up the sash. The window was locked. She found the catch and managed to turn it. Once again she tried to open the window, but it was stuck tight. Disappointed, she made her way down to the floor.

"Maybe I can find a pole and force the window up," she thought.

Her torch revealed an iron crowbar in one corner. She dragged it back beneath the window, climbed up again, and tried to force the sash open. As she struggled with it she could see the kitchen end of the house and the spring house.

Suddenly the window budged, and at the same moment, Nancy saw a gleam of light through a crack in the spring-house wall. With a gasp of surprise she let the crowbar fall, climbed out of the window, hung for a moment from the sill, then dropped several feet to the ground.

As she hit the earth there was a sharp yelp to her left, and Chief ran towards her, barking loudly. "Hush!" Nancy said.

She patted the dog and tried to quieten him. "Stay here," she ordered, and he sat down obediently while Nancy ran towards the spring house.

When she was halfway there, the light went out. As she reached the door, Mr Rawley came running from the kitchen end of the house.

"What is it, Nancy? What's the matter?" he asked.

Quickly she told him what she had seen. "No one came out," she concluded.

"Then whoever had a light there must still be inside," he declared, and pulled open the heavy wooden door.

Nancy shone her torch inside. The spring house was empty!

· 10 ·

Hidden Entrance

"I just can't believe it!" Nancy exclaimed. "No one could have come out. I could see the door all the time I was running towards it."

Ed Rawley looked at Nancy. "I'm sure you didn't imagine seeing the light. This worries me."

Nancy told him of the similar experience she had had the day before. "Perhaps there's a secret exit," she suggested.

Using her torch, Nancy examined the walls of the spring house, but found they were solid adobe. It occurred to her that there might be a wooden trap door and a passageway under the earthen floor. She looked for any sign of seams in the earth. There were none. Nancy gave a baffled sigh and glanced at the stone vat.

"No use bothering with that," said Mr Rawley. "It's too small to hide in and too heavy to be moved in a hurry. Whoever escapes from here does it in a twinkling."

As Nancy and the rancher left the spring house, she gazed uneasily towards the meadow. "The last time I saw the light, the phantom horse appeared out there," she remarked.

"I'll alert my men to watch for more sabotage," Uncle Ed said quickly. "And I'll take one off patrol duty to stand guard here at the spring house all night."

He hurried away. Nancy stood watching the dark meadow, puzzling over the problem of the disappearing light. The phantom horse did not appear and finally she returned to the house.

Nancy went to the living room, lit a lamp, and sat down alone to think over the mystery. How could someone disappear from the spring house without using the exit? Suddenly she remembered that a prowler had done the same thing from the cellar of the house.

Nancy jumped up excitedly. "Of course that's the answer," she told herself. "The spring house is next to the kitchen and the cellar is under it! There must be a hidden passage from one to the other."

She hastened out of the house and turned the corner, then stopped short. A shadowy figure was lounging outside the spring house. It was Dave on guard. Nancy decided against examining the spring house again that night.

On the way back she glanced into the kitchen. Mrs Thurmond was seated at the big table, reading a magazine. Next to her was Bud Moore. He saw Nancy at the door.

"Howdy," he said. "Mr Rawley changed me into a house guard tonight, so you gals can sleep easy."

"That's great. Thanks."

Nancy smiled, but inwardly she was disappointed. "Now I can't investigate the cellar, either," she thought, "with Bud around."

Nancy woke at dawn. She dressed quickly and slipped out of the house. To her relief, there was no longer anyone on guard at the spring house. She stepped inside and walked to the kitchen wall. Nancy lifted the lid of the vat and looked in. It was empty.

She knelt and began to feel the bottom of the vat. Along the front edge her fingers suddenly encountered a piece of cord and opposite it another piece. Nancy pulled on them and the bottom moved. As she yanked harder, the floor of the vat lifted a few inches. It was made of wood, which had been covered with grey plaster to look like stone!

Before Nancy could lift it higher, she heard footsteps outside. Quickly she dropped the bottom and closed the vat. She had just time to grab a tin cup and hold it under the stream of water before the wooden door opened. Nancy turned and saw Shorty standing there.

For a moment he was speechless with surprise. "Wal," he exclaimed, "you're sure up mighty early, miss!"

"Yes, I am," Nancy said with a smile, then excused herself and left the spring house. As she strolled off, she could feel Shorty's eyes on her.

Nancy knew that the ranch hands rose early. "Did Shorty intend to get a drink of water? Or did he see me go in and come to find out what I was doing?"

Excited by her discovery in the spring house, Nancy could hardly wait for her friends to waken so that she could tell them about it.

At the news George sat up straight in bed. "That's something!" she exclaimed. "You've found the secret entrance to the cellar!"

"I *think* so," Nancy replied. "It was still kind of dark and I raised the bottom only a few inches. There just might be a hidden compartment under the false floor. Let's not tell anyone until we're sure."

Bess said, "Good idea."

The girls dressed in jeans and shirts, hoping to

investigate the mysterious vat very soon. But at breakfast Foreman Sanders ruined the plan.

"Two of the men will be working on the pump most of the day," he announced. "It hasn't been right since the damage was done."

Before the meal was over, Nancy asked with a smile, "Who locked me in the tack room last night by mistake?"

There was silence in the kitchen. Nancy learned nothing. No one wore a guilty expression.

During the morning Mr Rawley asked the four girls if they would like to go with him to Tumbleweed. They all accepted eagerly and piled into the estate car, with Dave at the wheel.

On the way, Uncle Ed told them he was going to the stockyards to pick up a dozen fine palominos for breeding. He had ordered and paid for the horses some time before. "It's a big investment." He frowned. "I just hope nothing happens to them."

Dave drove straight through town and parked on the outskirts in front of the stockyards. As Nancy got out of the car she noticed a sign on the fence: TUMBLEWEED RODEO. BARBECUE AND SQUARE DANCE. SATURDAY.

Dave called her aside. "Will you go to the barbecue and square dance with me?"

Surprised, Nancy hesitated for a moment.

"Please do," he added earnestly. "Bess and George promised Tex and Bud they would go. We can make it a triple date."

"Okay. Thank you," she replied.

"Good," he said, then excused himself and hurried into the stockyard after Uncle Ed.

Meanwhile, the girls walked round the enclosures,

looking at the animals. The visitors were attracted to a small corral where a man was offering trained horses for sale. The girls walked to the fence and joined the cowboys and ranchers who were watching a little chestnut mare perform.

Her master stood in the centre of the ring and gave various whistles. In response the horse pranced, reared, and kneeled. At the final whistle the mare ran to him and took a piece of sugar from his hand.

"Isn't she a darling?" Bess murmured.

As the girls strolled away they saw Dave near one of the horse enclosures. Nancy asked him if she had time to take Bess, George, and Alice to Mary Deer's shop.

"Sure," he replied. "Go ahead. We'll pick you up there in the car."

The girls walked down Main Street and turned into the gift shop. A tall man was standing at the counter, talking to Mary. As he turned round, Nancy stopped short in surprise. He was the man in black she had seen near the shop after the attempted robbery!

Mary greeted the girls warmly and Nancy introduced Bess, George, and Alice. The Indian girl presented the tall man as Mr Diamond, one of her best customers.

He smiled at Nancy smoothly. "Miss Drew, I congratulate you. Mary tells me that she has given you that pretty little antique watch I have had my eye on. For weeks she has been refusing to sell it to me."

Mary spoke up. "I told Mr Diamond the history of Valentine and his treasure," she said. "Ever since then he has been most eager to have Frances Humber's watch."

Mr Diamond gave a deep chuckle. "I like to collect mementos of the romantic Old West."

"Do you live round here?" George asked.

"No, ma'am. I'm spending the summer in this area for my health. Staying at the Tumbleweed Hotel."

Mary smiled. "Mr Diamond spends most of his days riding in the mountains for exercise."

Nancy's thoughts went to the man in the black hat she had glimpsed in the ghost town—the one who perhaps had caused the rockslide. Had it been Mr Diamond? Nancy thought it possible, because of his knowledge of the treasure.

After chatting for a few minutes, Mr Diamond said, "Well, goodbye now, girls," and left the shop.

While the others selected a few souvenirs, Nancy took Mary aside and asked her if she had heard from the artist, Mr Bursey. When Mary said no, Nancy added, "If you do, please phone me right away." Mary promised that she would.

Dave pulled up in the car, so the girls hurriedly paid for their purchases and left.

"The horses are going to be delivered this afternoon," Uncle Ed said with satisfaction as they drove back to the ranch. "They're first-rate animals."

The estate car arrived home just as Mrs Thurmond was ringing the triangle for lunch. Nancy wondered how she would endure the long afternoon waiting for darkness so that she could investigate the vat in the spring house. Her attention was distracted, however, by vans bringing the new horses. The girls and Aunt Bet went outside and watched the men run the palominos into the big meadow.

Nancy hurried to the fence for a closer look. "Oh, they're just beautiful!" she cried out.

Dave, who was on horseback beside the meadow

gate, agreed. "They're just the way they should be—
the colour of a new-minted gold coin."

The last one, a little mare, trotted into the enclosure.
Dave wheeled beside her and herded the pony to the
fence. "Want to pat her?" he asked Nancy.

With a smile Nancy stroked the sleek nose of the
palomino. The mare whinnied and shook her head.

Dave laughed. "Okay, little lady," he said, "on your
way." He slapped the pony on the rump and she ran off
to join the others. With a wave to Nancy, Dave rode off.

She admired the confident way he did his job and his
kind, firm manner with the animals. "I do hope he's
not mixed up in the mystery." She sighed.

As soon as it was dusk, Nancy hurried to the stable
and saddled her mount in case the phantom horse
should appear that night. Then she asked Bess and
George to join her and investigate the spring house.
Bess inquired if they were going to take Alice along.

"She's writing letters in her room," George said. Not
knowing exactly what lay ahead of them, Nancy
thought it wise to leave the younger girl behind.

When it was dark, she took her torch and the three
girls hastened to the spring house. They went inside and
closed the door. Nancy turned on her light, raised the
vat lid and, with heart thumping, pulled up the false
bottom. A deep hole slanted downwards.

While George held the light, Nancy lowered herself
into it and felt her foot touch something solid. She
kicked lightly and a wooden panel moved. In a few
moments she dropped on to an earthen floor. She was in
the cellar! Through the hole came Bess. She landed
with a thud.

From above came the noise of the vat lid closing.

A moment later George appeared in the cellar, with her torch turned off.

For a moment they stood listening. A shiver ran up Nancy's spine. She thought she could hear someone breathing in the darkness.

Quietly Nancy took the torch from George and turned it on. The sweeping beam caught a crouching figure in the corner! Dave Gregory!

· 11 ·

A Rewarding Search

DAVE rose to his feet. "Well, Nancy, you caught me fair and square."

She noted the spade at his feet. It looked as though her suspicions about Dave had been right. "Are you digging for treasure?" she asked coolly.

"Yes," he said. "But I'm not pulling the phantom trick or causing the damage around here. Please believe me, Nancy. Let me tell you my story."

George advised, "It had better be good."

Dave said, "My brother and sister and I are the only remaining descendants of Frances Humber. I was born in Buffalo, New York, but our family moved to Phoenix when I was ten. We have Valentine's original will, and have always known the story of his treasure, but never bothered to hunt for it.

"However, since my father's death two years ago, things have been hard with us. I've been working my way through college, but will need more money to help educate my younger brother and sister. So I decided to take a summer job on Shadow Ranch and look for the treasure."

"How amazing!" Bess murmured.

Dave reached into his shirt pocket and pulled out a small piece of paper. In the beam of her torch Nancy saw that it was a faded photograph of a pretty woman. She also noticed that the corner was torn and the picture was just the right size to fit into the watch case!

"This is Frances Humber," she announced.

The cowboy looked surprised. "How did you know?"

Instead of replying, Nancy asked him where he had obtained the picture. He explained that after Frances Humber Dale's death, her friend in Tumbleweed, Miss Phillips, had removed the photograph from the watch and sent it to Frances' children in the east. "It has been handed down in our family since then."

Dave turned the picture over and on the back the girls saw the word "*cellar*", written in old-fashioned script. He told them that the tradition in his family was that the cellar was the location of the treasure.

Nancy was excited at this new clue, but before telling him about the note in the watch, she asked him why he had not told Ed Rawley what he was doing.

"I was afraid he wouldn't hire me. He might have thought I'd spend all my time searching." The cowboy assured Nancy that he had done all his treasure hunting in off-duty hours.

"How did you know of the secret entrance?" Bess asked.

"Stories about that have always been known in my family," Dave answered. "Originally the trees grew thickly around the spring house, and in times of Indian attack the occupants would escape by the secret exit into the woods and go to a hideout on the mountain slope."

Dave confessed that he was the prowler who had alarmed Mrs Thurmond in the kitchen. He had hoped to search for the treasure in the cellar that night just after his turn on guard duty.

"But you raised such a rumpus," he said to Nancy with a grin, "that I knew it was no use to go on. I sneaked out through the spring house and came round to the kitchen a little behind the rest of the crowd."

"I believe you, Dave," said Nancy. "But you must promise to tell Mr Rawley first thing in the morning what you have been doing."

The cowboy assured her that he would. "I'm sorry I was kind of rude to you girls. I just didn't want you hanging around and getting in the way of my treasure hunt."

"You were pretty awful," said George. "But maybe we'll forgive you."

"Of course we will," Bess agreed.

Nancy smiled at Dave and he chuckled. "From the start I couldn't help liking you," he said.

Nancy reached into her pocket and brought out the antique watch. She showed him how the secret lid opened. The picture of Frances fitted perfectly to the torn fragment on the empty side.

"You're amazing!" he said. "What a detective!"

Next, Nancy removed the picture of Valentine and turned it over, so that Dave could see what was written on the back.

"With the word on your picture, we now have a complete message!" Nancy said excitedly.

"*'Green bottle in cellar,'*" Dave read. "Surely the treasure would be too large for a bottle. But perhaps it's a clue to the real thing."

"That's what Nancy thought," George said, grinning. "Let's start digging!"

For half an hour Dave dug and the girls probed the loose soil for a bottle.

Suddenly Bess cried out. "I've found it!"

Nancy hurried to her side and pressed in the earth where Bess showed her. Her fingers touched the neck of a bottle with a cap on it.

Dave came over and dug carefully round the glass. When it was partly free, Nancy said, "Wait!" She brushed the dirt from the large bottle and shone her light on it. Bess exclaimed in disappointment. The bottle was black.

"No use bothering with that," Nancy said. "We're looking for a green one. This has been lying here for years and gradually became covered with dirt."

With grim determination the treasure hunters continued to dig and sift the earth. When they had worked over the whole cellar floor, the four stopped, exhausted, and sat down.

Bess expressed the thought that was in all of their minds. "Maybe someone has found it already."

"Shorty, perhaps," Dave said. "I've caught him snooping." He told the girls that he suspected the other cowboy of knowing about the secret entrance and of inflicting damage on the ranch. "I'm sure he's not working alone, either, but who else is in league with him I don't know."

Nancy pointed out that if Shorty and his accomplices had found the treasure, they would have left the ranch by this time.

The young detective said, "There's another person who might have found the bottle—Frances Humber herself. What do you know of her story, Dave?"

"Only that Dirk Valentine and Frances had met only once on Shadow Ranch. He sent her a message that he was coming and Frances slipped out of the house through the secret entrance and met him in the spring house. But the law was after Valentine as usual and he had to leave the territory. He wrote to Frances, however, during the summer of 1880, but her father intercepted the letter and sent Frances to friends in Montana.

"Then Valentine probably hid the bottle in the cellar while Frances was away, and sent her the watch with the location of the bottle written on the backs of the pictures."

"That's right," Bess declared. "The date on the watch is June, 1880."

Dave went on to say that Frances must have written to Valentine and told him on what day she would return, for that night the outlaw sneaked on to the ranch to see her.

"But the sheriff and the posse suspected that he would come. They were lying in wait and shot Valentine as he entered the spring house. A few minutes later the sheriff went to the living room to tell his daughter. He found her lighting a lamp. When he told her that her sweetheart had been killed, she fainted."

"Oh, no!" cried Bess.

"For many weeks she was ill," Dave continued. "During this time her father found the watch sent to her by Valentine and took it. When she was well enough to travel, he sent her to stay with relatives in Buffalo. There she married, had two children, and died while still a young woman," he concluded.

George sighed. "Poor thing! She never had a chance to come back here and hunt for her treasure."

Suddenly Dave stood up. "I must go now," he said. "I have to stand watch soon in the east meadow."

Quietly the foursome left the cellar by the secret entrance and parted outside the spring house. The girls went to have a shower and change their clothes.

As Nancy dressed, she mulled over the story Dave had told her. She tried to reconstruct the scene at the ranch house on the night of the outlaw's death.

"If Frances had returned home only that afternoon," Nancy reasoned, "she may not have had a chance to look in the cellar for the bottle until that night. No doubt she also knew or guessed that her sweetheart would come to see her at the place they had met before. When the shots were fired, Frances would surely have heard them."

Here Nancy came to the part of the story that puzzled her. Maybe Frances Humber was in the cellar and ran upstairs to light a lamp? But why? It would have been more natural for her to go outside to be with Valentine. But suppose Frances had already found the bottle? At the sound of the shot she dashed upstairs in a panic, then found that she still had the bottle in her hand.

"Of course! She hid it in the lamp!" Nancy said aloud. "Then when her father walked in, Frances lit the lamp to cover her action."

At the bewildered looks on the faces of Bess and George, Nancy chuckled. Quickly she told them her new theory. "We must ask Aunt Bet if any of the old Humber lamps are still on the premises."

The girls hurried to the living room and found Mrs Rawley seated in a rocking chair, mending her husband's socks. In response to Nancy's question, she told her that there was a lot of junk from former owners in a storeroom next to Alice's bedroom.

The girls hurried down the hall and entered the storeroom. Bess switched on the ceiling light. Amidst old trunks, baskets, and barrels they found a birdcage and a hatstand but no lamp. On the seat of a broken chair lay a ragged quilt with something wrapped in it. Nancy carefully unfolded the bedcover. Revealed was a large oil lamp with a deep ruby glass well.

Bess gave a gasp of excitement, and George said, "If only it's the right one!"

With anxious fingers Nancy removed the chimney and the wick. She reached into the well and pulled out a slender green glass bottle!

Lights Out

"WHAT wonderful luck!" Nancy exclaimed softly. "To think of finding this bottle after all these years!"

"Let's see what's inside it," Bess urged.

Nancy put her little finger into the bottle and slid out a curled-up paper. Carefully she unrolled it, then glanced at the signature at the bottom—a bold "V" and a heart.

"It's a letter from Valentine to Frances," Nancy said.

The girls crowded close and peered at the faded handwriting. The long-dead romance came alive for them as Nancy read aloud:

" 'My dear girl, I am writing this in haste to tell you that I truly love you. Would that we could marry! But the law pursues me and I doubt whether I will live much longer. Too late I am sorry for my misspent life.' "

"How sad!" murmured Bess.

" 'I want you to have my fortune,' " Nancy continued, " 'but many people are seeking it. I know my mail is seized. I have hidden instructions in this bottle. A little of my booty has been converted to gold and melted down into special pieces, dear Frances, made just for you.' "

"I wonder what he meant," said George.

As Nancy was about to read on, the ceiling light

96

went out. George gave an exclamation of annoyance. "What a time for the bulb to go! Wait here. I'll get one from the kitchen."

As George felt her way out of the room, a suspicion flashed across Nancy's mind. Slipping the letter into her shirt pocket, she said, "Come on, Bess!" and went down the hall with her friend at her heels asking what was the matter.

In the living room Nancy saw the shadowy figure of Aunt Bet standing by a table lamp. "The lights don't work," she said.

At the same moment Alice's voice came up the hall. "Did someone blow a fuse?"

Her fears growing, Nancy groped her way to the telephone and picked it up. The line was dead! She ran her hand down the wire. *It had been cut!*

Nancy returned to the living room as George hastened in from the kitchen.

"No lights there, either," she reported.

"And probably no water," Nancy added grimly. "The pump runs by electricity." She went on to say someone had probably damaged the generator or cut all the wires.

There was a moment of shocked silence.

"But why?" Alice asked in a frightened voice.

"I'm afraid our enemies are about to make more trouble. They think we're helpless without lights or a phone."

"What do you think they'll do?" Aunt Bet asked anxiously.

Nancy said she could not be sure, of course, but she expressed fears about the new palominos.

"We must report this to the men on patrol," said

Mrs Rawley. "They may not yet know anything about the power failure."

Nancy agreed. "But we must be very quiet about it. If the gang doesn't suspect we've guessed their plan, we may be able to catch them in the act."

Nancy suggested that Aunt Bet and Alice keep watch in the house while she and the cousins looked for the guards.

The three hastened to their room to get their torches. "Don't turn them on," Nancy warned, "unless you absolutely have to."

The girls walked out and paused at the edge of the veranda. Somewhere in the darkness men were ready to work more mischief.

"You two go to the east meadow and report to Dave," she said. "I'll locate the palomino guard."

"Be careful," Bess warned. "You may find the troublemakers instead. They struck at the pump house before. Remember? That's close to the big meadow."

"That's why I think they won't do it again," Nancy replied. "Probably they'll pick on a different place. Good luck! If you run into trouble, yell!"

George and Bess melted into the darkness and Nancy hurried in the opposite direction. As she gazed over the fence of the big meadow, she could see most of the palominos standing quietly together near the far end. One or two were browsing in the middle, but there was no sign of a mounted guard.

Quickly Nancy circled the stable and the adjoining tack room, but found no one. Puzzled, she looked across the yard to the corral. It was empty. Where was the guard?

"I must find someone," Nancy thought, but before

she could move, there came a loud whinnying from the stable.

Nancy wheeled and hurried to the door, then paused, well aware that it might be dangerous to go inside. She opened the door quietly and stood listening. Except for the whinnying of a restless animal, all was quiet.

Nancy stepped in and walked cautiously between the two rows of stalls. When she reached the one where her horse stood, it occurred to her that someone might have unsaddled him to prevent her from being first to go after the phantom. But she found the saddle still in place.

As Nancy walked quietly along the left side of the horse, he whinnied nervously. She murmured reassuringly to him and stroked his head. Then she felt the girth to be sure it had not been loosened and ran her hands over the bridle. All was in order.

She was about to leave the stall when there came a loud whinny from the other end of the stable and the sound of a hoof hitting a bucket.

Nancy froze. She heard a footstep!

Suppose it was one of the gang? "If he finds me," she thought, "I'll be trapped in this stall—unable to sound the alarm."

Nancy knew she must try to get out of the stable. The footstep had seemed to be near the excited horse. But exactly where was the intruder now? Nancy slipped out of the stall and, hugging the wall, moved towards the door.

The next moment she was seized from behind and a hard hand stifled her outcry. As Nancy struggled, there came a sharp exclamation and she was suddenly released.

"Nancy!" said a familiar voice. It was Tex! "Great jumpin' steers! I'm sorry! Are you all right?" the cowboy asked anxiously. "Shucks, girl, I thought you were one of the phantom gang!"

Nancy took a deep breath. "I thought you were, too," she said, and quickly told him her news.

The cowboy gave a low whistle. "Trouble's comin', that's for sure!"

"Where are all the guards?" asked Nancy.

"Mr Rawley and Walt Sanders have gone down the valley towards Tumbleweed to watch the road. Mr Rawley figured if outsiders are helpin' to do the damage they might come part way by car, park it, and sneak into the ranch on foot.

"If that's how it's done, maybe he and Sanders can nab 'em. Shorty took early watch, so he's probably sleeping in the bunkhouse.

"I'm set to guard the stable area," Tex went on, "but I figured I'd sure be less conspicuous on foot. A while ago I heard a noise from here and came in to check. It was nothin'—just Daisy thumpin' around. She's restless tonight."

"Who's watching the palominos?" Nancy asked.

"Bud."

"He wasn't a few minutes ago."

"Oh—oh!" said Tex. "Something's wrong there! He'd never leave his post. Come on!"

The two hastened outside. As they turned towards the meadow, from the far end, came a high weird whistle.

The signal for the phantom horse!

Tex stopped short, then raced towards the house, shouting the alarm. Moments later, the clanging of the iron triangle outside the kitchen filled the night.

Nancy, meanwhile, had sprinted into the stable and led out her horse. As she sprang into the saddle, she could see the mysterious glowing steed galloping from the trees into the meadow. It hardly seemed to touch the ground and it wavered in the wind.

"I'm going to catch it!" Nancy vowed, and spurred her horse to racing speed.

Straight ahead lay the meadow gate, but it was closed. Taking a deep breath, Nancy gathered her mount and cleared it.

As before, the phantom was heading straight across the meadow. Nancy rode hard to cut the animal off. She intended to seize the phantom's bridle should it have one on.

In a moment the apparition turned and raced down the meadow, straight towards the palominos. Shrilly whinnying, it plunged into their midst. Some palominos shied and reared, others ran wild.

Nancy's horse, trying to overtake the fleeing phantom, pounded through the scattered group. Suddenly one of the frightened palominos thundered across her path. Frantically Nancy tried to pull her own mount aside.

Too late! The two horses collided. Nancy flew from the saddle and hit the ground so hard she blacked out!

·13·

Missing Artist

WHEN Nancy regained consciousness, Dave was bending over her. "Are you okay?" he asked anxiously, helping her to sit up. "Any bones broken?"

"No," said Nancy. "I guess I'm just bruised. Have I been lying here long?"

"Only a few minutes," Dave replied. "I saw you smack into that palomino and go sailing off. You really reached for the moon!"

Dave lifted Nancy to her feet and steadied her for a moment. As she thanked him, she could hear horses whinnying and men shouting.

"That phantom sure spooked the palominos," Dave said. "Did you get a good look at it?"

Nancy shook her head regretfully. "I didn't get close enough to see how it was rigged."

A horseman reined up beside them. It was Walt Sanders. "Fences have been cut!" the ranch foreman barked. "We've got to round up those palominos. Could take all night or longer if they run into the hills."

He spurred off and Dave turned to Nancy. "Can you make it to the house by yourself?"

"Don't worry about me," she assured him. "I'm fine."

Dave looked around in the darkness, but there was

no sign of Nancy's horse. "I reckon he bolted," he said.

His own mount, a seasoned work animal, stood nearby, unaffected by the panic in the meadow. Dave swung into his saddle. "Keep clear of those running horses," he warned, then rode off after the foreman.

By the time Nancy had walked the length of the meadow to the ranch house, she no longer felt shaken from her fall. In the living room were the three other girls and Aunt Bet. On the table, lighted, was the oil lamp which had belonged to the Humbers. As Nancy walked in, Bess cried, "Did you catch the phantom?"

"Sorry. No."

"Was there any damage this time?" Mrs Rawley asked.

Nancy reported the bad news about the cut fences and the palominos.

Aunt Bet's voice was strained as she said, "If we lose those horses, it will be a crushing blow for us. I appreciate all you've done, Nancy. Bess and George told me how you found the letter."

"It was so clever of you to deduce what Frances Humber did," Alice said admiringly.

"But you didn't finish reading it," George reminded Nancy.

Nancy took the letter from her pocket, smoothed out the paper, and held it close to the oil lamp.

George said, "You left off where he said he had melted down some gold into special pieces."

"Yes, here's the place," said Nancy. She read the next sentence. " 'My treasure is hidden in the oldest dwelling on the ranch.' "

"That's this house," Aunt Bet exclaimed. "We were told that Sheriff Humber built it first."

"Read on," Bess urged. "Exactly where is the treasure?"

Nancy shook her head. "He doesn't say. Listen! 'I fear that I am followed and even this note may fall into my enemies' hands. Therefore, I will say only that you know the place I mean.'"

George groaned. "We'll have to search the whole house. We'd better get started."

"There's likely to be a space under a loose floorboard," said Nancy, "or a niche in a chimney flue, or perhaps a false wall in a cupboard."

She suggested that each of them take a section of the house to investigate.

Nancy herself went to the big fireplace in the living room. She thought that one of the stones in it might conceal a hiding place.

With the aid of her torch the young sleuth tried to peer between the rocks, but they were set close together and no space was visible. She pushed hard on each one, but none budged.

When she finished, Nancy turned her attention to the Indian grindstone. Because it was set in the middle, she thought there might be something special about it and tried hard to move the stone, but it was as tightly in place as all the others.

By the time Nancy had finished checking the living room, the rest of the searchers had straggled back. They reported no success.

Baffled, Nancy suggested that they go to bed. She felt sore and weary. "Maybe I'll be able to think more clearly after I get some sleep." She gave Valentine's letter to Aunt Bet for safekeeping.

At breakfast Uncle Ed was grey-faced and grim.

None of the men had been to bed the night before.

"Six palominos are missing and two are wire-cut," the rancher reported.

Tex snorted, "The meadow fence was wrecked! Some no-good varmint cut it in at least thirty places. We've been workin' on repairs all night. Dave is still out there finishin'."

Uncle Ed announced that he was driving into Tumbleweed to inform the sheriff of what had happened. "Maybe he can spare me a man or I could get some volunteers to help me round up the horses. We'll have to go up in the mountain and look for them. I'll also have the telephone company send a man to mend the wire."

"What about water?" Mrs Thurmond asked.

The rancher replied that the pump and the lights, too, would be working in a couple of hours. "The generator was damaged," he said, "but not seriously."

"The big mischief was the attack on the horses," Nancy remarked. "Whoever planned that wanted to be sure things would be dark and confused and you could not get help in a hurry."

The rancher quickly finished eating and was rising to go when Dave came in. The cowboy asked if he could see the Rawleys alone for a few minutes, and added, "You come, too, Nancy."

Uncle Ed led the way into the living room and closed the door. "Now what is it?" he asked.

Swiftly Dave told the couple about his search for the bandit's fortune. "If I do find the treasure," he added earnestly, "I certainly intend to turn over a share to you bo'h."

Mr Rawley smiled. "Thank you, Dave. But we wouldn't hear of it. I wish you luck."

Aunt Bet now told the men about Nancy's discovery of Valentine's letter.

Nancy pointed out that surely the treasure was linked to the trouble on the ranch. "Until it's found, I'm afraid the phantom horse will continue to appear."

Uncle Ed agreed. "You're a remarkable detective, young lady. Keep up the good work!"

Dave said that with Nancy on the case he thought they had a good chance of finding the treasure. "But I won't be able to do much today. We have those palominos to look for."

Nancy admitted that she did not know exactly where to search next for the hidden treasure.

Aunt Bet patted her shoulder. "You need a holiday from all this trouble. Why don't you girls drive into Phoenix for some fun?"

"That's a wonderful idea!" Nancy said.

As she had thought, her friends were delighted at the prospect. Nancy hurried to get the estate car. When she pulled up in front of the veranda, George was waiting with two vacuum flasks and a jug of water.

As she put them into the back of the car, Dave came hurrying past. He grinned. "I'm glad to see that you tenderfoot gals have turned into water-conscious Westerners."

Alice and Bess were approaching the car and heard him. When he was out of earshot, Alice said, "As for you, Nancy, he's really flipped!"

"And what'll poor Ned do?" George teased.

Nancy grinned. "We'll be home by the time he gets back from Europe."

"Just wait until the square dance tomorrow night," said Bess. "I'll bet Dave's a marvellous dancer."

"I wish," said Alice, "that there was somebody to take me."

There was a gleam in Bess's eye as she said, "Don't give up hope, Alice. You might meet somebody at the rodeo or barbecue."

George looked at her cousin quizzically and Nancy smiled. Both knew Bess loved playing the role of matchmaker!

"What have you got up your sleeve?" George demanded.

"Just my arm," replied Bess, but she grinned.

Nancy spoke up. "Let's do some shopping in Phoenix. I'd like to find something special to wear tomorrow."

"I know," exclaimed Bess. "Let's all buy Indian costumes!"

When they reached the city, George directed Nancy to a shop which sold a variety of Indian apparel and souvenirs. The sight of the colourful squaw dresses drove all thoughts of the ranch trouble from the girls' minds. Happily they tried them on and helped one another make selections. Alice was delighted and pirouetted in front of the long mirror to watch the wide skirts swing out.

Finally Nancy chose a turquoise-blue model with silver rickrack trimming. George's choice was a bold red which set off her short dark hair, and Bess selected one with a yellow skirt and black bodice. Alice picked out a pumpkin-coloured costume trimmed in black.

With their purchases in boxes the girls strolled down the street to a Spanish restaurant. Here they ate a delicious lunch of *tacos* and spicy chilli. For dessert they had iced fresh fruit.

Bess sighed. "Umm, that was super."

Afterwards, they walked to a wide street beside a park where an outdoor painting exhibition was being held. The group stopped now and then to admire and compliment the artists who sat beside their work.

As the other girls lingered over a painting, Nancy wandered ahead, then stopped before a lone picture. After a casual glance she suddenly realized that it was a pastel drawing of the old hotel in the ghost town on Shadow Mountain. Quickly she called her friends.

"That's the same hotel, all right," George declared. "The one where we hitched our horses and found that crushed crayon."

Alice was pale. "My father did that pastel! I know it!"

The artist's chair beside the picture was vacant.

"I must find him!" Alice cried out.

·14·

The Nettle Trick

NEAR the empty artist's chair a man sat sketching. Nancy walked towards him. "Pardon me, but do you know where the person is who drew that pastel?"

The man looked up from his work and pointed with his pencil. "There's the one."

Nancy turned and saw a stout woman in a blue dress coming towards them. "Want to buy that pastel, girls? It's the last one. The rest sold like hot cakes."

Alice's face showed keen disappointment. "This isn't your work."

The woman chuckled and sat down heavily. "That's right, dearie. I can't even draw a cow. I'm a dealer. I buy from the artists and sell their work."

"Where is the man who did this picture?" Nancy pressed.

"That I don't know. He told me he was a stranger— just visiting Phoenix. Seemed kind of close-mouthed— didn't say where he came from or where he was staying."

Alice asked, "Was he a slender grey-haired man?"

"Yes. Said his name was Bursey. Do you know him?"

"We think so," Nancy replied.

Alice looked longingly at the picture. "How much is it?" she asked the woman. When Alice heard the price, her face clouded. "I haven't enough money to buy it."

Exchanging quick glances, the other girls reached an agreement. "That's all right, Alice," said Nancy. "We'll make up the difference."

When the picture was paid for, Alice took it gratefully. She thanked the girls as they walked away from the dealer, then added, "Oh, Nancy, you've been so wonderful to me!"

Alice's eyes were misty with emotion. "I feel that we must be getting closer to my father." She thought that he might have returned to the mountain cabin and begged Nancy to go back there with her.

"I wish I could," said Nancy, "but it would be too late to make the trip today after we reach the ranch. Tell you what, though. I'll take you in the morning."

George had another idea. "There's just a chance our Uncle Ross Regor might be around this exhibition somewhere. He might have come to see how his pictures are selling."

The others agreed that George had a point. And for a while the four girls strolled through the park, keeping their eyes open for the slender grey-haired man. They did not see him.

Near mid-afternoon Nancy treated everyone to cool lemonades from a passing vendor and they sat on a bench to drink them. Bess glanced at her watch and suggested they start for home. George drove.

They crossed the desert without trouble and arrived at the ranch in time for supper. At the table they learned that the telephone, lights, and water had been restored, but four of the palominos were still missing.

"The critters are up on Shadow Mountain somewhere," Bud remarked gloomily as he passed the biscuits to Nancy. "We have our work cut out to track 'em."

"And we might as well face it," said Uncle Ed, "they might be badly hurt."

To lighten the conversation, Aunt Bet reminded everyone of the barbecue next day. "It's customary for us ranch folks to take a dessert. Any suggestions?"

Tex grinned. "I sure do cotton to chocolate cake."

"Nancy makes scrumptious ones," said Bess.

"Then I guess she's elected," Mrs Rawley said with a smile.

Nancy laughed. "Thank you for the job, my friends! Now, who's going to help?"

"I will!" chorused Dave, Tex, and Bud.

"Good," said Nancy. "You boys can shell the walnuts for topping the icing—that is, if you have any, Mrs Thurmond."

"We have plenty of everything," the cook declared. "Just step right up and take hold!"

"We'll all help," Bess said happily. "Let's make it an extra big cake."

After supper the girls dried the dishes for Mrs Thurmond. Then Nancy put all the cake ingredients on the big kitchen table. The cook gave her several large bowls.

Tex grinned as he picked up a nutcracker. "Boys, we hired out to punch cows and here we are peelin' nuts!"

While Nancy and her assistants worked, they talked

about the phantom. Mrs Thurmond listened intently.

"Where do you think the ghost horse is kept?" Alice asked.

"Folks say Valentine had a hideout on Shadow Mountain," Mrs Thurmond spoke up, "and I figure that's where the critter stays now—same as it did in life."

The girls tried to convince the cook that the apparition was a mere trick, but they could not do it.

Nancy changed the subject. "If Valentine did have a hideout in this area, very likely he kept his horse in a corral there. It's possible that the people who are attacking the ranch have discovered the place and are using it for their trick horse."

Mrs Thurmond shook her head gloomily. "If it was real folks doin' the damage, I'd face right up to 'em," she declared. "But I've seen that spook with my own eyes. I tell you it's too much for my nerves!"

By the time the baking was finished, Mrs Thurmond had excused herself and gone to bed.

"Now for the icing," said Nancy.

When the cake was cool enough, she covered it with thick creamy swirls of dark chocolate and studded the top with whole walnuts.

Bess sighed. "It's too bad we can't have just a teeny piece now, isn't it?"

"I sure could go for a slab," Tex agreed hungrily.

"Come on, cookie," Dave coaxed Nancy.

"Think how good that would taste to us poor riders out on the midnight watch," Bud said in his soft drawl. "Saddlesore, weary—"

"You're breaking our hearts," George said cheerfully.

"Plain biscuits and milk tonight," Nancy announced

"Hang on, Nancy!" Tex shouted

with a chuckle. "You'll get your cake tomorrow."

In the morning Alice could hardly contain her excitement over the trip to the cabin. Not wanting their destination known, Nancy had warned Alice to say nothing of her hopes at the breakfast table. When Aunt Bet asked the girls about their plans, Nancy said, "Alice and I would like to go for a ride in the mountains."

George had letters to write and Bess said she wanted to wash and set her hair.

"I'll saddle up for you," Shorty volunteered. Nancy was surprised at his friendly gesture. She and Alice thanked him, then hurried to change into riding clothes.

When they were dressed and waiting on the veranda, Tex walked up, leading Nancy's bay. Just behind him came Shorty with a sorrel for Alice. Nancy stepped into the yard and mounted easily. With a shrill whinny, the horse reared.

"Hang on!" Tex shouted.

Nancy gripped the pommel tight and hung on to the reins. The horse pitched high and landed stiff-legged on all fours!

Tex seized the bridle and held the bay down, giving Nancy time to fling herself from the saddle.

"Hey, boy! Easy now!" Tex said as he tried to calm the excited animal.

"Nancy, are you hurt?" Alice asked worriedly.

"I'm all right," Nancy replied breathlessly. "But what's the matter with the horse?"

Shorty had hurried to Tex's assistance, and now the snorting steed was standing still. The red-haired cowboy's eyes narrowed with suspicion as he loosened the saddle girth and reached up under the blanket.

"I thought so!" He brought out his hand and held it open for the others to see. In his palm lay a nettle.

Shorty's eyes grew wide. "Well, what do you know about that!" he drawled.

Tex looked at him levelly. "What do *you* know about this?"

"Me!" exclaimed Shorty. "Some mean coyote pulled that trick, not me!"

"You saddled the animals," Tex retorted and turned to Nancy. "I was passin' the stable when Shorty came out with these mounts. He asked me to bring this one over to you."

"Now hold on thar a minute," Shorty put in. "When I went to the stable after breakfast I found this bay already saddled. I throwed the saddle on the other one and brung 'em out. That's all I know about it. You got no call to accuse me. No sir! Not me!"

Tex's face flushed with anger. "*If* you're tellin' the truth, Shorty Steele, I apologize."

Before the stocky cowboy could answer, Nancy suggested that Tex check Alice's saddle blanket. He did and reported that it was all right. The girls mounted and rode towards the meadow.

"I don't believe Shorty was telling the truth," said Alice.

Nancy said nothing, but she was inclined to agree. Aloud she said, "Someone has not given up trying to get me out of the picture."

When they finally sighted the cabin, Nancy reined up behind the clump of big boulders. She swung from the saddle and hitched her horse to a rock, but was not so quick as Alice. The younger girl dashed to the cabin and knocked on the door. As Nancy ran up, it was opened by a slender grey-haired man.

With a shock Nancy recognized him. He was the one who had put the snake's rattle into her knitting bag and dropped the warning note into the car!

·15·

A Perilous Ride

ALICE was on the verge of tears. The man in the cabin doorway was not her father!

He scowled at the two girls. "What do you want?"

Nancy was sure the man must have recognized her, but he gave no sign of it, so she pretended not to know him. Quickly she thought of an excuse for coming. "Are you Mr Bursey?" she asked.

"Yes. Why?"

"We'd like to buy one of your pastels," Nancy replied.

"My what?"

"Pastels—your pictures," Nancy said.

"Oh," The man paused. "I haven't any more. How did you know I was here?"

Nancy explained casually that Mary Deer had told them the artist lived on the mountain. "Several days ago we happened to see this cabin and we thought perhaps it might be where you live."

He gave Nancy a long, hard look. "My paintings are all gone," he said. "No use coming back."

Nancy apologized for bothering him, and as the girls turned to walk back to their horses, he closed the door.

Alice was deeply upset. "I just can't believe that man drew those pictures."

"I'm sure he didn't," Nancy replied as the girls

mounted. "He's no artist. He didn't know what I meant by pastels and he called the pictures paintings. He should have known they're drawings made with special crayons."

She told Alice how she, Bess, and George had encountered the man before.

Alice was excited. "Maybe he's holding my father prisoner somewhere!"

Nancy agreed that was possible. But where? she wondered. There had been no one else in the one-room cabin. Recalling how Chief had appeared mysteriously from behind it, Nancy surmised there was a hiding place nearby.

"What shall we do, Nancy?" Alice asked.

"Report to the sheriff as fast as we can."

Nancy added that if Alice's father was a prisoner of Bursey, the grey-haired man and his pals might very well be the Chicago bank robbers. "And since Bursey is also mixed up with the ranch trouble, his gang is probably responsible for the phantom horse."

As the girls rode down the trail, Nancy's thoughts dwelt uneasily on the man who said his name was Bursey. Could he possibly believe that she had not known him? "I'm afraid my trumped-up story didn't fool him," she decided. "He must know I'll report him to Sheriff Curtis. But why didn't he try to stop me?"

The answer was plain. The man believed that people knew the girls' destination. "He doesn't want us to disappear at his cabin," Nancy told herself, "so he'll arrange an 'accident' for us on the way down the mountain."

She turned in her saddle and warned Alice to keep

alert for signs of pursuit. A little farther along they came to a fork in the trail.

"Let's follow this other path," Nancy suggested.

They soon found the new route a hazardous one, however, and were forced to slow down. The horses were picking their footing on the narrow trail which wound back and forth across a sheer cliff.

Alice glanced up. "Uncle Ed says that Westerners call this kind of path an 'eyebrow trail'. I can see why."

A few minutes later the girls rode under a rock overhang, which prevented them from seeing the turn of the path above them. Suddenly pebbles and dust started falling from above. Someone was following them!

Nancy signalled to Alice, who nodded her understanding. The riders sat in tense silence as their horses slowly proceeded to the bottom of the cliff, where the trail became less steep. But it was narrow and precarious. The girls urged their horses to go as fast as they dared. Soon they heard the clatter of a horse's hoofs behind them.

Nancy knew they had no defence against the surprise attack she feared was coming. It would take only a few boulders rolling from above to scare the horses and cause the "accident".

Nancy looked ahead for shelter. Some distance below, the trail disappeared among high rocks. "If we can reach that spot before our enemy strikes," she thought, "we may have a chance!"

Again the girls urged their mounts on and rode desperately towards the screen of rocks. Jolting hard, Alice clung to the saddle horn all the way.

"We made it!" she gasped as they rounded a curve

and were hidden between huge boulders which lay on either side.

Swiftly Nancy dismounted, signalling her companion to do the same. The younger girl followed as Nancy led her horse into a cluster of the giant rocks. Alice held her mount firmly and kept one hand soothingly upon his nose. If only the animals would stand quietly! One jangle of the bridle, or a hoof scuffing a stone, and their hiding place would be revealed!

Hardly breathing, the girls heard the clatter of stones as their pursuer approached. The sounds came closer, then suddenly stopped.

"He sees we're not on the trail ahead," Nancy thought. Would the rider guess that they had rounded the next curve but were hiding? For a long moment there was silence from the other side of the boulders.

"He's listening!" Nancy thought.

The girls stood frozen. Then came the creak of a saddle and the sound of hoofs as the rider moved on.

Nancy and Alice gave sighs of relief, and, after waiting a few minutes, led their horses out of the boulders. Quickly the two remounted.

Alice said fearfully, "When he reaches open mountainside again, he'll see that he has missed us and come back. We'll meet him head-on!"

"I know," Nancy replied. "We must look for another branching trail."

Presently she spotted a side path among the boulders and the girls guided their horses on to it. The way downwards was narrow and rough, but the two riders were sheltered first by rocks, then by tall fir and tamarack trees. They reached the valley a mile from where the other trail came down.

"We made it safely!" Alice cried in relief. "Oh, Nancy, how can I ever thank you?"

Her companion smiled. "Don't think I wasn't scared myself!"

It was noon when the girls dismounted at the stable. They hurried to the living room where they found the Rawleys chatting with Bess and George.

While Alice excitedly reported all that had happened to them, Nancy telephoned the sheriff. She told him her suspicions of the man calling himself Bursey, and also the possibility that Ross Regor, Alice's father, was being held prisoner on the mountain by the same gang responsible for the phantom-horse trick.

Sheriff Curtis said, "I'll go up to the cabin at once with two men and arrest this hombre Bursey and his confederates."

Nancy hastened back to the living room and reported the conversation.

"That's great!" exclaimed George. "If the sheriff catches the bank robbers, it will mean the end of the damage on the ranch."

"But they must have another hideout, where they keep Uncle Ross," Bess objected, "and we don't know where that is. Besides, the sheriff may find only Bursey."

"But if he talks, we'll get to the bottom of the mystery," Nancy reminded her.

Suddenly the door to the veranda burst open and Dave came in. "Mr Rawley, we found the missing horses!"

Amid the girls' exclamation of joy, the rancher beamed and asked. "Where are they?"

"Tex, Bud, and I put them in the meadow. We found them up on Shadow Mountain, grazing by a creek."

Dave hesitated. "The only thing is, they're hurt."

Mr Rawley's jaw tightened. "Bad?"

"Three of 'em are wire-cut and one mare is limping. We'd better call the vet."

The rancher agreed and Dave hurried to the telephone. "Could be worse," Uncle Ed said. "Maybe everything will be all right—provided there's no more damage."

Aunt Bet smiled cheerfully. "Nothing more is likely to happen. After all, the sheriff is on his way to round up the gang—thanks to Nancy."

In a happy frame of mind, the girls hurried away to dress in their squaw outfits before lunch. While she had a shower, Nancy's thoughts were on the treasure. Where could the outlaw have hidden it? Still puzzling, Nancy slipped into her blue costume. She brushed her titian hair until it gleamed, then put on a pair of small silver earrings and added a touch of lipstick.

The other girls were not ready yet, so Nancy went into the living room to wait for them. As she seated herself in one of the rocking chairs, her glance fell on the fireplace. Once again, the Indian grinding stone caught her attention. She recalled what Aunt Bet had told her about it and about the other stones. Suddenly her eyes lit up with an idea and she jumped forward in excitement.

"Bess! George! Alice!" she called, running to the door.

"What is it?" asked George as the three girls came hurrying down the hall.

Nancy's eyes sparkled with excitement. "I think I know where the treasure is!"

·16·

The Sheriff's Quarry

A BURST of excited questions met Nancy's announcement. She chuckled and George said, "Quiet, everybody. Now tell us where the treasure is."

Nancy led her friends into the living room, shut the door, and announced, "In the cliff houses down the valley."

"They're certainly the oldest dwellings around here," said George. "But they are not on the ranch."

"They were when Valentine wrote his letter."

"Nancy, how do you know?" Alice asked.

"Because Aunt Bet told us that every stone in this fireplace came from somewhere on the ranch. It stands to reason that the Indian grinding stone came from the cliff dwelling." She reminded the girls that Sheriff Humber had been obliged to sell that part of his property after Valentine's death. "It's natural that he would get rid of the outlying section first."

"Nancy," declared George, "that's a great piece of deduction."

Just then the triangle clanged for luncheon. As the girls hurried to the kitchen, Nancy requested them to keep her theory a secret.

"We won't be able to check it before tomorrow, and we don't want anybody else to get there before us."

As the group hurried into the kitchen, they stared in amazement. Mrs Thurmond, ladelling out stew at the stove, was wearing her big white apron as usual, and on her head was perched a black straw hat bedecked with artificial roses. Instead of being amused, the cowboys stood about looking uncomfortable and Aunt Bet's face was strained.

"I'm leavin'!" announced the cook, without turning from her work. "I've fixed my last dinner in this place. As soon as it's over, I'm ridin' into Tumbleweed with you young folks and takin' the three-o'clock bus for Phoenix."

Mr Rawley said soothingly, "Things have been pretty rough around here, Mrs Thurmond. But we think they'll be getting better pretty soon."

Mrs Thurmond faced the rancher squarely. "Mr Rawley, I can take rough times with the best of 'em, but phantom horses—that's too much for me." She picked up the big bowl of stew and walked towards the table.

Aunt Bet followed her, pleading. "Mrs Thurmond, please reconsider."

"Nope!" said the woman, and set the bowl down with a thump.

Nancy knew that the loss of the cook would be an added hardship for Aunt Bet, who not only had ranch-house duties, but was needed to help her husband.

This new crisis threw a pall over the meal. At the appearance of a magnificent lemon meringue pie, the gloom became even deeper, for it seemed likely to be the last time any of the diners would taste Mrs Thurmond's fine baking.

When the dessert was gone, the men pushed back their chairs and rose. Immediately the cook asked Dave what time he would be driving the car to Tumbleweed.

Before he could answer, Nancy spoke up. "Not for half an hour yet, are you, Dave?"

He caught the urgent message in her eyes and nodded. "I'll honk the horn when I'm ready to go," he promised.

As soon as the men had left the kitchen, the girls and Aunt Bet gathered round Mrs Thurmond and pleaded with her to remain. The little woman shook her head regretfully, but steadfastly refused. "That phantom has me scared out o' my skin," she declared.

"If I could prove to you that the phantom is a real horse, Mrs Thurmond," Nancy asked, "would you stay?"

" 'Course I would! I'm not afraid of a live critter."

"Then just let me have a little time. I feel sure I'll be able to show you how the trick is done."

The others chimed in, cajoling the cook to give Nancy a chance. Bess added, "I don't know how we'll get along without you and all those wonderful pies."

Mrs Thurmond considered a moment. "All right. One more night." At their delighted thanks she flushed with pleasure and marched off to remove her hat. When she returned, the girls and Aunt Bet helped her clear the table. Before long, the horn of the car sounded and Nancy left with her friends.

Dave, Tex, and Bud were in the yard talking to Uncle Ed. Bud was holding a guitar in a case. A short distance away Shorty lounged against the horse trailer, which had been hitched to the back of the estate car.

As the girls came up, they heard Uncle Ed say, "You go ahead, boys, and have a good time. You've earned a holiday."

"You might need help with those palominos when the vet comes," said Dave. He glanced uneasily at Nancy and she understood at once how he felt.

"I'll be glad to excuse you, Dave, if you feel you ought to stay," she said.

"No, that's not necessary," Ed Rawley said.

As Dave thanked him, Nancy noticed Tex talking quietly to Alice. Flushed with excitement, she smiled happily and hurried to Nancy's side. "Tex's brother Jack is going to be in the rodeo and Tex says Jack would like to take me to the barbecue and dance. He's fifteen—Jack, I mean. Is it all right, Uncle Ed?" she asked, blushing.

The rancher nodded and chuckled. "I've met the young man. Go ahead."

As Alice went back to tell Tex, Nancy and George looked knowingly at Bess, who dimpled.

"Now how did you fix that, Miss Cupid?" her cousin asked.

"It was easy," Bess replied. "I remembered Tex had mentioned his brother was coming into Tumbleweed for the rodeo."

"Come on!" called Tex. "Let's roll!" The others hastened to the car.

Bud, carrying his guitar, climbed into the back of the car, and Shorty joined him. Tex, George, and Bess sat in the middle, while Nancy and Alice took seats next to Dave, who was at the wheel.

"I've never been to a rodeo," Alice said as they started out. "What's it like?"

Tex grinned. "Well, Dave here is going to flip some fancy loops and so's Bud."

"He means they're going to rope cows," said Bess.

"Steers," Tex corrected.

Bess asked Tex what he was going to do. "Dog a steer," was his reply.

Dave chuckled at Alice's puzzled look. "He'll ride his horse alongside a running steer and leap aboard."

"Then he'll bite the dust," Bud teased.

"Not Tex!" Dave rejoined. "He's a real salty bulldogger!"

"And Shorty there is a broncobuster," Tex added.

"And I'm fixin' to win, too," Shorty declared. "Wouldn't be the first time." He went on to brag about several occasions when he had won prizes in rodeos.

While he talked, Nancy was quiet, thinking hard about the phantom horse. "Oh, how I wish Chief could talk!" she said to herself. "He's been closer to it than anyone." She wondered again why the dog had been held prisoner.

Suddenly Nancy thought of the light she had seen in the spring house shortly before the ghost horse had appeared. With a thrill of excitement, Nancy suddenly hit on how the trick could have been done! It was all she could do to keep from exclaiming aloud. She decided to say nothing to the other girls until she had an opportunity to prove her theory. "And I can't do that until after dark," she thought.

When they reached Tumbleweed, Dave drove slowly through the streets crowded with visitors. Many of the men had on fringed buckskin jackets and some of the women wore long pioneer dresses with sunbonnets. Others wore graceful squaw dresses.

Suddenly Nancy spotted a drably dressed grey-haired man standing in the doorway of a store—the man who called himself Bursey! At that moment his eyes met hers and he darted away into the crowd.

Nancy's heart sank. The sheriff, who was on his way to or from the cabin, had missed his quarry!

Nancy wondered what to do—get word to the authorities? Dave interrupted her thoughts by saying that the rodeo would not start for an hour. "We have to go and check in," he said. "What do you girls want to do in the meantime?"

"Oh, we'll keep busy," Nancy replied.

When the cowboys had left, she suggested that Bess take Alice and hunt for Bursey. She and George would go in another direction. "Let's meet at Mary Deer's shop."

They all arrived half an hour later. There had been no trace of the man. "He probably left town in a hurry," George declared.

The store was crowded and Mary Deer had an assistant working behind the counter. While the other girls looked at jewellery, Nancy beckoned her Indian friend aside and asked if she would keep a secret. When Mary promised, Nancy told her that she hoped to find the treasure in the cliff dwellings, and inquired the best way to get to them.

"There are stairs up the front," said Mary, "but they are not safe. You had best come down from above."

She explained that at the far end of the cliff apartments there was a huge slab of rock which had been used as a lookout point by the ancient Indians. Stairs led from the rock down to the top row of dwellings. Nancy thanked Mary and promised to let her know if she discovered anything.

By this time the other girls had bought Indian

jewellery, and after Nancy had purchased a turquoise pillbox hat for Hannah, they left the shop. The foursome followed the arrows to the far end of town where they found the rodeo arena, a short distance from the stockyard. Nancy bought tickets at the front gate, and they all found seats in the stands.

Bess sighed. "I'm so hot, I'd like to have a cold drink and I think I need a hot dog to go with it."

George grinned. "Eating is really a very fattening hobby, dear cousin."

Before Bess could retort, a voice came from the loudspeaker. "Telephone call for Miss Nancy Drew in the booth next to the refreshment stand."

The girls looked at one another in amazement. Afraid that something had gone wrong at the ranch, Nancy excused herself and hurried off. She made her way through the crowd to the first telephone booth beside the hot-dog stand. As she reached it, the door opened and Bursey stepped out with a grin. At the same moment a tall figure in black glided to her side—Mr Diamond!

Bursey's strong fingers closed on Nancy's wrist. "You're coming with us!" he growled. "And don't yell or you'll be sorry!"

·17·

An Interrupted Programme

BEFORE Nancy could say anything to the two men, Bess's voice rang out. "She is *not* going with you!"

"Let her go!" George ordered.

As Bursey whirled in surprise, Nancy jerked her wrist from his grasp. Diamond's startled look changed to a scowl and the two ran away fast, disappearing under the grandstand.

"Girls, you were wonderful!" Nancy exclaimed, recovering from her shock. "But those men must be caught!"

The three friends dashed after the fugitives, all the while looking for a deputy but seeing none. Finally they gave up the chase—the two men had vanished.

"I'll go to the sheriff's office and report this," Nancy said.

"Not alone!" George declared. "We're sticking close to you for the rest of the afternoon. It's a good thing I let Bess talk me into coming down for a hot dog."

Bess thought she had better go back to Alice, who was holding their seats in the grandstand. George accompanied Nancy to Sheriff Curtis' office, where the young sleuth left a note for the absent lawman about the kidnapping attempt.

When they returned to the rodeo arena, they heard a burst of cheering. "Dave just won the roping contest!" cried Alice as Nancy and George took their seats. The delighted girls clapped loudly.

"Bud was good too," Bess put in loyally, as Dave walked to the judges' stand. Modestly he accepted the first prize, a pair of silver spurs, and left the arena to another burst of applause.

Next came the broncobusters. The girls watched, thrilled, as one after another of the contestants hurtled into the arena on the bucking horses.

Shorty came last. Shrill whistles filled the air as he tried to stick in the saddle for the required number of minutes.

"Look at 'im sunfish!" came a shout from the stands as the frantic horse pitched high into the air, his back arched.

Suddenly a shot rang out from the judges' stand. "Time's up! Shorty won!" George exclaimed.

The stands erupted into cheers. At the same time, the bronc shook his rider loose. The winner rolled over in the dust, picked himself up, retrieved his hat and waved it at the spectators. As the bronc was taken out of the arena by attendants, Shorty strode to the judges' stand. He claimed his prize, a silver buckle, and held it up for all to see. Then he swaggered out of the arena.

After the rodeo the girls met their dates outside the front gate. Tex introduced his brother Jack, a tall freckle-faced boy, whose friendly manner immediately put Alice at ease. Quickly Nancy warned the boys about Bursey and Diamond.

Dave looked worried and Jack spoke up. "I don't know what this is all about, but no one will get Alice away from me until I turn her over to Nancy after the dance!"

Nancy and Dave led the way to the car. "Shorty said he'd come along later," he remarked.

On the drive to the barbecue grounds, Nancy quietly told him her deduction about the treasure. Dave was excited and said he hoped she was right.

About a mile beyond Tumbleweed he parked in a grove of willow trees beside a narrow stream. The grounds were set with many long wooden tables and benches, and overhead were strings of small electric lights.

"Come on, gals," said Tex. "We're goin' to put on a big feed!" He led them towards a long serving table. Four men passed by, each carrying a shovel bearing a big canvas-wrapped parcel. These were dumped on to the table.

"There goes the meat," said Bud. "It's been buried in the barbecue pit since last night."

"Cookin' nice an' slow over hot stones," Tex added.

"When the canvas fell away, the fragrance of the steaming meat was irresistible. All the girls enjoyed generous servings, with a spicy sauce and potato salad.

By the time they had finished their desserts of ice cream and Nancy's chocolate cake, the coloured lights overhead came on. A stout middle-aged man mounted the dance platform in the centre of the grove and announced that he was master of ceremonies. Seeing Bud's guitar, he called on him for some cowboy songs.

Bud played "I'm a Lonesome Cowboy", and everyone joined in enthusiastically. He followed with a number of other old favourites. Finally he strummed some Gold Rush songs, including "Sweet Betsy from Pike".

The cheers and applause had not yet died down when Shorty stepped on to the platform. Ignoring the master of ceremonies, he leaned towards the microphone and said, "Folks, how'd you like me to do my imitations?"

At the scattered handclapping and whistles, the stout man nodded and stepped back. Shorty cupped his hands around his mouth, closed his eyes, and the long mournful hoot of an owl filled the night.

"He's really good," Bess whispered.

"I'll bet he can also do a whining dog," Nancy said meaningfully.

Next, the cowboy announced a coyote and produced several realistic howls. Suddenly in mid-howl he spotted Nancy in the audience. His jaw dropped and he stood silent before the microphone. Staring at her, he stammered that his act was over and left the platform. The girls exchanged baffled glances.

Dave grinned. "That was one surprised coyote, all right! He thought his pals had got rid of you, Nancy."

Just then a band of three musicians began tuning up and a square-dancing contest was announced. Alice suggested that the four couples enter as a set, and the others agreed enthusiastically.

Of the four groups in the contest, Nancy's was called first. The young people lined up on the platform, facing each other in couples. At the sound of the lively music they began to dance. The fiddle player called the steps and played his tunes fast.

"Swing your partners and a do-si-do!"

Whirling past the edge of the platform, Nancy glimpsed Shorty glowering at her.

When the breathless dancers returned to their table, Nancy told the others of the incident. "It's going to be hard to shake Shorty from now on. I'm afraid he and his pals will watch us so closely we'll have no chance to go after the treasure."

While the other sets of dancers competed, Nancy pondered on how to make sure the girls were not followed to the cliff houses.

At the end of the contest, the crowd voted by applause and the Shadow Ranch group won easily. Nancy was sent to the platform to claim the prize.

The master of ceremonies handed her a pink slip of paper. "You take this to the food table over yonder, young lady, and they will give you and your friends a big ice-cold watermelon!"

Nancy thanked the man, then turned to the audience and said, "I would like to make an announcement that I believe will interest everybody in this area. My friends and I think we know where the famous long-lost Valentine treasure is hidden."

An excited rustle ran through the crowd and cries of "Where?"

Nancy smiled. "I won't say anything more about it now, but tomorrow a few Shadow Ranch men are going out to do some digging."

As Nancy hurried from the platform, she saw Sheriff Curtis making his way towards her. He spoke of his futile search on the mountain and his regret that the desperadoes were still at large. "I'm sure glad you outwitted 'em this afternoon. Watch your step."

Then he joined the young people at their table.

George asked Nancy, "What was the meaning of that announcement you made?"

In a low voice the young detective said, "Everybody look happy—not as if we're talking about anything important—and I'll explain."

Dave obligingly gave a broad grin. "I'll collect our prize."

He soon returned and began cutting and serving the watermelon. Meanwhile, the others listened, smiling and laughing as Nancy told them that the Shadow Ranch cowboys were to act as decoys while the girls went to the cliff dwellings to search for the treasure.

"Shorty will no doubt alert Bursey and Diamond and they'll be keeping an eye on the ranch."

Sheriff Curtis praised Nancy for her plan and said he would follow the decoy group. "I'll nab the varmints when they move against the cowboys."

His blue eyes were sober as he said, "I can see you're a capable gal, Miss Drew, but you've got to be extra careful from now on, 'cause those thievin' hombres'll want to keep all o' you tenderfeet quiet."

"We'll stay close to the girls," Dave promised, and the cowboys permitted no one to cut in during the dancing that followed.

When the party was over, Jack said good night to Alice at the ranch wagon and promised to telephone her soon. As Nancy and her friends climbed into the car, Shorty came hurrying up to join them.

Dave drove to the corrals behind the arena where Tex and Bud coupled up the horse trailer. Shorty got out, too, and walked into a phone booth at the edge of the parking area. He did not stay long.

"I'll bet he called Diamond and Bursey to tell them what I said," Nancy declared.

As Dave started the drive home, Shorty questioned Nancy about her announcement. She laughed and replied that he would see later what she meant. Before he could ask any more questions, Bud struck a chord on his guitar and started a cowboy song. Shorty gave up talking and sat sullenly while the others sang all during the ride.

Although she joined in the songs, Nancy's thoughts dwelled on the plan she had made for proving to Mrs Thurmond that the phantom horse was a trick. She was pleased to note that the moon had gone behind heavy clouds and the night was very dark.

When they reached the ranch, the cowboys hurried off to relieve Ed Rawley and the foreman who had done guard duty during their absence. The girls went to the house where they found Mrs Rawley in the lighted living room. Chief lay by the fireplace.

"I felt safer with him in here," Aunt Bet explained.

Nancy asked the others to accompany her to the kitchen. There they found Mrs Thurmond seated at the big table reading a magazine.

"I believe I can show you now how the phantom was made to appear," Nancy said.

The cook looked sceptical, then exclaimed nervously as Nancy turned out the lights. With a mysterious smile, she slipped outside and hurried down the veranda. Soon she returned. "All set? Look through the screen door."

Her friends complied and stared into the darkness. Suddenly Mrs Thurmond gave a scream and Mrs Rawley gasped. Bobbing towards them, about three feet above the veranda, were tiny glowing specks!

"Oh!" moaned the cook. "Phantom spots! Take 'em away!"

Nancy opened the door and the shining specks floated into the room!

·18·

The Black Phantom

As the watchers stared amazed, the glowing specks stopped moving and hung in the darkness.

"Oh!" Mrs Thurmond quavered. "They shine just like the ghost horse!"

Nancy switched on the light. Before them stood Chief, a large rubber ball clutched in his jaws.

Smiling at the flabbergasted onlookers, Nancy said, "Do you see how the phantom trick was worked?"

"I do," George said promptly. "Phosphorescent paint on the dog's teeth."

"Where are the specks now?" Mrs Thurmond asked as Chief dropped the ball.

"They don't show when the lights are on. At the time Chief disappeared—after he chased the phantom horse—the spots were on his teeth," Nancy explained. "I thought perhaps he had bitten the ghost, but when I examined him in daylight, of course I found no evidence."

"The gang must have washed him," remarked Bess.

"But they never thought of his teeth," Nancy said, "and fragments of the paint remained."

"How did you get on to the idea?" Aunt Bet asked.

Nancy reminded the others of her suspicion that Chief had been muzzled and taken away because the gang feared there was a clue to the apparition on him.

"I learned in chemistry class that phosphorescent paint glows in the dark after it first has been exposed to light," she went on. "I remembered that each time I'd seen the phantom horse there had been a light in the spring house just before. I put two and two together and decided that the apparition was a real horse. He was covered with a soft thin material which had been coated with phosphorescent paint and exposed to light in the spring house by one of the gang members."

Mrs Thurmond drew a deep breath and turned to Nancy. "You're a downright marvel, that's what you are, young lady!"

Nancy blushed. "You'll stay now, won't you?" And the others all added their pleas.

" 'Course I will," Mrs Thurmond declared stoutly. "You just show me the varmint that's been doing this no-good trick and I'll give him a piece o' my mind!"

Before going to bed, Nancy told Aunt Bet and Uncle Ed of her plan for the following day. The rancher assured her he would co-operate. At breakfast the girls talked lightheartedly of their all-day horseback ride.

"Where you gals fixin' to go?" Shorty asked.

"We'll start up Shadow Mountain," Nancy replied vaguely. "After that, we'll see."

Mr Rawley broke in to appoint Tex and Bud as his helpers on the "treasure" expedition.

When the meal was over, Nancy took Dave aside and told him that if she and the other girls found Valentine's hoard, they would light a fire on the lookout rock.

"Good," he replied. "Then I'll drive down the valley in the truck and climb up to the cliff houses by the front steps to help you bring the treasure back to the ranch."

Half an hour later Uncle Ed, Tex, and Bud saddled up for their trip. Shorty hung around, eager to help as two pack horses were led out. One was loaded with digging tools and other supplies.

"What's the second animal for?" asked Sanders, who had been told the secret.

The ranch owner grinned. "For the treasure."

The trio headed down the valley away from Tumbleweed. Shorty watched them for a minute, then hurried into the woods behind the ranch house. Strolling towards the stable, Nancy suspected that Bursey and Diamond were hiding among the trees, waiting to see which way the "treasure" party had gone.

In the tack room, Dave helped Nancy pack small digging tools into a saddlebag and wrap a spade in a blanket. The cowboy then saddled the girls' horses and slung the gear aboard two of them. Mrs Thurmond brought lunches which Dave added to a pack as Nancy called to her companions that everything was ready.

Before they mounted, Nancy suggested that they cross the big meadow. "We'll ride up Shadow Mountain from there."

"But it's in the opposite direction from the cliff dwellings," Alice whispered.

"That's the idea," Nancy replied. "Just in case Shorty suspects a trick and decides to follow us."

Dave pulled out a stub of pencil and drew a map for Nancy on the back of an envelope. It showed a trail going east across the mountain to the cliff dwellings.

Twenty minutes later the girls were heading up Shadow Mountain. As they jogged along the trail, Nancy studied the map and noted that Dave's route began not far from the cabin.

"We can go there first," she said. "If the gang is off on a wild-goose chase, now would be a good time to search for their hiding place."

Though the girls were eager to go on with their real purpose, they spent the morning wandering over various trails. "If anyone is following us, I hope he'll think we're just out for pleasure and give up the chase," Nancy remarked.

In early afternoon they stopped beside a stream to eat their lunch, then rode straight for the cabin. After half an hour, however, they were brought up short by huge boulders on the path.

"A rockfall!" George exclaimed. "We'll have to detour."

The riders backtracked, then crossed a steep stony slope, so treacherous that they were forced to dismount and lead their horses slowly. Finally, they reached clear trail again. It was mid-afternoon when Alice cried out, "There's the cabin! I see the roof."

The foursome rode up the slope and hitched their horses to pegs in the ground. Cautiously they made their way towards the cabin. The door was open and no one was inside.

Nancy led the way behind the cabin and noticed again how close the back window was to the brush screen and rock wall.

"What a funny place to put a window!" Bess remarked.

"Yes. That's one of the reasons I feel sure a hiding place is back here somewhere," Nancy replied. "I think the window was used as an escape exit from the cabin."

The girls examined the close-growing chaparral. A

few feet to the side of the window, George discovered a break in the thorny brush.

Nancy slipped into it, and one by one the girls struggled through and entered a narrow cleft in the rock wall.

A few yards inside the opening Nancy pointed out horseshoe, paw, and shoe prints. "Let's follow the prints," she suggested. "I have a hunch this path might lead to Valentine's hideout."

The girls hurried to their mounts, and soon were riding through the narrow pass with only a strip of blue sky visible above them.

After a while even that was blotted out by an overhang. The path grew gloomy and wound sharply round jagged outcrops.

By the time the riders saw daylight again, the sun was low in the sky. They rode up a gentle slope and found themselves on a high plateau. Some distance ahead was a long, straight rocky parapet about twelve feet high.

Nancy reined up sharply. "Look!" she cried out. Built against the wall was a three-sided stone enclosure with an old wooden gate. Inside pranced a handsome black stallion.

"The phantom horse!" Nancy exclaimed.

As the four riders approached, the animal whinnied and reared, backing towards a crude lean-to stable.

"Maybe the trick trappings are in there," George said.

Nancy dismounted quickly, opened the wooden gate, and slipped into the enclosure. The black steed whinnied nervously and shied away, but Nancy talked soothingly to him as she walked forward.

There was a pile of hay in a corner of the stable. Nancy felt under it. In a few moments her fingers encountered something soft and she pulled out a bundle of white material. She carried it outside and closed the gate behind her.

"The phantom costume!" Bess exclaimed as Nancy shook out the filmy cloth.

"It's thin silk material used for theatrical effects," Nancy told the girls. She tucked the cloth into her saddlebag.

"This stable looks old," Bess remarked. "I don't think the gang built it."

"You're right!" Alice exclaimed, and pointed to a barely discernible heart scratched on the gate.

"Then Valentine's hideout must be near here," Nancy said.

As the girls looked round, Nancy noticed a huge rock jutting from the far end of the parapet. With a thrill of excitement she recognized the lookout point. "We're on top of the cliff houses!" she exclaimed. "Let's get the wood ready for the fire, then start searching for the treasure."

Beyond the lookout rock the girls could see a grove of trees. They rode over and tethered their horses. The wind moaned through the fir trees and Nancy shivered. She took her sweater from the saddle horn and threw it over her shoulders. It was nearly dusk, so the girls hung torches on their belts.

Then they collected wood for the signal fire and carried it to the lookout rock just as the sun set. Nancy was the last to make her way off the rock. To one side of it was a short flight of worn steps going down to the top row of cliff houses.

Nancy was about to lead the descent when they heard the howl of a coyote. She stopped short.

"What's the matter?" asked Alice.

"Sh—listen!" Everyone froze. "I hope that's a real coyote," said Nancy.

Bess gasped. "You mean Shorty—"

"If the gang has discovered our ruse, they may have backtracked and traced us here," George said.

Nancy nodded. "We'd better not turn our lights on."

Hugging the parapet, the girls went down the steps to the narrow walk which ran in front of the houses. To their left was a sheer drop.

For a moment they stood still, breathless at the height and the silence. Suddenly there came a *thump* from the first room.

Bess grabbed George's arm and Alice gasped. Quietly Nancy stepped to the open doorway and peered into the gloom.

A man was lying on the floor!

The Cliff's Secret

"HELP!" called a feeble voice as Nancy shone her torch into the dim room.

"Daddy!" cried Alice and brushed past Nancy. She threw herself beside a thin grey-haired man who was bound hand and foot.

"Uncle Ross!" exclaimed Bess and George.

The older girls swiftly untied his bonds. Crying for joy, Alice helped her father sit up and the two embraced.

After introductions, Mr Regor explained that he had made the thumping noise by kicking his heels. "My throat was so parched I couldn't yell out to you."

Then Alice's father told his story. "I've been a prisoner in the cabin for six months—ever since they kidnapped me at the time of the bank robbery. But this morning the gang intended to go after the Rawley treasure party, so they moved me here, where they thought I wouldn't be discovered."

"Why did you go to the bank the night of the robbery, Daddy?" Alice asked.

"To get some important papers I had left there. I was working at home and needed them." He said he had interrupted the robbery, and the gang took him along to keep him from identifying them.

"They're Westerners," he went on, "and have used

this cabin hideout before. The idea was to stay here for a cooling-off period."

"How many are in the gang?" Nancy asked.

"Three. At first Shorty and Sid Brice stayed in the cabin with me while Al Diamond lived in Tumbleweed and brought us supplies."

"Who's Sid Brice, Uncle Ross?" Bess asked.

"The grey-haired fellow who looks like me."

"He calls himself Bursey," Nancy told him.

"I know," said Mr Regor. "One day Al Diamond came to the cabin all excited. He'd talked to an Indian girl named Mary Deer and learned all about Valentine's treasure. So Diamond decided that the gang should go after it and sent Shorty to get a job on the ranch. He was supposed to spread the phantom horse story and drive the Rawleys off."

Nancy looked troubled. "Mr Regor, what happened to the bank loot?"

"It was hidden in the cabin until Shorty reported that you girls had spotted the place.

"The next day Diamond and Brice moved the money to the ghost town and made me go along. They had just finished hiding the loot in the old hotel when we heard your horses approaching. Brice hustled me down the hill. All I could do was drop one of my crayons and hope somebody would find it."

"Oh, we did, Daddy!" exclaimed Alice.

Mr Regor said Diamond had remained in the ghost town to spy on the girls. "Later he told us he had caused a rockslide."

Nancy mentioned finding the coffee cups on the table in the cabin.

"Yes. We heard your horses clattering up the slope,

so Brice forced me out through the window at the back and into the little rocky passage. He had the dog on a rope and made him go too. But later he broke loose."

"We found one of your pictures on the table, Uncle Ross," said George.

The man smiled. "I've been drawing pictures to keep myself busy. Brice has been selling them and keeping the money for himself," he added.

"Those terrible men! Have they mistreated you, Daddy?"

The bank president said he had not been hurt, but had been underfed and was weak. "I once heard Brice say there was time enough to get rid of me when they left Shadow Mountain."

While Alice told her father all that had happened so far, Nancy, Bess, and George flashed their lights about Mr Regor's prison.

The floor was littered with pieces of broken pottery and rock. Beside the door Nancy noticed a flat-topped boulder. "The Indians probably used it for a table, or a seat," she thought. Nearby was a large rectangular chunk of stone.

The three girls switched off their lights and stepped outside. With Nancy in the lead, the three friends walked close to the wall of the cliff dwellings. They searched one apartment after another for the treasure, but always found the same thing: shards and crumbled rocks.

As the girls emerged from one of the middle rooms, Nancy noticed a crude wooden ladder resting against the wall and leading to the roof.

"It's just an old ladder—probably put there by the cliff dwellers," said Bess.

Nancy did not agree. "There are nails in this. Perhaps Valentine brought it here. I'd like to climb up."

"Let's finish searching the rooms," George said.

"Okay."

As they neared the end of the row, the young detective exclaimed, "Look!" The last doorway was neatly blocked with an enormous stone.

"Valentine's hideout!" exclaimed George. "He must have put that rock there to keep intruders out!"

"But how did he get in?" Bess asked, puzzled. "The stone's too big to be moved much on this little ledge."

"I know!" exclaimed Nancy. "Come on!" She hastened back to the ladder. Swiftly she attached her torch to her belt and slipped her arms into her sweater.

By the time Bess and George caught up to Nancy, she had begun to climb. Breathlessly they watched her as she cautiously tested each rung. One splintered before she finally reached the roof.

"Nancy, be careful!" Bess cried fearfully.

Shading the beam of her torch, Nancy moved towards the end chamber and found a column of ancient footholds to the plateau above.

"Probably there's another set like them on the other side," she reasoned. "The ladder was Valentine's extra escape route."

Playing the torchlight over the surface, Nancy walked a dozen steps towards the end of the roof. Suddenly she spotted a large hole.

Shining her light into it, Nancy saw a pile of broken rock directly below. She gripped the sides of the opening and lowered herself into the chamber.

"O-oo, it's musty in here!"

In one corner lay a mouldering blanket and saddle.

Nearby was a pick-axe. On the wall above these Nancy found an indistinct carved letter. She brushed away the dust.

V—for Valentine!

Nancy's pulse pounded with joy and excitement.

But where was the treasure? "It can't be buried," she thought. "The floor is solid stone."

When Nancy lifted the blanket, it fell into shreds at her touch. There was nothing beneath it. Her eyes fell upon a large pottery vase in the corner. The vessel was nearly three feet high and had a wide mouth. Nancy beamed her light into it.

Standing on end and level with the top of the vase was a metal box!

"This might be it!" Nancy exulted. She put down her torch, reached in, and lifted out the heavy box. It slipped from her grasp and hit the floor, jolting off a rusted padlock.

Nancy pulled open the lid. Before her lay hundreds of small shining gold hearts!

"Oh!"

Beneath the layer of gold pieces lay stacks of United States bank notes and a chamois leather bag. It contained an assortment of precious jewels!

"It can't be real!" Nancy said aloud. "I'm dreaming!"

But Nancy's mind clicked back to reality. "I can't get this chest back through the ceiling, that's for sure." She eyed the pick-axe. "Maybe I can pry the rock away from the door."

Nancy worked the point of the pick-axe beneath the rock. She pulled hard. The slab moved a trifle! She tried again. This time the rock moved about a foot.

Nancy pushed the treasure box through the opening, turned off her torch, and squeezed outside.

"George! Bess!" The girls came running and Nancy told of her find. "Take the treasure back to Alice and Mr Regor," she directed. "I'll light the signal fire."

Cautiously Nancy crawled out on to the jutting rock and took a packet of matches from her pocket. She struck one, shielding it from the wind, and held it to the kindling.

As the smoke rose, a gruff voice behind her suddenly barked, "Put out that fire!"

· 20 ·

Daring Tactics

THE voice was Al Diamond's. Nancy was trapped on the jutting rock, far above the valley!

"Stamp out that blaze!" the man repeated sharply, "or I'll knock you off there!"

"All right!" Nancy's brain was in a whirl. She delayed until Diamond bellowed again, then she kicked the pile of smouldering wood from the rock. It burst into a shower of sparks and flame on the way down.

Diamond snarled, "Come here!" When Nancy made her way back to the cliff, he said gloatingly:

"You think you're smart. As for those phoney treasure hunters, we cut out of that trap when I spotted the sheriff trailing us."

Nancy's spirits sank as Al continued to storm. "You've made it too hot for us here, and you'll pay for it."

He said the gang was on its way to the ghost town to pick up the bank loot when they stopped at the cabin. Shorty found fresh horse tracks and guessed the girls had a line on the treasure.

"He saw you gathering wood and gave us his coyote signal."

Nancy's captor bragged that he and his partners had

hurried to the top of the steps and watched from above. Seeing the girls emerging from Regor's prison, the three men had sneaked down into one of the cliff-dwelling rooms to spy on them.

"Finally we saw you hurry by, and then your friends showed up, carrying something heavy. I said to myself, 'There goes the treasure. How nice to have Nancy Drew do all the work for us!' "

"You didn't harm Bess and George!" Nancy said hotly.

"Oh no," came the sarcastic reply. "My boys let 'em get to Regor's prison, then they closed in."

Nancy fumbled for her torch and switched it on.

"Turn that off! I don't want anybody getting nosey. Hurry up! Get going!"

Nancy hoped desperately that Dave had seen the signal fire. In order to give him time to make the treacherous ascent, Nancy hugged the wall and moved as slowly as possible.

"Step on it!" Diamond barked. Finally he pushed her into the prison room. In one corner she saw the red glow of a torch shaded by a cloth, and near it the dark figures of two men. But she could see nothing else in the room.

"We're okay, Nancy," came George's voice. "They made us sit on the floor."

"And smashed our torches," said Bess.

Diamond spoke up sharply. "Shorty, where's that treasure?"

"Can't see it, Boss. You told me to keep the light covered."

Diamond fumbled about before giving an exclamation of disgust. "Regor, are you hiding it?"

"Leave my father alone!" Alice cried out. "He doesn't have anything."

Instantly Nancy's foot reached for the large chunk of stone she had seen near the door. Quickly she shrugged her sweater from her shoulders and it dropped over the stone.

"All right, Mr Diamond. Here it is!"

As she spoke, Nancy stooped and gathered the rock into her sweater.

"I'll take it!"

"No, you won't!" With a mighty lunge Nancy hurled the stone through the door and over the side of the cliff. Seconds later it crashed on the rocks below.

For a moment there was a stunned silence. Then Diamond exploded. "You've played your last trick on me, Nancy Drew. Brice! Shorty! Tie 'em up!"

Nancy sat on the stone bench beside the door and waited coolly while Shorty lashed her ankles together.

Diamond said, "Brice, you and I'll go down to the valley and find the treasure. Shorty, guard these girls till you get my signal."

At this Nancy chuckled. "Poor Shorty! By the time you reach the valley, your pals and the treasure will be gone."

The cowboy stopped his tying and turned to Diamond. "Let Brice stay. I'm through stickin' my neck out!"

"Yes," Nancy declared, "suspicion was on you from the beginning. You wrecked the pump and cut the telephone wire."

"All right," Shorty said resentfully. "And I put the generator out of action and pulled the nettle trick."

"Shut up!" Diamond ordered.

George spoke up. "They kept you busy, Shorty.

After you imitated poor Chief you found the clue in Nancy's watch and later stole the green liniment bottle."

Out of the darkness came Bess's voice. "Who ransacked our room?"

"Brice," replied Shorty, "and that's about all he did!"

"What do you mean?" Brice interrupted. "I cut the fences and knocked down the windmill!"

"Is that so!" Diamond spluttered angrily. "Without my brains, you'd both be nowhere!"

Now the men's voices shrilled in anger as each claimed importance for his part in the conspiracy.

Diamond's voice rose with fury. "Listen," he raged, "I got the idea for the phantom horse. I bought the silk and paint and trained the stallion to come to my whistle."

"We helped you!" Shorty retorted. He reminded Diamond that he and Brice had put the trappings on the stallion for the phantom performance.

Ross Regor cut in. "You almost caught them at it one night, Nancy. Scared them so badly they called off the phantom. I heard Brice say he had to slip from the spring house into the cellar through the secret opening."

"Quit wasting time," Diamond shrieked. "We've got to clear out of here!"

"Now take it easy, Diamond," Shorty said with a ring of authority. "It's me and Brice agin you. We'll go for the treasure. You stay here."

Diamond fumed. "Okay. But don't try any funny business. And come right back."

Without a word, the other two men went out of the door, taking the light with them. The captives heard Diamond make his way through the darkness to the back of the chamber, then heard the creak of a hinge.

A soft laugh came from the gang leader. "In case you're wondering, I'm opening a wooden box where we keep dynamite and fuses."

Gasps came from the prisoners. "You can't do that!" George cried out.

"I'm forced to. Ross Regor knows too much, and I can't afford to let him go. Too bad, Nancy Drew, that you butted into my affairs."

"I'll stay," Mr Regor cried out. "But don't harm these girls!"

"No! And as soon as I light the fuse, I'll get out of here."

Crack! A match flared in Diamond's hand.

"Wait!" Nancy exclaimed. "You'll blow up the treasure!"

The match hovered in mid-air. "What?"

"That was just a big stone I threw over the cliff," Nancy admitted.

She turned on her torch and swept it about the room, making certain the beam hit the entrance several times. Someone just might notice it.

"Here! Give me that!" Diamond snatched the light. "Now where's the thing you girls carried?"

"Here," said Bess, "we're sitting on it."

Diamond pushed her and George aside and flipped open the chest. "Well I never!" He grabbed a handful of the gold hearts and let them run through his fingers. Then he closed the lid and began to carry the box towards the entrance.

Just then the rattle of falling stones came from below. Flushed with success, Diamond called out, "Shorty! Brice! I have the treasure! Fellows, we're rich!"

Voices! Then a light flashed into the room.

"Hold it, Diamond!"

"*Dave!*" Nancy cried out.

Diamond made a break for freedom, but George put out her foot and the criminal fell into the strong arms of Sheriff Curtis. Handcuffs clicked shut.

The girls and Mr Regor gave shouts of joy at the sight of Dave, the sheriff, his deputy, and Mr Rawley. As the captives were untied, Ross Regor told how cleverly Nancy had played for time.

Dave smiled. "She's the smartest little tenderfoot I ever saw." Then he related how the decoys and the sheriff's party had lost the gang and gone back to Shadow Ranch.

"When we saw the fire falling, I figured something like this had happened."

Mr Rawley said, "We didn't want to give ourselves away, so we drove up the valley with our lights off."

Dave added that Brice and Shorty had been caught on the way down. "But where's the treasure?"

"Here." George grinned.

Half an hour later, the party reached the valley floor just as the moon rose. Dave put Valentine's fortune in the estate car while Nancy gave Sheriff Curtis a brief report. It was agreed that he would recover the stolen bank money from the ghost-town hotel in the morning and the cowboys were to bring in the girls' horses and the "phantom". The sullen prisoners were driven off in the sheriff's car.

As Dave headed the car down the valley, he said he thought Nancy should have a share of the treasure. "I know the gold must be turned over to the state," Dave added. "But the jewels and bank notes should be worth a good sum. Nancy, since you found them, I feel a share rightfully belongs to you."

The young detective smiled, then graciously but firmly declined to accept any part of the find. "It was fun," she said.

The grateful cowboy grinned. "My brother and sister sure will be excited by the news."

A little later they turned into the gate. The ranch, bathed in silvery moonlight, looked peaceful.

Alice squeezed her father's hand. "Everything has turned out happily!"

"Thanks to Nancy Drew." Mr Regor smiled.

"What are you going to do now, Nancy, without a mystery to solve?" Bess teased.

Her friend smiled. "Work on the sweater I'm knitting for Ned." She did not know then that soon she would become involved in the thrilling *Mystery of the 99 Steps*.

But George knew that Nancy and mystery were never far apart. She gave a sigh of mock sadness. "Poor Ned! I hope he doesn't need that sweater in the near future!"

The Nancy Drew Mysteries

The Mystery of
the 99 Steps

Carolyn Keene

CONTENTS

·1·

The Strange Dream

"How exciting, Nancy! Your dad really wants Bess and me to go to France with you?" Nancy's tomboy friend exclaimed over the telephone.

"Yes, George, to help us solve a couple of mysteries. How about you girls having dinner with me tonight and I'll tell you the details."

"Give me a hint," George begged. "I can hardly wait!"

Nancy Drew laughed. "My case involves a weird dream."

"A dream!" George exclaimed. "Jeepers! And what's your dad's case about?"

"Too confidential for the phone," Nancy replied. "Be here at five so that we can talk it over before dinner. I'll call Bess."

Bess Marvin and George Fayne were cousins. Like Nancy, they were eighteen, and had been friends of the attractive, titian-haired girl detective for a long time. They arrived promptly. Blonde Bess's warm smile revealed two dimples. George, with close-cropped dark hair, was slim and athletic—the exact opposite of her slightly plump cousin.

"We both have permission to go to France, Nancy," said Bess, "but please, *please* don't get me into any scary

9

situations the way you have in your other mysteries."

Nancy grinned and put an arm affectionately around Bess. "I can't promise, but—"

"Of course you can't," George interrupted. "Besides, that's what makes solving mysteries so exciting. Now tell us all about everything."

The three girls went into the living-room where a cheerful blaze crackled in the fireplace. This was an unseasonably cool June day. Bess and George seated themselves in comfortable chairs, but Nancy remained standing, her back to the fire. Her blue eyes glistened excitedly.

"Begin!" George urged. "From your expression I'd say we shouldn't waste a minute getting these mysteries solved."

"How'd you guess?" said Nancy. "Dad has already gone to Paris on his case. We're to meet him at a hotel there and after a couple of days in Paris we girls will go for a visit to a large château in the country."

Bess's face glowed. "A real château! Divine!"

"Not only that," Nancy went on, smiling, "we're having dinner guests tonight—they live in the château."

"We'll be staying with them?" Bess asked.

"No, they're visiting the States for a few weeks and are staying in this house. You girls and I will be exchange guests."

George chuckled. "Will I be in exchange for a boy?"

Laughingly Nancy replied, "They're girls—Marie and Monique Bardot." She explained that arrangements had been made between her father and an aunt of the Bardot sisters. Carson Drew was a prominent attorney, who often was called upon to handle difficult cases. Frequently his daughter helped him.

"The girl's aunt, who is a few years older than their mother," Nancy continued, "lives here in River Heights. Marie and Monique are with her now. But her apartment is too small to accommodate overnight guests. Mrs Blair is the person with one of the mysteries—mine. She asked me to solve it."

Nancy went to stand by the fire. "You both know Mrs Josette Blair, don't you?"

"Of course!" said Bess. "She's that lovely woman who lives in the apartment house near us. Don't tell me she's having more trouble and so soon after her husband and son were killed in that car accident. Now she has a sprained ankle! Poor Mrs Blair," Bess added sympathetically.

"This is another kind of trouble," Nancy told the cousins. "It's weird. Every night Mrs Blair has a horrible nightmare and wakes up with her heart pounding. In her dream she's blindfolded and is about to fall down a long flight of stairs as someone whispers, '99 steps'. "

"How horrible!" Bess murmured.

"But," put in practical George, "at least it's only a dream. What's the mystery?"

"The mystery of the 99 steps," Nancy answered. "You see, Mrs Blair lived in various places in France as a small child, and actually had this frightening experience, but she can't remember where or anything else about it. For years she did not think of what happened but recently had the dream again. Then something occurred that has really frightened her."

"What was it?" George asked.

Nancy said that Mrs Blair had received a letter from Paris, written in French. "Unfortunately, in a moment of panic she destroyed the message. There was only one sentence in it. 'Tell no one about the 99 steps. Monsieur Neuf'!"

"Mr Nine, eh?" Bess murmured, and Nancy nodded.

"It's our job," she continued, "to find Monsieur Neuf and where the 99 steps are, and—well, solve the mystery so that poor Mrs Blair can sleep peacefully again.

As Nancy stooped to poke the fire and put on another log, Bess groaned. "I can see danger ahead with this mysterious Mr Nine."

Suddenly the three girls were startled by a loud whirring noise. "A helicopter!" George cried out. "It's awfully close!"

The girls listened tensely, knowing it was against a River Heights ordinance for any aircraft to fly so low over the residential area. Was the pilot in trouble?

An instance later a strong downdraught of air burst from the chimney. It sent sparks, soot and ashes over Nancy and into the room.

"Oh, Nancy!" Bess screamed.

She rushed forward with George to help Nancy. They patted out the sparks in her hair and on her sweater. Then George trampled some burning fragments on the carpet.

The scream had brought Mrs Hannah Gruen, the Drews' housekeeper, running from the kitchen. She was a kind, pleasant-faced woman who had helped to rear Nancy since the sudden death of Mrs Drew when the girl was three years old.

Hannah exclaimed, "What happened? Oh, my goodness!" she added, seeing Nancy covered with soot and ashes.

George and Bess rushed forward to help Nancy

"That helicopter?" George exclaimed. "I'll bet it caused this mess!"

While Bess told Mrs Green about the chimney episode and Nancy went upstairs to bathe, George dashed outdoors. She could see the helicopter in the distance, apparently getting ready to land at the River Heights airport.

"That pilot ought to be reported!" George thought angrily.

When Nancy came downstairs, George mentioned this and Nancy agreed. "I'll drive out to the airport tomorrow morning to see about it."

"In the meantime, Detective Drew," put in Bess, "tell us more about your mystery. For instance, how did Mr Nine find out where Mrs Blair is?"

"I suppose from her relatives in France. We'll ask Marie and Monique when they come. Maybe they can give us some other clues too."

At that moment a taxi drove up and two attractive, dark-haired girls alighted. Each carried a large and a small suitcase. Nancy went to the door to meet them.

"You are Nancy Drew?" asked the taller of the pair, smiling. She had a musical voice with a delightful accent.

Nancy smiled. "*Oui*. And you are Marie, *n'est-ce pas*?" She turned to the shorter girl. "Hello, Monique. Please come in, and welcome!"

As soon as the Bardots were in the hall, Nancy introduced Bess, George, and Mrs Gruen. Then the visitors' bags were carried upstairs.

"What a charming house!" exclaimed Monique when all the girls were seated in the living-room. "You are very kind to invite us, Nancy. We do not want to be any trouble. Mrs Gruen must give us something to do."

Conversation turned to Mrs Josette Blair's mystery. The sisters felt sure none of the family in France had given their aunt's address to anyone. Marie and Monique were worried about the mysterious message she had received.

"Perhaps Tante Josette should go away," said Marie.

"I'm sure Mrs Gruen would be glad to have her stay here," Nancy offered. "Perhaps she wouldn't be so frightened if she weren't alone."

"*Merci bien*," Monique said gratefully.

Presently Hannah announced dinner. At the table the group continued to discuss the mystery of the 99 steps, but the French visitors could shed no light on the subject. Nancy did not refer to her father's case. Bess and George, though disappointed, realized that it was a confidential matter and Nancy would tell them about it later.

Nancy herself was thinking, "I'll drive Bess and George home and tell them Dad's mystery then."

A luscious lemon meringue pie had just been served by Hannah Gruen when the front doorbell rang.

"I'll get it," said Nancy. "Excuse me."

At the door Nancy was startled to see a man wearing a half mask! "This is the home of the Drews?" he asked in a strong French accent.

"Y-yes," Nancy replied. Fearful that he would force his way inside, she held the door firmly.

The masked man did not try to enter, and Nancy made quick mental notes of his appearance. He was tall, with exceptionally long arms and feet.

The stranger, who wore heavy leather gloves, handed Nancy a sealed envelope, turned on his heel, and left. She noted that he walked with a slight limp and wondered if this was genuine. He disappeared down the winding driveway and Nancy closed the door. The typewritten address on the envelope was to Mr and Miss Drew.

"Why was the man wearing heavy leather gloves—in June? This could be a dangerous trick," Nancy thought, her detective instinct for caution aroused.

She carried the envelope upstairs. To be rid of any possible contamination from it, Nancy washed her hands thoroughly, then put on leather gloves.

Using a letter opener, she carefully slit the envelope. A single sheet fell out with a typed message:

STAY OUT OF FRANCE!
MONSIEUR NEUF

"Monsieur Neuf!" Nancy thought in dismay. "Was he the man who brought this?"

·2·

The Frightened Financier

AT ONCE Nancy rushed to the telephone in her father's bedroom and called Mrs Blair. She told her of the warning note and asked if the first message from Monsieur Neuf had been typed also.

"Yes, on a French typewriter. You know many of the keys have different characters."

"Then the warning I just received was typed on another machine—an American one," Nancy said. "Monsieur Neuf probably has a confederate in this country. By the way, Mrs Blair, we were going to suggest that you stay here with our housekeeper and your nieces while Dad and I are away."

"That's sweet of you," said Mrs Blair. "Let me think it over. It's you I'm worried about—not myself. I don't want you to take any undue risks for me."

Nancy replied in as lighthearted a tone as she could muster, "Oh, don't worry, Mrs Blair, I must take risks when solving a mystery."

Some traps and dangerous situations in which she had found herself flashed through the young detective's mind.

"I'm sure you do take risks," Mrs Blair said. "But I beg of you, be careful."

When Nancy returned to the dining-room, she told

18

the others about the masked man who had left the warning note. Everyone looked worried.

"Oh dear! You are in danger, Nancy, because of Monique and me," Marie burst out. "We will leave."

"No indeed you won't," Nancy replied firmly. "Monsieur Neuf is trying to keep me from going to France. But I'll go just the same. Dad wants me there. Besides, I have a job to do. I must solve your aunt's mystery. After I leave, I hope you people won't be bothered again."

Marie and Monique glanced at each other, as if unconvinced, but finally they smiled. Monique said, "Nancy, you are brave as well as kind. We will remain."

All the girls thanked Mrs Gruen for the delicious meal, then insisted that she watch television while they cleared the table and tidied the kitchen. Shortly afterwards, when Marie and Monique excused themselves to unpack, Bess and George declared they must leave. Nancy offered to drive them home.

As soon as the three girls were on their way, George said, "Now tell us about your father's case."

Nancy chuckled. "He calls it 'The Case of the Frightened Financier.' "

Bess giggled. "Who is this money man?" she asked. "And what's he frightened about? The stock market?"

"His name is Monsieur Charles Leblanc. We don't know why he's frightened."

Bess murmured dreamily, "Frenchman. Mmm!"

Nancy went on, "He lives in a château in the Loire valley, and his office and a factory he manages are in Paris. He's wealthy and influential in business circles but inherited most of his financial empire. Lately he has become very secretive—is drawing large sums of cash from banks and threatens to close up his factory."

"And put all those people out of work?" George broke in.

"Right. He has sold large holdings of stocks and bonds, too, which isn't good for the country's economy."

"Nancy, how does your dad fit into this picture?" Bess asked.

"Monsieur Leblanc's business associates have engaged Dad to find out what has scared him into doing this. An American lawyer on vacation in France wouldn't be suspected by the 'frightened financier' of trying to learn what's going on."

As Nancy finished speaking, she pulled up in front of the Marvins' home. The girls said good night and Nancy went on to the Faynes'.

"By the way," said George, "when are we taking off?"

"Day after tomorrow. Meet you at the airport eight-thirty A.M. sharp. Good night."

During the drive home Nancy's thoughts dwelt on the mystery. On a deserted street she was suddenly startled when a man stepped off the kerb directly into her path! He limped forward, then fell. Nancy jerked the steering wheel hard and jammed on her brakes to avoid hitting him. Shaken, she stared out at the prone figure.

"Help!" he cried, with a French accent. "I am sick!"

Nancy's first instinct was to assist him, but instead she reached for the door locks and snapped them. *The man on the road was the masked messenger who had come to her house earlier.* This must be a trick! He had followed her and probably knew the route she would take home!

Quickly Nancy pulled the car near the opposite kerb

and drove off. In the rear-view mirror she could see the man picking himself up and limping to the pavement. On a chance she had been wrong, Nancy stopped a patrol car and told her story.

"We'll investigate at once, miss," said the driver.

A little while after arriving home Nancy telephoned police headquarters and learned that the suspect had vanished. The young sleuth, convinced the man had been feigning illness, told her French friends and Hannah of the incident.

Mrs Gruen sighed. "Thank goodness you're home safe."

Marie and Monique looked concerned, but made no comment. Nancy felt sure they were wondering if all American households were as full of excitement as this one!

The trying events were forgotten temporarily when the visitors offered to sing duets in French. Nancy and Hannah were delighted.

"These are old madrigals from the Loire valley where we live," Monique explained. "You will hear them often while you are there."

"The songs are beautiful," Nancy said, clapping.

Mrs Gruen applauded loudly. "This is just like having a free ticket to a lovely concert," she said, smiling.

Before the group went to bed, Nancy invited the visitors to accompany her to the airport the next day. She told them about the helicopter incident.

The three girls arrived there in the middle of the morning. Nancy spoke to the man at the regular service counter and was directed to the office of a private helicopter company.

A young man at a desk had to be prompted twice before replying to Nancy's question. He kept staring with a smile at the two French girls.

"Oh, yes," he finally said to Nancy, "a man was up with me yesterday—the one who's going to build the helipad on your roof."

Nancy stared at the young pilot, speechless. Then she said, "You're kidding!"

"Kidding, the girl says!" He rolled his eyes and shrugged his shoulders. "No, this is true."

Suddenly Nancy realized the pilot had been the victim of a hoax that perhaps tied in with Monsieur Neuf. She decided to be cagey in her questioning.

"Who told *you*?" she asked.

"Why, the man I took up. Guess you know him—James Chase."

"Was he from the—er—company that's going to build the helipad on our roof?" Nancy asked.

"Yes. He showed me a letter from the A B Heliport Construction Company signed by the president. I don't remember his name. It said what they were going to do and asked if I'd fly him low over your house. I got permission to do it."

"Next time you fly low you'd better be more careful," Nancy warned. "We had a fire going and you caused a downdraught that could have set our house on fire."

"Gosh, I'm sorry about that."

"I don't know this James Chase," Nancy said. "What does he look like?"

The pilot grinned. "Queer-looking duck about fifty-five years old. Real long face and arms and feet. Limped a little."

"Anything else?" Nancy asked, her pulses quickening.

"Well, he spoke with a French accent."

Nancy thanked the pilot for his information and left with her guests. When the three were out of earshot of his office, Nancy said excitedly, "James Chase is the masked man who came to the house!"

Marie and her sister exchanged quick glances. "Nancy," Marie burst out, "we think we know who this man is. His name is not James Chase!"

·3·

The Green Lion

"You know who the masked man is?" Nancy cried out unbelievingly.

"We are not acquainted with him," Marie answered. "But I'm sure he was a gardener at the château of friends of ours. He was discharged for being dishonest. In fact he was later suspected of stealing large sums of money from several shops."

Monique spoke up. "We remember him because he was so odd looking, although I don't recall he limped. His first name was Claude. We don't know the rest."

"And," Nancy said, "he could be Monsieur Neuf! But if Neuf is trying to keep people away from the 99 steps, why would he leave France? Girls, you've given me a very valuable clue, anyway. Since you say Claude was not honest, and he's using an assumed name and sent that warning note to Dad and me, I think our police should be alerted."

When they reached headquarters, Nancy took the Bardot sisters inside to have them meet Chief McGinnis. The middle-aged, rugged-looking officer, a good friend of the Drews, greeted them all with a warm smile.

"I'm glad to meet your French visitors, Nancy," he said.

"You'll be doubly glad," said Nancy, "when they

tell you about the man who is trying to keep me from going to Paris."

After Chief McGinnis had listened to the story, he nodded gravely and turned to the Bardots. "Will you young ladies compose a cable to your friends and ask for Claude's last name and his address in France. I'll send it, but the reply will come to your house, Nancy."

The officer winked, adding, "I wouldn't want the Bardots' friends to think Marie and Monique are having trouble with the River Heights' police!"

"Oh, no, no," said Marie, and the sisters laughed.

Everyone was pleased at the quick response that came from France. The three girls, after a sightseeing trip on the Muskoka River, arrived home at five o'clock. Hannah Gruen had just taken the message over the telephone. It said:

Name Claude Aubert. Whereabouts unknown.

"Good and bad news at the same time," Nancy remarked. "Apparently Claude the gardener has disappeared from his home town. But won't *he* be surprised when our River Heights police pick him up!"

She dialled headquarters at once. Chief McGinnis was still there. Upon hearing Nancy's report, he said, "I'll get in touch with immigration authorities in Washington at once to check if Aubert entered this country legally. Most offices will be closing, but I'll call anyhow." He paused. "My men are out looking for this Frenchman. When do you leave, Nancy?"

"At eight tomorrow morning,"

"Well, if I have any news before then I'll let you know. Goodbye now."

"Goodbye, and thanks!"

Monique turned to Nancy. "Oh, I hope the police

catch Claude! He may try to harm you again before you leave."

The telephone rang. Nancy answered. "Hi, Bess! What's up?"

"You must help us out—tonight."

"How?"

"By performing anything you like. Play the piano, do tricks, tell a mystery story."

"Bess, what *are* you talking about? Is this some kind of gag?"

"No, indeed, Nancy. This is the night the Teeners Club entertains the Towners Club, remember? You had to decline because of your trip."

"Sorry, Bess," said Nancy. "I'm afraid I must decline again for the same reason. I haven't finished packing yet, and I told Mrs Blair I'd drop in to see her. She was trying to find some clues for me from old diaries of her mother's."

"But, Nancy, we need one more number. We Teeners can't disappoint the older folks. Couldn't you just—?"

"Bess," Nancy said suddenly, "I just had a brainstorm. Maybe Marie and Monique will sing some madrigals."

"Marvellous!" Bess exclaimed. "Oh, Nancy, you're a whiz. Hurry up and ask them."

At first the French girls demurred, feeling that they did not sing well enough to perform in public. When Nancy, backed by Mrs Gruen, assured the sisters they sang beautifully, the girls consented.

Monique said happily, "Marie and I brought old-time costumes used by singers in the Loire valley. We thought Tante Josette would like to see them."

"That's great," said Nancy, hugging the girls.

When she told Bess the good news, there was a squeal of delight from the other end of the wire. "I'll pick up Marie and Monique at seven-thirty," said Bess.

Nancy requested that the sisters come last on the programme. "I'll try to finish my visit with Mrs Blair in time to hear them."

A little later when Marie and Monique came downstairs in their costumes, Nancy and Mrs Gruen clapped in admiration. The long-skirted bouffant dresses with tight bodices were made of fine flowered silk. Marie's was blue and trimmed with narrow strips of matching velvet. Her sister's was rose coloured festooned with shirred white lace.

The girls' hair was piled high on their heads and they had powdered it to look like the wigs worn by the elegant ladies of the eighteenth century. On one cheek of each singer was a tiny black patch, another custom of that time.

"You will make a great hit," Mrs Gruen prophesied.

"*Merci beaucoup*," said Marie, her cheeks flushed with excitement. "Mrs Gruen, are you not going?"

"I hadn't planned to, since Nancy was not perofrming," the housekeeper replied.

At once the three girls urged her to attend. Hannah beamed. "All right. It won't take me long to change."

She hurried to her room and soon returned in a becoming navy-blue dress. A few moments later Bess arrived for her passengers and they left. Nancy set off in her car for Mrs Blair's apartment.

The attractive woman, about forty years old, opened the door and said eagerly, "I found some notes in Mother's diary that may help us."

She sat down beside Nancy on a low couch in the living-room and opened a small red-velvet-covered book. The writing was precise and quite faded in places.

"I've had a hard time deciphering this," said Mrs Blair. "It tells mostly of my parents' travels, and mentions that I went along sometimes. But I was always with my governess."

"Then the experience you dream about," Nancy guessed, "could have included your governess. Is she still living in France?"

"I really don't know. To me she was just 'Mademoiselle' and that is what she's called in the diary. She was very kind, I remember. I was only three years old at the time."

Mrs Blair gave the names of several famous châteaux they had visited. Another was where Marie and Monique lived.

Nancy's eyes sparkled. "Now we have something to work on! We'll go to each château and look for the 99 steps!"

"Another place mentioned in the diary, Château Loire, was mostly in ruins," Mrs Blair went on. "It says the place was haunted by a ghostly alchemist who carried on his work there. You know, Nancy, in olden times people were superstitious about chemists and their experiments and they were forbidden by law to work their 'miracles'. "

"But they did it in secret?" Nancy asked.

"Oh, yes. They had all kinds of signs, and symbols and special words to indicate to other people in their group what they had accomplished."

"How clever—and daring!" said Nancy.

Mrs Blair arose and took a book from a shelf. It too

was in French. She showed it to Nancy. "One of the interesting sets of symbols includes a Red King, White Queen, Grey Wolf, Black Crow, and Green Lion. The Red King stood for gold; the White Queen, for silver. I don't understand the meaning of the crow, but the Green Lion—he's a bad one. He devours the sun—or in other words, he's acid making the silver or gold look green."

"That's fascinating!" Nancy exclaimed.

"Yes, it is," the woman agreed. "And it's hard to realize that the forbidden art of alchemy finally became the basis for our modern chemistry. In the sixteenth century alchemists believed that minerals grew, so certain mines were closed to give the metals a chance to rest and grow."

Nancy listened intently as Mrs Blair went on, "For a long time people laughed at this idea. But today chemists have discovered that metals do literally grow and change, though very slowly. My goodness!" the woman exclaimed. "We have wandered off the subject of our mystery, Nancy. But actually I didn't find any other clues to my dream or the 99 steps incident of my childhood."

Nancy glanced at her wrist watch. She was reluctant to leave, but would still have time to hear Marie and Monique perform. She invited Mrs Blair to accompany her, but the woman declined because of her sprained ankle.

Nancy rose. "You have given me a lot to work on, Mrs Blair. I'll certainly be busy in France! *Au revoir*, and I hope I'll soon have good news for you."

Nancy hurried to the school auditorium where the Teeners were giving their show. She slid quietly into a rear seat in the dim light.

The Bardot sisters had just been announced and came out before the footlights. Standing with their heads close together, they began to sing. At the end of the number the applause was terrific.

As it died down, and the sisters started the second madrigal, Nancy's eyes wandered over the audience. Suddenly she caught her breath. Directly across the aisle in the centre of a row sat Claude Aubert!

"I must get the police before he leaves!" Nancy thought. Quickly and unobtrusively she made her way outside.

·4·

Backstage Scare

WHEN Nancy reached the street she looked back to see if Claude Aubert were following, but evidently he had been unaware of her presence in the auditorium. She ran to a nearby street telephone and called police headquarters.

The officer on duty promised to send two plain-clothes detectives to the school at once. Nancy said she would meet them in the lobby, and hurried back to the school. As she entered the lobby she heard enthusiastic clapping and assumed Marie and Monique had finished their act.

"Oh, I hope Claude doesn't come out here before those detectives arrive," Nancy thought worriedly. She peered inside the auditorium. He was still in his seat.

Fortunately the audience insisted upon encores. Just before the show ended, Detective Panzer and Detective Keely walked into the lobby.

Nancy quickly led them aside and pointed out their quarry. Suddenly Claude Aubert rose, pushed into the side aisle, and, without limping, hurried towards the stage.

"Come on!" Nancy urged the detectives. "He may be planning to harm the Bardots!"

The three hurried after the French ex-gardener. He

went through the door that led up a short flight of stairs to the stage. To the left of the steps was an exit to the car park. When the pursuers reached the spot, the suspect was not in sight.

"Where did he go?" Nancy asked in dismay.

Detective Panzer yanked open the exit door and reported, "I don't see him." He and Keely dashed outside.

The next instant a scream came from somewhere backstage. Electrified, Nancy raced up the steps where a throng milled about on stage. Many persons were asking, "What happened?"

A sob could be heard above the noise. Nancy went to investigate and found Monique in hysterics. Marie was trying to comfort her.

Seeing Nancy, they cried out together, "He threatened us!"

"Claude Aubert?"

"Yes," said Monique. "He grasped my arm so hard I screamed. Then Claude said in French, " 'If you sisters let Nancy Drew go to France, you will suffer and she will too!' "

"He *must* be Monsieur Neuf!" Marie added fearfully.

"Where did he go?" Nancy asked.

Marie pointed to the opposite side of the stage from where Nancy had entered. When Nancy reached it, she found an exit to a walk that ran behind the building to the car park.

Nancy was elated. Mr Nine was trapped! The walk ran between the school and a high concrete wall. There was no way out except through the car park. By this time the detectives must have nabbed the suspect!

Nancy dashed along the walk and stared ahead. A

large crowd was making its way to their cars and some of them had already started to move out. The detectives were not in sight. Neither was Claude Aubert.

"*Oh great!*" Nancy groaned in disgust. Then she took heart. "Maybe he's already been captured and is on his way to jail!"

Nevertheless, Nancy searched thoroughly among the cars, but saw neither Claude Aubert nor the detectives. She returned to the stage. By this time Monique had calmed down and with her sister was receiving congratulations for their excellent performance.

"You certainly made a hit," said Bess, coming up with George. "Just as Hannah said."

"Oh, thank you." The Bardots smiled.

George added, "Someone told us a fresh guy came up and bothered you. Who was he?"

"A Frenchman who threatened Marie and me if we let Nancy make the trip."

"Such nerve!" George exclaimed. "What's his name?"

Nancy whispered it, then brought Bess and George up to date, telling of her suspicion that Aubert was Monsieur Neuf.

"Wow!" said George. "Mr Nine must be worried you'll solve the mystery."

In a low tone Nancy said, "We'd better go home, and I'll call headquarters to see what happened to the detectives."

They found Mrs Gruen waiting in Nancy's convertible. After bidding good night to Bess and George, Nancy drove off. The housekeeper was astounded at the story of the threat.

"Starting tonight, I'm going to keep the burglar

alarm on all the time!" she declared. "I'm glad we had it put in."

Nancy grinned. "Marie and Monique, be careful not to come home unexpectedly. You may scare Hannah."

"Just the same," said Mrs Gruen, "I don't like this whole thing. Nancy, perhaps you ought to postpone your trip for at least a few days."

"I can't," Nancy replied. "Dad and Mrs Blair are counting on me. Let's not worry until we find out if Claude Aubert has been captured."

As soon as she reached home Nancy telephoned the police. The suspect, she learned, had not been brought in. Furthermore, Detective Panzer and Detective Keely had neither returned nor phoned a report.

"We assume they're still tailing their man," the desk sergeant added.

Nancy hung up, her mind in a turmoil. How had Claude Aubert escaped? Where would he show up next?

"I'll bet," she thought, "that it will be right here. I'm glad the burglar alarm is on."

After a pre-bedtime snack, Mrs Gruen and the girls went upstairs. Nancy, who had some final packing to do, was the last one to retire. Some time later she was awakened abruptly by a loud ringing.

The burglar alarm had gone off!

Instantly the young detective was out of bed and pulling on her robe and slippers. She dashed to a window and leaned out, hoping to spot the intruder. Seeing no one, Nancy sped to her father's room in the front of the house and peered below.

"Oh, they've caught him!" she exulted.

In the rays of a flashlight, the two plain-clothes-men

were holding a tall, long-faced man. Aubert? Just then Mrs Gruen, Marie and Monique rushed in.

Nancy cried out, "The detectives got the burglar! Hurry! Let's go down!"

She quickly led the way, turning on lights as she went, and flung open the front door. The detectives marched their prisoner, now limping, into the hall. Claude Aubert!

"Hello, Miss Drew," said Detective Keely. "We saw your lights go on and thought you'd like to know we got this fellow."

"Bud here and I had a wild chase," Panzer told Nancy. "We got clues to Aubert from people all over town who saw him, but we missed him every time. We figured he might come here, so Bud and I hid near your house and waited. We let him try to force the window, then nabbed him red-handed."

Nancy expressed the theory that the fugitive had eluded them at the school by running in front of the stage curtains, jumping from the platform, and mingling with the crowd leaving the auditorium. The policemen agreed. "That's why we all missed him," said Detective Keely.

The prisoner was prodded into the living-room. His black eyes glared malevolently at the three girls. The man's lips moved but no intelligible sounds came through them. A quick search of his pockets by Keely revealed no passport or other identification.

As soon as Mrs Gruen and the girls were seated, Detective Panzer ordered, "Okay, Aubert. Talk! Tell everything from the beginning. Why and how did you sneak into this country and under what name?"

Silence.

Nancy spoke to the detectives. "I haven't introduced my friends from France—Marie and Monique Bardot. Perhaps they can act as interpreters."

"Good idea," Detective Keely agreed.

Marie was spokesman. She relayed questions from Nancy and the police to the prisoner about the threatening letters to Mrs Blair and the Drews; the helicopter ride; the faked illness in front of Nancy's car, and his inconsistent limping. No answers from Aubert.

Finally Detective Panzer said, "We'll go now. A night in jail may loosen this man's tongue. He'll learn he can't run around threatening people."

After the men had left, Mrs Gruen said, "We should all be thankful that awful man is in custody. Nancy— you, Bess, and George can go to France with nothing to worry about."

Nancy merely smiled. She was not so sure! The group exchanged good nights again and retired. Soon Nancy began to dream. She kept chasing after a man who carried a large sign reading:

BEWARE M. NEUF

Then a great crowd of people in old-fashioned costumes came swarming from the ruins of a château. They carried large bells which they were ringing lustily.

Suddenly the dream ended. Nancy was wide awake. Bells, bells! Then she realized what was happening. The burglar alarm had gone off again!

· 5 ·

Prowler Without Footprints

WHEN Nancy reached the top of the stairway Mrs Gruen was there. Marie and Monique appeared a few seconds later. The group hurried down and flooded the first floor with light and turned off the alarm. No sign of a prowler.

"Let's divide up and search," Nancy suggested. "Marie and Monique, will you examine the windows? Hannah, please try the doors. I'll search for anyone hiding."

The four separated. There was tense silence as the hunt went on. Nancy looked in cupboards, behind curtains and furniture. She found no one.

"I guess the intruder was scared away," she thought. "At least we know he wasn't Claude Aubert!"

At that moment Marie called from the dining-room, "Please come here, everybody!"

The others rushed to her side. She was pointing to a side window which had been forced between the sashes and the lock broken. The intruder probably had been frightened by the burglar alarm before he had a chance to climb in.

"There will be footprints outside," Mrs Gruen spoke up.

"We'll look," Nancy said, and went for a torch.

The quartet trooped outdoors to the dining-room window. A few feet away from it they stopped and Nancy beamed her light over the area.

"No footprints!" Hannah exclaimed. "If somebody tried to get in the house from here, he must have been a ghost!"

Nancy had been studying the ground. Now she pointed to a series of evenly spaced holes. "I think they were made by stilts."

"Stilts!" Monique exclaimed. "You mean the person who tried to get into your house was walking on stilts?"

"That's my guess," Nancy replied.

Mrs Gruen gave a sigh. "It seems to me that every time we have a chance to pick up a clue, somebody outwits us."

Nancy smiled. "Stilts might be a better give-away than footprints," she said cheerfully. "I'm sure there aren't many thieves who use them."

Monique asked, "Then you think the intruder meant to steal something?"

Hannah Gruen answered. "He was either a thief or intended to harm us."

Nancy's own feeling was that the stilt walker might be linked with her mystery. She returned to the house and called the police. The sergeant at the desk was amazed to hear of the second attempted break-in.

"Two alarms in one night!" he exclaimed. "But this one sounds like some boy's prank," he commented. "Probably a town hoodlum. I'll make an investigation and see if anybody on our list of troublemakers owns a pair of stilts. Miss Drew, perhaps you have some ideas yourself about who the person was and why he wanted to break in."

"No, I haven't," she answered, "unless there's a connection between him and Claude Aubert."

The officer whistled. "In any case, I'll speak to the chief about having a detective watch your house every night until this prowler mystery is solved."

"Thank you and I'll hunt around our place for more clues," she offered.

Again Nancy organized a search party. Marie and Monique were assigned to the house. The sisters frankly admitted they did not know what to look for.

"Oh, anything that seems odd to you," Nancy replied. "For instance, table silver missing or disturbed." Even though she felt that the intruder had not entered the house, Nancy did not want to miss an opportunity to track down the slightest piece of evidence.

She and Mrs Gruen began searching the grounds. A single set of stilt marks came from the street, ran along the curved driveway, then turned towards the window.

"There should be two sets of marks," Nancy said. "One coming and one going."

She asked Hannah to go into the house and put on the back porch and garage lights. As soon as this was done, Nancy extinguished her torch and stared intently at the ground.

She noticed that the top branches of a bush near the forced window were broken. Nancy looked beyond the shrub and saw that the stilt marks went across the rear lawn towards the garage.

"I guess the man stepped over the bush," she thought.

As Nancy hastened forward to follow the marks, the housekeeper joined her. Side by side the two hurried to the double garage. The door behind Nancy's convertible had been left open. As she and Hannah approached it, they stared in astonishment. Propped against the inside of the rear window of the car was a large cardboard sign. On it, printed in green crayon, were the words:

BEWARE THE GREEN LION

"How strange!" Mrs Gruen murmured.

At that moment a patrol car came up the driveway and an officer stepped out. He introduced himself as Detective Braun. "Are you Miss Nancy Drew?"

"Yes. And this is Mrs Gruen who lives with us."

The headlights of the police car had shown up the warning sign vividly. "For Pete's sake, what's that all about?" the detective asked.

"We just found it," Nancy told him. "I think the person who tried to get into our house intended to leave the warning in some room. When he was scared away, he put it here."

"Do you know what it means?" Detective Braun asked.

"I'm not sure, but the message may have something to do with a mystery I'm trying to solve." Nancy told about the old alchemists' codes, some of which Mrs Blair had shown her.

"One man used the Green Lion as a symbol that he had discovered how to make gold look green."

Detective Braun shook his head. "This wasn't the stunt of a kid on stilts," he said. "It's a real warning."

Mrs Gruen nodded. "I'm afraid you're right and this means trouble for Nancy in France after all. She's leaving early tomorrow morning."

"How strange!" Hannah murmured

Nancy, seeing how worried the housekeeper was, tried to sound lighthearted. "Not *tomorrow* morning, Hannah dear," she said teasingly. "It's already morning! Do you realize I'll be leaving home in about four hours?"

Hannah gasped. "You're right. What a terrible night you've had—just when you need a good rest!"

Braun said he would take the sign back to headquarters and have it examined for fingerprints.

"Good night," Nancy said. "And thank you."

At eight o'clock the young sleuth was ready to leave. She and Hannah Gruen and the Bardots drove to the airport in the convertible. The housekeeper would bring the car back. Marie and Monique were sad when the time came to say goodbye at the departure gate.

Marie said, "I want to see Tante Josette's mystery solved, but please don't let yourself be harmed, Nancy dear."

Monique added, "Do not spend all your time on your detective work. France is so lovely to see, and please have some fun."

"I will," Nancy promised.

She had begun to worry about Bess and George, who had not yet arrived.

But a minute later the two girls came dashing up with their parents. The cousins said quick hellos and goodbyes. Then the three travellers waved adieus and walked to the aircraft that would take them to New York. There they would change planes.

Nancy motioned Bess to a window seat while she took one next to her on the aisle. George sat across from her. Seat belts were fastened and in a few minutes the aircraft taxied down the runway and took off.

As soon as the lighted "Fasten Your Seat Belt" sign was turned off and the girls had unbuckled their straps, Nancy said to George, "Sit on the arm of my chair. I have something exciting to tell you and Bess."

When she finished her recital of the night's adventures, both her friends gaped unbelievingly. Then Bess said worriedly, "More trouble—now with a green lion!"

George snorted. "Sounds ridiculous to me. The alchemist who worked out that code lived hundreds of years ago. Somebody came across it just by chance and is using those words to try to scare you, Nancy."

The girl detective frowned. "What puzzles me is, where does everything fit? I have a feeling it'll be some time before I put this jigsaw together."

As she spoke, Nancy could hardly hold back a yawn and slept during most of the flight to New York. Here the girls boarded a larger plane and took off for Paris. After they had been cleared through customs the next morning, Mr Drew met his daughter and her friends. The tall handsome man beamed in delight at seeing the girls.

"I've been mighty lonesome without you, Nancy," he said. "I'll enjoy showing this beautiful city to you. Now tell me, how is your mystery coming along?"

Nancy chuckled. "I have one villain in jail already." She was amused at her father's upraised eyebrows and quickly reported all that had happened.

"I can hardly believe it," the lawyer said. "Well done, Nancy. You're way ahead of me."

In lowered tones, Mr Drew continued, "I haven't learned yet why Monsieur Leblanc is acting so strangely. Whenever I meet the man I find him very pleasant but not a hard worker, though he goes to his office regularly. He hasn't given a hint as to why he is selling his investments at such an alarming rate."

Mr Drew remarked that he was very much interested in the warning *Beware the Green Lion*.

"Dad, I've been assuming the warning was linked with my mystery," she said, "but now I wonder if it was meant for you, too. After all, the first one from Monsieur Neuf was addressed to both of us."

"You could be right."

When the travellers reached the heart of Paris, they were delighted by the wide boulevards with their beautiful buildings and the spectacular Eiffel Tower.

"What would you girls like to visit first?" Mr Drew asked.

George responded at once, "Notre Dame. I want to see those ugly gargoyles."

The lawyer laughed and nodded. "Notre Dame it shall be, as soon as we have checked into our hotel on the Rue de la Paix and you girls have unpacked. I have reserved a large room for you with three beds."

In an hour they were ready for the sightseeing trip. Mr Drew called a taxi and they drove directly to the street called Double D'Arcole in front of the famous old cathedral.

As they stepped from the cab, Bess exclaimed, "Oh, it's gorgeous! Goodness, look at all the carvings and statues! There must be hundreds!"

"There are," Mr Drew agreed. "Would you girls like to climb to the top of one of the two towers? You can get a better look at some of the gargoyles and also a magnificent view of the city."

"Yes, let's," George urged.

Mr Drew led the girls round the corner into a side street with several pavement cafés opposite the north wall of the cathedral. A narrow doorway opened on an even narrower circular stone staircase. The steps were precipitous and on one side there was barely toe room.

"I hope we don't meet anyone coming down," Bess remarked, frowning.

Nancy went first, with Bess directly behind her. George came next and Mr Drew brought up the rear. The stairway was rather dark in places where light could not filter through the tiny square openings in the outer wall.

Nancy was silently counting the steps. "I may as well begin my sleuthing and see if there are any clues on the 99th step," she thought.

Slowly she and the others spiralled their way upward. Nancy had just passed the 99th step without having seen anything significant, when she started round a sharp turn. Coming down towards her was an enormously fat woman, who blocked the entire width of the staircase.

Without regard for those below her, she descended swiftly and thoughtlessly, not moving sideways to give Nancy any room. Dismayed, Nancy stood on her toes and tried to hug the wall which was too flat to give any handhold.

"*S'il vous plaît*—" Nancy began.

The fat woman paid no attention. She pushed against Nancy so hard that the girl lost her balance! She fell against Bess, who in turn dropped backwards onto George. Unable to keep her balance, George desperately clawed the air!

Would they all go tumbling to the bottom?

· 6 ·

Double Take

As the three girls stumbled down the circular stairway, Mr Drew braced himself to try to stop them. He held one hand firmly against the inner wall and leaned forward. As the impact came he teetered, but only momentarily. The girls, too, had pressed against the stone side and this had helped to break the fall.

"Oh, thank you!" Bess cried out. "I was never so scared in my life!"

She, George and Nancy regained their balance. The fat woman who had caused the accident had paused for only an instant. With a curt *pardon* she went on down the stairway.

The Americans laughed off the incident, but all of them sincerely hoped they would not meet any more overweight people on the steps!

"How much farther to the top?" Bess asked, puffing a little.

Mr Drew said that the Notre Dame tower was 226 feet high. "You should be glad you're not going to the tip of the spire," he said with a chuckle. "That's 296 feet from the ground."

"It's a tremendous building, isn't it?" Nancy remarked.

Mr Drew nodded. "And some outstanding historical events have taken place here, including two corona-

47

tions full of pomp and ceremony—of Henry V of England and Napoleon I."

By this time Nancy had reached the top step and walked out onto the platform of the tower with its shoulder-high stone railing. A few feet ahead of her a massive stone gargoyle protruded from the roof. It looked like some strange prehistoric bird overlooking the swift-flowing Seine below.

As Bess reached Nancy's side, she commented, "This gargoyle and the others I can see around this tower are so ugly they're almost handsome!"

George turned to Mr Drew. "Who ever thought up gargoyles and what does the name mean?"

"I understand," Mr Drew replied, "that these figures are really rainspouts. Gargoyle is derived from a medieval French word meaning gurgle or gargle. As to why they were made to look so grotesque, it's thought this was a whim of the designer and the architects."

Mr Drew and the girls walked from one end of the platform to the other viewing as much of Paris as they could. The thing they noticed particularly was that practically all the buildings except churches had flat roofs.

"They were also in vogue in our country around the turn of the century," said Mr Drew, "but we went back to the gabled variety. Now the flat ones are becoming popular again for large buildings. Give you one guess why."

"So helicopters can land on them," Nancy replied. Smiling, she said, "Dad, will we have to change our roof for the helipad?"

George chuckled. "Paris is ready for the future. A helipad on every roof! And the Drews won't be far behind!"

Nancy glanced down at the street from which they had entered the tower. Suddenly she grabbed her father's arm.

"Dad! That man down there! He looks like Claude Aubert!"

Mr Drew was surprised and Bess and George dashed to Nancy's side. The man in the street was gazing upwards directly at the group.

"But you said Claude Aubert was in the River Heights' jail!" Mr. Drew exclaimed.

At that moment the man apparently sensed that they were looking at him. He turned on his heel and walked away quickly.

"He's not limping!" Bess exclaimed.

As George gazed after him, she said, "Hard to believe he escaped from jail and got over here so fast!"

Nancy remained silent, but her father spoke up. "It's possible Aubert had someone put up bail money for him, then he jumped bail and managed to catch an overseas plane somewhere."

When Nancy still did not put forth an opinion, Mr Drew asked, "What's your theory?"

"Rather startling," she replied, "but I have a hunch this man is Claude Aubert's brother, perhaps an identical twin."

"Then which one," said George, "is the real Monsieur Neuf?"

Nancy frowned. "I don't know, but I believe they're working together—Claude in the United States, this man over here. It's my guess we've been followed ever since we arrived."

A frightened look came over Bess's face. "Then we didn't leave the danger behind. Nancy, supposing the men are brothers, do you think one calls himself the Green Lion?"

"Possibly. In any case, we should find out at once if Claude Aubert did escape, or jump bail. I'll phone Chief McGinnis as soon as we leave here."

Mr Drew approved and the four left the tower immediately. When they reached the street, Nancy suggested that Bess and George go into the cathedral while she and her father looked for a telephone.

"There's a delightful little garden at the back of Notre Dame," said Mr Drew. "Suppose we all meet there in half an hour."

The group separated. Nancy and her father found a restaurant which had a telephone booth and Nancy put in a call to River Heights. She was told there would be a delay of fifteen minutes.

"I'll wait," she said in French. "Will you please ring me at this number?"

The operator promised to do so. Nancy and her father sat down at a nearby table and ordered some French pastry and hot chocolate. When the food arrived, Mr Drew chuckled and said, "Wouldn't Bess be goggle-eyed over this pastry?" Nancy grinned.

Ten minutes later the telephone rang and she jumped to answer it. "Chief McGinnis?"

"Yes. You're calling from Paris, Nancy?" he said. "It must be important."

It is. Tell me, is Claude Aubert still in jail?"

"Sure. Why?"

Quickly Nancy told him about the man she had seen. "Could you find out from Aubert if he has a brother who looks like him, perhaps a twin?"

"Hold on!" The chief was gone for several minutes.

Finally McGinnis came back and said that Aubert had refused to answer. "That makes me think you may have guessed correctly," the officer told Nancy. "By the way, we've observed that his limp is phoney. Anyhow, I will report your suspicions to the Paris police."

Nancy told the chief where she was staying and thanked him for his help. She asked about the stilt walker. The man had not been found yet.

As Nancy emerged from the booth and rejoined her father, she was beaming.

"Don't tell me," said Mr Drew. "I know from your expression you're on the right track."

Nancy laughed. "I shouldn't wear my secrets on my face." Then she remarked softly, "If this other man is Claude Aubert's brother and is following us, we should turn the tables and follow him."

"A neat trick if you can do it," the lawyer said. "But we'll keep our eyes open."

The Drews made a tour of the breathtaking interior of Notre Dame. Nancy was awed by its vastness and the beauty of the stained-glass windows and the many statues. She paused before one of the Virgin Mary whose lovely face looked down at arms which had once cradled an infant.

"The baby's statue was mysteriously taken away," her father explained. "Stolen apparently."

"How dreadful!" Nancy exclaimed. "And how sad!"

She and her father left the cathedral and walked down the side street to the open garden at the rear. Bess and George were waiting for them and admiring the colourful beds of zinnias and petunias. The four sat down on chairs and Nancy told the cousins of her talk with Chief McGinnis. She urged that wherever they all went, each one was to try to spot the man she thought was Claude's brother. A few minutes later Mr Drew suggested that they go back to the hotel and have lunch.

"That's a grand idea," Bess spoke up. "I'm starved!"

She arose, and before heading towards the street, turned slowly in a complete circle, hoping she might see the suspect. Suddenly her eyes became riveted on a black lamppost which stood near high bushes and trees at the back of the garden. She had spied a figure crouching behind the post.

"Nancy," Bess whispered quickly, "I think I see Mr Nine!"

·7·

Exciting Steps

As Bess pointed towards the lamppost, the man crouching behind it seemed to realize he had been discovered. He sprang up and plunged into a mass of bushes and trees behind him.

"Let's chase him!" Nancy urged, and the whole group took off in pursuit.

George reached the other side of the shrubbery first. She cried out, "I see him! He's heading for the back street!"

When they came to the Rue du Cloître they could see their quarry running to the south.

"We mustn't let him escape!" called Mr Drew. "You girls go on. I can't run as fast as I used to."

Nancy soon caught up with George. But at the corner of the Quai de l'Archêveché, they were stopped by a policeman wearing a tight-fitting, dark-blue tunic suit, white gauntlets, and a high-crowned, peaked cap.

"Why are you in such a hurry?" he called out in French.

Nancy pointed down the street towards the fugitive. "He is a suspect trying to get away from us!"

The officer's eyebrows lifted. "Suspected of what?" he asked.

For a moment Nancy was stumped. What did she

53

suspect the man of? Only of being Claude Aubert's brother. Finally she said, "He has been watching and following us. We want to find out why."

By this time Mr Drew and Bess had reached the group. The lawyer introduced himself and the girls and showed his identification.

"I beg the pardon of the Americans," the policeman said, and waved them on.

But Nancy shook her head. "Too late. Look!"

At that moment the long-armed man was jumping into a taxi. Disappointedly his pursuers watched it drive out of sight.

The policeman said cheerfully, "If the man is following you, he will be seen again. What is his name?"

"We do not know," Nancy replied. "We think it may be Aubert. By any chance, have you ever heard of a Claude Aubert?"

The officer stared at her. "*Mais oui*, mademoiselle! Claude Aubert is a well-known forger. Some time ago he faked the signature on a large cheque and was nearly caught by our captain, but he got away. You mean, that man you were chasing is Claude?"

"No, he's in jail in the States," Nancy replied, then added that Captain McGinnis was going to get in touch with the Paris police. On a hunch she asked whose signature Claude Aubert had forged. The group was astounded to learn it was that of Charles Leblanc! The "frightened financier"!

Nancy and her father were elated over this clue, which might prove a strong link between his case and Nancy's.

As calmly as she could, Nancy asked the officer where Claude Aubert had lived at the time he vanished. The policeman gave her the address of a house in the section of Paris known as the Left Bank.

The Drews thanked him for the information and walked back towards Notre Dame. Mr Drew suggested they have lunch at one of the sidewalk cafés instead of returning to the hotel, then go to Aubert's house.

"That would be fun," Bess said eagerly. "Some fine French food will step up my brainpower. You'd like that, wouldn't you, Nancy?"

Her friend laughed. "This mystery is becoming so complicated, I can use all the help you can give me."

Mr Drew selected a pleasant café and they all sat down at a small table. After their luncheon orders of cheese soufflé had been given, the lawyer said in a low tone, "Monsieur Leblanc's office building is not far from Aubert's apartment."

George asked, "Do you think that fact has a bearing on your case, Mr Drew?"

The lawyer shrugged. "At least it's a strange coincidence."

When they finished eating, Mr Drew suggested that on their way to the Left Bank, they should stop at the famous Louvre to look at some of the paintings and statues. A taxi took them to the great museum which once had been a palace.

Bess sighed. "It would take us a week to see everything," she commented.

Mr Drew smiled. "You're right, Bess, but there are certain priceless art objects you must not miss—for instance, the Winged Victory."

George grinned. "She's the lady with the wings but no head, isn't she?"

"That's the one," Mr Drew answered.

"The Venus de Milo is here too," Nancy said.

"That's right."

George chuckled. "She's the beautiful lady without any arms. Where did she lose them?"

"I haven't heard, " the lawyer said with a grin, "or I might look for them."

Bess announced, "One thing *I* want to see is Leonardo da Vinci's portrait of Mona Lisa."

Mr Drew said that this was considered to be the most valuable art treasure in the Louvre, since it was more heavily protected than any of the other pieces.

When the group reached the famous painting, they found it guarded by an iron rail and two uniformed men, who carefully watched each visitor.

"Mona Lisa's face is lovely," Nancy remarked. "Just looking at her portrait gives me a peaceful feeling."

The River Heights visitors stayed for an hour in the Louvre. Then, weary, they decided to stop walking and drive across the Seine to Claude Aubert's former home. The concierge in charge of the building was a rather gruff man of about fifty. At first he seemed unwilling to answer any of their questions about the forger.

"It was bad enough having the police come here disturbing me!" he complained, growing red in the face. "Who are you?"

Nancy smiled disarmingly. She decided to shoot a direct question at him. Could she get him to answer?

"What's Claude Aubert's twin's name?" she asked.

Without hesitation, the concierge replied, "Louis."

Nancy could hardly keep from shouting her delight. Mr Drew, Bess, and George also found it difficult to maintain calm expressions.

"Oh, yes," Nancy said nonchalantly. "Let me see, where does Louis live?"

The man did not answer at once, but finally he said, "It is out in the country. I do not know the name of the place." Suddenly he went on, "You know, Louis is the bright one. Claude is a bit slow. He just does what his brother tells him."

Mr Drew put in casually, "Louis keeps busy, no doubt. We saw him today from a distance. What's he doing now?"

"Oh, he is some sort of scientist. That business with formulas and flasks and such is beyond me."

Nancy's intuition told her they were getting nearer and nearer to an important clue. Again she smiled at the concierge. "Would it be possible for us to see where Claude used to live?"

Actually Nancy did not expect to find any clue in the apartment. What she did want to do was count the number of steps to Aubert's living quarters. It was just possible there might be 99 and there would be some significance to this!

"I can show you which apartment it is," the concierge replied. "But I cannot admit you because a young man and his wife occupy it now."

As he led the way up the stairs, Nancy moved backwards to the front door. Then, as she walked forward again, she began to count. It took her ten steps to the stairway. She added each tread as the group climbed. On the second floor there were ten steps to the next stairway. The concierge went on, and Nancy continued to count. When they reached the top, she found there were 69 steps in the two stairways.

"Maybe—just maybe—" Nancy told herself.

Would there be ten steps to the Aubert apartment? There were. The total was 99!

"But now that I have the information, how can I use it?" Nancy thought. "The number may have been a signal between Louis and Claude or between Claude and some friends of his to meet here in connection with his forgeries. But where does it fit in with Mrs Blair's dream?"

Meanwhile, the Drews and their companions had pretended to gaze with interest at the apartment door, then returned to the front entrance. Mr Drew thanked the concierge, hailed a taxi, and they all went back to their hotel.

"I have a surprise for you girls this evening," said Mr Drew. "We're invited to a soirée. It's being held by friends of mine especially for you girls to meet Monsieur Charles Leblanc and to see what you can learn."

"It sounds wonderful!" Bess remarked.

The lawyer turned to his daughter and smiled. "If you can get as much information from Monsieur Leblanc as you did from the policeman and the concierge, I'll buy you a special gift from Paris!"

Nancy laughed. "I'll do my best to win it!"

After tea and a short rest, Mr Drew and the girls dressed and went by taxi to a beautiful mansion near the Bois de Boulogne. The large stone building had several steps leading up to a massive carved doorway. The house was brilliantly lighted, and strains of music floated from inside to the ears of the arriving guests.

"How divine!" Bess murmured.

Mr Drew alighted first. He was just helping Nancy

out when a car came up behind their taxi, and without braking, smashed into it. Despite her father's efforts to save Nancy, she was knocked off-balance and thrown full force to the pavement!

·8·

Dancing Sleuths

THE impact snapped Bess and George against the rear seat of the taxi, then bounced them onto the floor. The driver was also jolted, although less severely.

A stream of furious French issued from his lips and he scrambled out, shaking his fist. But the car responsible for the crash had quickly backed, then roared off down the street before anyone could get the licence number.

By this time Mr Drew had gently helped Nancy to her feet and the taximan assisted Bess and George from the car. Although badly shaken, the cousins' first concern was for Nancy.

"Are you hurt?" they asked.

At first she did not answer. The breath had been knocked from her and she had fallen heavily on one shoulder. Nancy admitted it hurt.

"Nothing's broken, though. I'll be all right. How about you girls?"

"Okay," George said gamely, rubbing the back of her neck. "We're lucky."

Mr Drew was greatly concerned for his daughter and her friends. "We'd better give up the party and go back to the hotel."

"Oh, no!" Nancy insisted. "I just wish we'd seen the

person who crashed into us. It was certainly deliberate!"

Grim-faced, her father agreed. No one had caught even a glimpse of the culprit. Mr Drew paid their fare and the taxi rattled off.

The door of the mansion had opened and the doorman, who evidently had heard the crash, came hurrying down the steps. Upon learning that Mr Drew and the girls had an invitation to the soirée, he said quickly:

"I will take you to bedrooms so that you can refresh yourselves." When he saw Nancy rubbing one shoulder, he told her there was a doctor at the party. "I will send him upstairs."

Nancy protested, but the doorman was insistent. "I know Monsieur Tremaine—your host—would want me to do that."

He escorted the American guests to elegantly furnished bedrooms on the second floor. Heavily carved furniture was set off by velvet flower-patterned rugs and large tapestries which hung on the walls. The one in the girls' room showed a hunting scene with women seated sidesaddle on their horses. The costumes made the girls smile. The women wore bodiced dresses with long skirts and large hats with plumes.

"I wonder if those women ever really did any riding or whether they just sat on the horses and posed," Bess remarked.

A few moments later the doorman brought in the physician and introduced him. He was very gracious and seemed glad that Nancy and the others spoke French, since he said he spoke little English. He examined her shoulder thoroughly and reported that it was neither broken nor strained.

"But you have a bad bruise. I suggest that an ice

pack be put on it at once and that you get some rest."

Then the doctor examined Bess and George. He found that their injuries were minor and also prescribed ice packs for their bruises.

Mr Drew summoned a maid, who quickly brought some ice and the girls lost no time in applying it.

Presently Nancy declared, "I feel all right now. Let's go down to the party."

Bess helped her put on fresh make-up and combed her hair. George brushed the dirt off Nancy's dress and used some water to remove a couple of spots.

"Thanks a million, girls," she said. "All set?"

With a smile Mr Drew gave Nancy his arm and they led the way downstairs. News of the accident had spread among the guests and many had gathered in the reception room to meet the newcomers. Beyond, the girls could see a ballroom gleaming with crystal chandeliers.

Monsieur and Madame Tremaine were most solicitous, but Nancy and the cousins assured them they felt fine. "We are grateful to you for inviting us to the soirée," Nancy added, not revealing she knew why the party was being given.

"I should like to introduce you to some of our other guests," Madame Tremaine said.

After she had presented them to various friends, she escorted the four Americans into the ballroom where Monsieur Leblanc was standing, and introduced them. A tall slender man with iron-grey hair and moustache, he spoke English fluently.

Nancy thought, "He is handsome and has a charming smile."

"Mr Drew," said the financier, "you are fortunate to

have such a lovely daughter." His eyes beamed with admiration as he looked at Nancy. Then, turning, he smiled at Bess and George.

"Ah! We Frenchmen pride ourselves on the good-looking women in this country, Mr Drew, but if Mesdemoiselles Drew, Fayne, and Marvin are examples of the young women in America, perhaps our women have to take second place, *non*?"

Nancy, Bess, and George as well as Mr Drew carried on the banter. Then Nancy adroitly brought the conversation round to another subject with the question, "You are alone this evening, Monsieur Leblanc?"

"Unfortunately, yes," he replied. "Madame Leblanc is at our house in the country. She did not feel well enough to attend."

"I'm so sorry," said Nancy. "I would have liked to meet her."

She had the feeling he might have invited the group to do so, but at that moment they were interrupted by an announcement from the leader of a small string orchestra. He introduced a young woman soprano who had just joined the Paris Opera Company. The listeners were spellbound by her clear silvery voice, and after she had finished two solos, the applause was thunderous.

Directly afterwards, Monsieur Leblanc murmured "*Pardon*" to the girls and Mr Drew and went off. The young opera singer graciously gave an encore, then said she must leave.

As the orchestra resumed playing, Nancy, Bess, and George began to talk in subdued tones to Mr Drew about Monsieur Leblanc. "He seemed attentive to the music," Nancy remarked, "but I did notice that once in a while during the singing he had a faraway look in his eyes."

Bess said dramatically, "Maybe he's been hypnotized and is being coerced into selling his securities!"

"At any rate," George declared emphatically, "I have a hunch it won't be easy to get information out of him!"

Mr Drew nodded. "I've already learned that. But I really think you girls may have better luck."

Some of the guests they had already met began introducing the River Heights group to others. Two debonair young men asked Bess and George to dance. Another young man was just making his way towards Nancy when Monsieur Leblanc returned.

Bowing low, he said, "May I have the pleasure?"

Nancy did not want to dance—her shoulder was aching—but she felt she should not miss this opportunity to talk to the financier. As they circled the floor of the ballroom, he began to query her about her trip to France. Instantly she wondered if he suspected something, but if he did, Leblanc gave no evidence of it.

She said, "Whenever Dad's away from home he misses me very much. My mother died when I was a child and he and I have always been close friends. He asked me to join him here. Bess and George often go on trips with me."

"I wish," Leblanc said, "that I might have the honour of showing you and your friends round. But I am very busy and unfortunately have little time to myself."

When the music stopped, the Frenchman escorted Nancy to a chair, then excused himself. A few minutes later George made her way to Nancy's side, saying:

"I have something terribly important to tell you. I told my partner I'd be back in a few minutes. See that man in Arabian dress standing in the doorway?"

When Nancy nodded, George went on, "Well, what do you think of this? After Monsieur Leblanc left you, I heard him say to the Arab—in the doorway to the palm garden, where I was—'I told you not to come here, or anywhere else, unless we were alone!' "

Nancy sat straight. "Go on!" she urged.

"The Arab replied, 'But 9 is coming up. You must meet me.' "

"This is exciting!" Nancy remarked. "What else happened?"

"Monsieur Leblanc answered, 'Tomorrow—99.' Then the men separated."

"Ninety-nine!" Nancy echoed softly, her eyes lighting up. "I'd like to follow the Arab!"

At that moment Mr Drew walked over and Nancy repeated what George had told her. He too was extremely interested but said he would not permit Nancy to do any more sleuthing that evening.

"Don't forget your shoulder. You must get back to the hotel and go to bed. I'll make a bargain with you, though. Tomorrow we'll follow Monsieur Leblanc."

"All right, Dad. Now, may I make a bargain with you?"

He smiled. "What is it?"

"I'd like to shadow the Arab here just for a few minutes and see what I can find out. Please!"

Mr Drew agreed to give his daughter twenty minutes. "Be very careful," he warned her. "We don't want anyone becoming suspicious."

Just then a young man, Henri Durant, came up and

asked Nancy to dance. She accepted and as the music started he led her onto the floor. The young sleuth glanced about as casually as possible. Suddenly her gaze fixed on the far end of the ballroom which opened onto the indoor garden full of palm trees and exotic plants. She spotted the Arab in the garden!

An idea came to Nancy. "I hope it works!" she thought.

As they moved along to a lively tune, Henri complimented Nancy not only on her dancing but also on her ability to speak French so well.

Nancy laughed. "You dance very well yourself." Then, seconds later, she said, "Would you mind going into the garden and sitting out the rest of this dance? My shoulder is aching."

Henri was most solicitous and at once led her to a bench in the garden. At first she could not see the Arab. Then suddenly she spotted him among the palms. He was staring intently at her!

Did he know who Nancy was? Had he guessed that she was trying to solve the mystery of the 99 steps? Was this man a new enemy of hers?

Turning to her companion, Nancy asked, "Do you know who that Arab is?"

"No, but I'll be glad to find out," Henri answered.

He arose and started towards the man. But instantly the stranger turned and hurried off to the far end of the garden where there was another entrance into the ballroom.

Nancy followed Henri, thinking, "That Arab certainly acts suspiciously. I mustn't let him get away without finding out who he is!" Smiling, Nancy said to

Henri, "I want to speak to that Arabian man and I thought he might be leaving."

This seemed to satisfy Henri and he accompanied her to the edge of the dance floor. Nancy caught sight of the Arab's turban as he disappeared out the doorway which led to the hall. She and Henri made their way through the crowd of dancers as fast as they could.

By the time they reached the hall, however, the Arab was going out at the front door. Apparently he had not bothered to say good night to the Tremaines. Hurrying to the doorman, Nancy asked him who the stranger was.

"I do not know the gentleman," he replied. "He had a proper invitation, so of course I admitted him."

"I must speak to Monsieur!" said Nancy, and the servant opened the door.

She ran outside and from the top of the long flight of steps gazed up and down. The Arab was striding quickly towards a long, dark car parked further up the street. There was a driver at the wheel and the motor was running.

"Come on, Henri!" Nancy urged.

Startling Headlines

TOGETHER, Nancy and Henri dashed down the steps of the Tremaine mansion. By this time the mysterious Arab had jumped into the car. The driver pulled away and the car shot forward.

Suddenly, in the glare of two street lamps in front of the Tremaine home, the Arab took off his turban. With it came a wig and false whiskers.

"Oh!" Nancy gasped.

The man was Louis Aubert!

"Is something the matter?" Henri asked.

"That man was in disguise. I have an idea he had no right to be at the party. We should tell the Tremaines."

"Do you think he is a thief?" Henri looked perplexed. "Is that why you wished to stop him?"

Nancy hesitated, then answered truthfully, "I'm not sure. But I do have reason to suspect that the man is dishonest."

Henri accepted her reply, sensing that Nancy did not wish to divulge anything else. The couple re-entered the house.

Monsieur and Madame Tremaine were at the back of the hall saying good night to several guests. Nancy waited until they had departed, then asked her host who the Arab was. He and his wife exchanged glances, then Monsieur Tremaine replied:

"We did not catch his name. He suddenly appeared and told us he was a friend of Monsieur Leblanc's. Do you wish me to ask him?"

"He has already left," Nancy told them. "He seemed to be in a great hurry."

The Tremaines frowned. Obviously the man had displayed very bad manners! Nancy was saved from explaining the reason for her query because Bess, George, and Mr Drew joined them. The lawyer said he thought they should leave now.

Henri smiled at Nancy and said good night. Monsieur Leblanc then came up to the group. His manner seemed perfectly natural as he expressed the hope of seeing them all again some time in the near future.

Nancy's brain was in a whirl. She wondered if the financier might be staying in town and planning to meet Louis Aubert early in the morning. Smiling, Nancy asked Leblanc, "Will you go out to the country tonight?"

"Yes, indeed. I love it there. I sleep much better."

George had caught on to Nancy's line of questioning. She spoke up. "Do you commute to your office every day, Monsieur Leblanc?"

"Yes. I will be at my desk by nine o'clock tomorrow morning, as usual," he replied.

Nancy had come to a conclusion. He would meet Louis Aubert either in Paris during the daytime or in the country the next evening. "I can't wait to follow him," she thought.

The girls collected their wraps, and after thanking the Tremaines for a delightful evening, left with Mr Drew. Nancy, although bursting with her news, decided not to tell it until they were alone at the hotel.

Once there, she asked her father to come to the girls' room.

Nancy told about the Arab being Louis Aubert and added her suspicion that the invitation might have been obtained fraudulently.

"It could even have been forged," she said. "Remember, his brother Claude is a wanted forger. Louis could be one, too."

George in turn repeated the conversation she had overheard between Louis and Leblanc.

"Well done girls!" the lawyer exclaimed. "This may tie in with something I heard this evening from Monsieur Tremaine. He is one of the people who is greatly alarmed about Monsieur Leblanc's irresponsibility in business affairs."

Nancy asked eagerly. "Can you tell us why?"

"Oh, yes. Today Leblanc received a very large sum of money—thousands of dollars in francs—for the sale of certain securities. He had insisted upon having it in cash. I assume that he had the sum with him tonight."

Bess's eyes grew wide with excitement. "You mean that perhaps the poor man is being blackmailed by Louis Aubert?"

The lawyer smiled wryly. "I'm not making any definite statement yet, but what we've heard and seen tonight seems to add up to some kind of secret dealing."

He and the girls continued to discuss every angle of the mystery for nearly an hour. In the end, all agreed that the whole thing remained very puzzling.

"I still can't fit Mrs Blair's strange dream into the picture," Nancy remarked, "yet I'm sure there's a connection."

One by one the four began to yawn. Mr Drew stood

up and said he was going to bed. "I'll see you all at breakfast," he added, then kissed each girl good night.

As Nancy undressed she looked woefully at her bruised shoulder. There was a large black-and-blue area. Bess asked if she wanted more ice, but Nancy shook her head.

"The doctor said I was all right and I think a good night's sleep will help a lot."

In the morning her shoulder did feel better, although it was still tender. Nancy smiled. "Just a little souvenir of Paris."

When the girls joined Mr Drew in the hotel dining-room, they found him reading the morning paper. As he laid it down, a headline caught Nancy's eye and she gasped.

"Monsieur Leblanc robbed on the way home!" she repeated. "And of thousands of dollars! It must have been the money he received from the securities!"

Her father nodded. "I'm afraid so."

"Have you read the whole article?" George asked Mr Drew.

"Yes. Leblanc's car was waylaid by two men on a lonely stretch of road not far from his home. The bandits did not harm Leblanc or his chauffeur, but they did take every penny which each of them carried."

"How dreadful!" Bess exclaimed. "Have the thieves been caught yet?"

Mr Drew said No, and there was probably little chance the police could do so. After the hold up, there had been rain and any footprints had been washed away.

"Mr Drew," Bess asked, "could one of the hold up men have been Louis Aubert?"

"I confess I'm baffled," Nancy's father replied. "If

that make-believe Arab is blackmailing Leblanc and was going to meet him today, why would he rob him last night? On the other hand, he may have feared Leblanc would change his mind so he decided to get the money right away."

Nancy spoke up. "One thing we haven't followed up about Louis is his being a scientist. My hunch is he's a chemist."

Bess sighed. "It's going to be hard to find out about his work if nobody knows or will tell where Aubert lives. I'll bet if Monsieur Leblanc has the address he isn't going to reveal it."

The others agreed and felt that pursuing this lead would have to wait. Nancy said, "I'd like to find out if Monsieur Leblanc plans to stay at home because of the robbery."

"Why don't you call up and find out?" Bess suggested. "You can act terribly upset and sympathetic over what happened."

"I'll do that," Nancy said. "I'll phone his office."

Shortly after nine, Nancy put in the call. She learned from the operator that Monsieur Leblanc was there, and appeared to show no ill effects of the incident. "He is busy in a conference," the girl told her. "Would you like to leave a message?"

"No, thank you. I just wanted to make sure that Monsieur Leblanc is all right." Nancy rang off before the operator might ask who was calling.

When Mr Drew heard his daughter's report, he decided to get in touch with Monsieur Tremaine and suggest that a private detective be retained to watch Leblanc's office building that day and follow the financier wherever he might go.

Mr Tremaine readily agreed and asked if the detective should continue his assignment that evening also.

"Thank you, no. The girls and I will take over then."

Nancy was eager to pursue her sleuthing, but she went sightseeing with her friends and had lunch aboard a pleasure boat on the Seine. Later, while buying some souvenirs, Nancy said, "Look! A musical coffeepot! I'll buy it for Hannah!"

Late in the afternoon Mr Drew and the girls picked up a car he had rented earlier. They drove to Monsieur Leblanc's office building and parked nearby.

Immediately a man in street clothes walked up to them. Smiling and tipping his hat to the girls, he inquired, "Monsieur Drew? Monsieur Carson Drew?"

When Mr Drew nodded, the man presented a card identifying him as the detective assigned to watch Leblanc.

"Monsieur Leblanc has not come out all day," the detective reported. "Do you want me to stay longer?"

"No, that won't be necessary," Mr Drew replied. "We'll relieve you now."

Not long after the detective had left, the financier emerged from the building. He walked briskly to a car with a chaffeur at the wheel and got in.

A few seconds after Leblanc's car started, Mr Drew pulled out and followed him easily, but for only half a block. Then the dense rush-hour traffic closed in making it impossible for Mr Drew to keep close to their quarry. In a few moments he had lost sight of the financier's car completely.

Nancy sighed. She was very disappointed. "What if Monsieur Leblanc stops for a rendezvous at the 99 steps!" she thought. "We'll miss a perfect chance to find out where they are."

As the Drews were debating what to do next, Bess spoke up. "I'm absolutely famished. Couldn't we stop somewhere for just a quick bite—and then look for Monsieur Leblanc?"

Nancy started to agree when a sudden idea struck her. "First let's go back to Claude Aubert's old apartment!" she exclaimed.

"Why?" Bess asked.

"Monsieur Leblanc might be heading there right now—to meet Louis!"

· 10 ·

A Sinister Figure

MR Drew threaded his way through the Paris traffic to the Left Bank. When they reached the apartment, the travellers scanned both sides of the street. Leblanc's car was not in sight.

"I guess he didn't come here after all," the lawyer said.

Before leaving the area, however, Mr Drew drove around the two adjoining blocks. Still no sign of Monsieur Leblanc.

"He probably went straight home," Bess remarked. "Do we eat now?" she asked hopefully.

Mr Drew chuckled. "Right away."

Soon he had pulled up at a small cheerful restaurant which was willing to serve dinner earlier than was customary in Paris. Bess regarded the menu suspiciously.

"Snails!" she exclaimed. "And fish served whole—I just can't stand to look at the eyes of a fish on a dish!"

Mischievously Nancy pointed to another item. "Why not try this, Bess? It's very popular here—raw beef mixed with chopped onions and an uncooked egg."

Bess was horified. "That's even worse!"

The others laughed and George said, "Why, Bess Marvin, I thought you were a gourmet!"

"Sorry," said Bess. "I'll stick to good old cream of tomato soup, medium-well-done roast beef, potatoes, asparagus, salad, some cheese, and then fruit."

George looked at her cousin disapprovingly. "You'll be bursting out of your clothes within three days if you eat like that!" As a compromise Bess said she would not have the soup.

The food was delicious, and everyone enjoyed the meal immensely. It was seven o'clock before they left the restaurant.

"How far away does Monsieur Leblanc live?" Nancy asked her father.

"About twenty miles outside Paris."

On the way, Nancy did not talk much. She was mulling over the various angles of the mystery. There was no doubt now that both her case and her father's revolved round the 99 steps. Her one clue to them so far had faded out.

"If I could only unearth another clue to the right steps!" Nancy said to herself.

Mr Drew had come to an area of handsome houses, most of them standing in extensive grounds. The girls exclaimed over their attractiveness. In a little while they reached an estate which Mr Drew said belonged to Monsieur Leblanc. It was surrounded by a high stone wall and the entranceway was almost hidden by a grove of sycamore trees. Nancy's father pulled in among them and stopped.

"I'll hide the car here," he said. "It will be easy to take out and follow Leblanc if necessary."

"What if he doesn't come outside?" Nancy asked. "Shall we go up to the house when it's darker?"

"We'll have no choice."

They waited in the car for over fifteen minutes, then George burst out, "I need exercise! Let's do some walking!"

The others agreed and Nancy added, "We can try a little sleuthing too."

Mr Drew locked the ignition and took the key. As the four passed through the driveway entrance, they noticed a great stone pillar on either side. Tall iron gates were attached to them, but they stood open.

"Just put here for decoration," Mr Drew observed. "I imagine they're never closed."

Nancy suggested that the group separate. "Bess and George, suppose you take the right side of the driveway up to the house. See if you can pick up any clues as to what Monsieur Leblanc is frightened about. Dad and I will take the other side and meet you there."

Mr Drew added, "If you two girls see Leblanc leaving, give our bird call warning and run as fast as you can back to the car so that we can follow him."

Bess and George set off among the trees that grew along the driveway. It was dark under the heavy foliage and they kept stumbling over roots.

"I wish we'd brought torches," Bess complained.

"We couldn't have used them, anyhow," George retorted. "Someone would spot us right away."

They went on silently for a few minutes, then Bess whispered fearfully, "I don't like this. There may be watchdogs prowling around."

"Oh, don't be silly!" said George and hurried ahead.

Suddenly Bess let out a scream. George dashed back. "What is it?"

Bess, ashen-faced, stammered out, "There! Hanging from that tree! A—a body!"

George turned a little squeamish herself, but decided to investigate. She went over, felt the object, and then laughed softly.

"It's only a stuffed dummy," she declared.

"Why is it hanging there?" asked Bess, still trembling. "It must be some kind of sinister warning. I'm not going another step. Let's go back to the car."

"And run out on Nancy? Nothing doing," George replied firmly. "Do you know what I think this figure might be? A punching bag!"

"You mean, like football players use in practice?" Bess asked.

George nodded.

Finally Bess summoned up enough courage to go on, and presently the cousins found themselves at the top of the driveway. On the far side stood a large and imposing château. The girls would have to cross an open stretch to reach it. They discussed whether or not it was wise to do this.

The front of the mansion was well lighted. Several windows stood open but not a sound came from inside.

"I wonder if Monsieur Leblanc is at home," George murmured.

Before she and Bess could make up their minds what to do, the front door opened. A tall, slender woman, holding a mastiff on a leash, walked down the short flight of steps. Hastily the cousins ducked back among the trees as the woman turned in their direction. Had she heard Bess's scream and was coming to investigate?

"I told you they'd have a watchdog!" Bess groaned. "We'd better go before she lets that beast loose!"

George did not argue, and the two girls began to retrace their steps hurriedly.

Meanwhile, Nancy and her father had made their way cautiously towards the rear of the big house. A little way behind it was a five-car garage, filled with cars. The Drews recognized one as the car in which Leblanc had ridden earlier.

"Dad, this must mean he's at home," Nancy said.

Directly behind the house was a large flower garden. The Drews entered it and walked along a path. Fortunately it was dark enough and their figures would not be seen in silhouette. They passed what Mr Drew said were the kitchen and dining-room. Just beyond was a brightly lighted room with a large window, partly open, that overlooked the garden.

The room was lined with bookshelves and comfortably furnished. In the centre stood a mahogany desk. The Drews could see no one.

A moment later a telephone on the desk began to ring. The door to the room opened and a tall man strode in.

"Monsieur Leblanc!" Nancy whispered excitedly. "He *is* home! Now we can follow him if he leaves!"

Her father said, "Remember, he may already have met the man we think is Louis Aubert. Let's wait and see what happens."

Monsieur Leblanc did not lower his voice and through an open window his part in the phone conversation came clearly to the Drews.

"I told you the money was stolen!" the financier said. "If I did not have the money, what was the use of my coming?"

Another long pause. Then Leblanc said firmly, "Now listen. People are beginning to be suspicious. I will have to be more careful."

There followed a long silence. At last he spoke again. "It is against my better judgment. Let us not do anything more for a few days."

Nancy was hardly breathing. She did not want to lose one word that the financier was saying.

Leblanc's voice grew angry. "Why can't you wait? I know you said 9 was coming up, but even the thought of it brought me bad luck. Every cent I had with me was taken."

The next pause was so long that Mr Drew and Nancy began to wonder if the caller had hung up. But finally they heard Monsieur Leblanc say in a resigned tone, "Very well, then. I will go to the orange garden." He put down the telephone.

· 11 ·

Clue From Home

NANCY squeezed her father's arm and whispered, "The orange garden! Do you think it's here?"

Mr Drew shook his head. "I know every inch of these grounds."

The two became silent again as they wondered where the orange garden might be and if the telephone caller had been Louis Aubert. "I'm sure he was," Nancy thought, and hoped Monsieur Leblanc would start out immediately.

The Drews watched him intently. Leblanc did not leave the study, however. Instead, he took off his jacket and slipped on a lounging robe. Then he sat down at the desk and wrote for several minutes.

"It doesn't look as if he's going out tonight," Nancy remarked.

At that moment the Frenchman picked up a book from his desk and went to a large leather easy chair. He sank into it and began to read.

"I guess this settles the matter," said Mr Drew in a low voice. "We had better go."

His daughter lingered. "Maybe Monsieur Leblanc is going out later."

Mr Drew smiled. "I think it's more likely he'll stop at this mysterious orange garden on his way to the office. But we can't stay here all night. Remember, you girls leave for the Bardots' château tomorrow."

Reluctantly Nancy started back with her father. Just then they heard a series of deep-throated barks. "That's the Leblancs' guard dog," Mr Drew said.

"Oh!" Nancy cried out. "It may be after Bess and George! We'd better find out!"

The Drews hurried from the garden and raced quickly down the driveway. The barking continued. When Nancy and her father reached the entrace, the gates were locked.

There was no escape!

"This is bad!" Mr Drew exclaimed. "Nancy, I'll boost you to the top of the wall. The dog won't harm you there."

"But how about you?" Nancy argued. "And where are Bess and George?"

At that moment the cousins appeared, running like mad. The mastiff's barks were closer now.

"Quick! Over the wall!" Nancy said. "The gates are locked!"

Bess and George did not say a word. Quickly Mr Drew helped them to the top of the stonework, then he he boosted Nancy up. She and George lay flat on the wall and grasped the lawyer's hands. The dog, his leash trailing, had reached the scene and managed to tear one trouser leg before the girls yanked him to safety.

Out of breath the group dropped to the ground and returned to their car. As they headed for Paris, Mr Drew remarked, "I guess we got what we deserved. We *were* trespassing."

Bess said, "Thank goodness we escaped. Two scares in one night are two too many for me."

She and George told the story of the figure hanging from a tree. When Mr Drew heard George's idea that the dummy was a punching bag for Monsieur Leblanc, he laughed heartily. "I've been calling him the frightened financier, but maybe I'll have to change it to the fighting financier!"

The girls giggled, then George eagerly asked what Nancy and her father had found out. When they were told about the orange garden, the cousins agreed it was an excellent clue.

"How are you going to follow it up, Nancy?" Bess queried.

"Right now I don't know. But I intend to find out where the orange garden is."

Nancy went on to say that one thing was very puzzling: Why did Louis Aubert have such a hold over Monsieur Leblanc when his name had once been forged by Aubert's twin, Claude?

Her father said this mystified him too. "I'm afraid we'll have to wait for the answer to that question, Nancy, until you turn up more evidence about the exact relationship between Louis and Monsieur Leblanc."

Next morning, when the girls came downstairs to breakfast, Mr Drew said, "I've rented a car for your trip to the Loire valley, girls."

"Wonderful! Thank you, Dad," said Nancy. "You think of everything."

The lawyer smiled. "I have another surprise for you." He pulled a letter from his pocket. "Some news from Hannah Gruen."

Nancy excused herself and read the letter. Marie and Monique were having a good time in River Heights.

The sisters were popular and they had made several friends. There were two special messages for Nancy. One was from Chief McGinnis. The River Heights police had caught the stilt walker! He had been paid, he said, by a James Chase to do the job.

"Claude Aubert again!" Nancy murmured, then quickly told the others about the stilt walker's arrest. She read on. Suddenly she said excitedly, "Oh, listen to this, everyone!

" 'Here's the other special message for you, Nancy. Just after you left, Mrs Blair phoned to say she'd had the dream about the 99 steps, as usual. But this time she was a child, playing with her governess. Presently the woman tied a dark handkerchief over the child's eyes for a game of blindman's buff. Later, Mrs Blair came across another clue in her mother's diary—the name of the governess. It was Mlle Lucille Manon.' "

Nancy looked up from the letter and burst out, "How's that for a marvellous clue?" Mr Drew, Bess, and George were elated by the information.

The girls had packed before leaving their room, so soon after breakfast they checked out of the hotel and were on their way to the Bardots. Nancy, at the wheel of the small French car, found it took some time to make progress. The morning rush hour was in full swing, with its hurrying crowds and hundreds of taxis dashing recklessly in and out of traffic.

The route to the Bardots led past the famous palace of Versailles. Nancy paused briefly so that the girls could view the huge building and gardens.

"Let's see," Bess mused, "wasn't it Louis XIV who built Versailles?"

Nancy nodded. "It has a fascinating history.

Imagine a German emperor being crowned here! You remember that Germany once controlled all of France."

"But the French finally got their country back," George remarked.

Suddenly Bess chuckled. "The thing I remember is that Louis XIV was supposed to have had over a hundred wigs. He never permitted anybody to see him without one, except his hairdresser."

Presently the girls came to the Bardots' house. Set far back from the street, it was approached by a curving driveway. The stone dwelling was in the style of an old French period when buildings were square and three storeys high. It had a flat roof with a cupola for a look-out.

"Isn't it lovely here?" Bess remarked as she looked round at the green lawns, the well-trimmed shrubs and the flowering bushes.

As Nancy stopped the car at the front entrance, the door opened and Monsieur and Madame Bardot came out to greet them. At once the girls could see that Marie resembled her mother and Monique her father. The couple were most gracious in their welcome and led the visitors inside.

The furnishings were charming but not elaborate. They gave the château an atmosphere of warm hospitality, which was enhanced by vases of beautiful flowers.

The Bardots spoke perfect English, but upon learning that the girls could converse in French, Monsieur Bardot advised them to speak only in French during their visit. "I believe it will help you in your sleuthing," he added.

No further reference was made to the mystery at the

moment, for suddenly excited barking came from the rear of the house. The next moment a miniature black poodle raced into the living-room. She jumped up on the girls, wagging her tail briskly.

"Fifi! Get down!" Madame Bardot commanded.

"Oh, we don't mind," said Nancy. "She's very cute."

The girls took turns to pat Fifi. When she finally became calm, Nancy said, "Monique told me that the dog sleeps in an antique kennel."

Madame Bardot smiled. "Actually, we should call it a bed, since we keep it in the house. Would you like to see it?"

She led the guests across the central hall into a combined library and game room. In one corner stood the most unusual dog bed the Americans had ever seen. The square frame surrounding a blue satin cushion was of gilded wood with an arched canopy of blue velvet. The headboard was covered in blue-and-white-striped satin.

"This was built in the early eighteenth century," Madame Bardot explained.

"How charming!" Bess commented. "Does Fifi really sleep in the bed? It looks so neat."

Monsieur Bardot laughed. "Every time Fifi comes into the house she is brushed off and her feet washed!" His eyes twinkled as if he were teasing his wife, who pursed her lips in pretended hurt.

The visitors' baggage was brought in and the girls were shown to Marie's and Monique's bedrooms. They loved the wide canopied beds and dainty gold-and-white furniture. Bess and George said they would share the same room.

Conversation during luncheon was confined to Marie and Monique and their trip to the United States. Nancy told about the madrigal singing and how the people of River Heights loved it. The Bardots beamed with pride.

When the meal was over, their hostess arose. "Shall we go out to the patio?" she suggested.

The Bardots led the girls to the rear of the château and through a garden filled with roses, mignonettes and lilies.

As soon as the group was seated in comfortable chairs, Madame Bardot leaned forward. "Now please tell us, Nancy, have you had any success with my sister Josette's mystery?"

Nancy had decided it would be wise not to mention her father's case and had instructed Bess and George not to. She and the cousins described the various warnings received by Nancy, the helicopter incident and the Aubert twins.

"I think," Nancy went on, "that Claude, the one in the United States, left the warnings at the request of his brother Louis."

"And," said Bess, "Louis calls himself Monsieur Neuf."

George put in, "We thought we had found the 99 steps but we were wrong."

"We may have a new clue to them," Nancy added. "Do you know of an orange garden in this area?"

After some thought, Monsieur Bardot replied, "At Versailles a double flight of steps leads down from a terrace to L'Orangerie, the orange orchard."

"You mean," Nancy said eagerly, "that there are 99 steps in them?"

The Frenchman smiled. "Actually there are 103 in each flight, but they are called the *Cent-Marches.*"

"The hundred steps!" Nancy exclaimed.

"That's close enough to 99," George declared.

"It's worth investigating," Nancy agreed.

Her host suggested the girls drive to Versailles that very afternoon. "I'm sorry that my wife and I cannot accompany you, but we have an engagement."

Within an hour the trio set off. When they reached the palace of Versailles, Nancy parked the car and the girls walked up to the huge, sprawling edifice. They went to the beautiful gardens at the south side, exclaiming over the pool, palms, orange trees, and velvety grass.

Nancy spotted the imposing double staircase leading down from the broad terrace of the palace. Excitedly the girls mounted the steps, counting them.

Presently Bess gasped and called out, "Look!"

On the 99th tread was a black chalk mark—M9!

"M9—Monsieur Neuf!" George exclaimed. "Then what you overheard at Leblanc's last night, Nancy, was true! Louis Aubert must have come here. But when and why?"

"Maybe," Bess spoke up, "it has nothing to do with Louis Aubert after all."

Nancy shook her head in disagreement. "I believe Aubert chalked this M9 here as the spot where Monsieur Leblanc was to leave something—probably money. Let's do a little sightseeing in the palace and then come back in case Leblanc stops here on his way home."

The girls went down the steps again and walked to the main entrance. Inside, they stared in wonder at the grandeur of the palace. Walls, ceilings and floors were ornate, but what amazed the girls most was the lavish décor of Louis XIV's bedroom.

"It's absolutely magnificent but it sure doesn't look like a man's room," George said.

"At least not a modern man." Nancy grinned. "Don't forget, back in the seventeenth and eighteenth centuries this was the way people in power liked to live, men as well as women."

When the girls came to the famous Hall of Mirrors, a guide told them it was here that the peace treaty between the United States, the United Kingdom, and France on one side and Germany on the other had been signed after the First World War.

"They couldn't have picked a more beautiful spot," Bess murmured.

When the girls left the palace, Nancy glanced at her wrist watch. Very soon Monsieur Leblanc might be stopping at L'Orangerie. The three friends went back to the steps and waited. Minutes dragged by.

Finally George said, "I can't stand this inactivity another second. Nancy, I'm going to climb these steps again."

The next instant George was running up the flight of steps. When she reached the 99th, George stared in amazement, then turned round and called down to the others:

"The M9 mark is gone!"

The words were barely out of her mouth when she noticed a door in the palace being opened. No one came out, and she wondered if the girls were being spied upon.

"I must find out!" George said determinedly as she sped across the terrace.

Just as she reached the door a man's arm shot out. In his hand was a cane with a large curved handle. Suddenly the crook of the cane reached around George's neck and she was yanked inside the building!

• 12 •

The Red King Warning

As the door of the palace closed, Bess shrieked and Nancy gasped. George was a prisoner! Whose? And why?

"M9 has kidnapped her!" cried Bess. "What'll we do?"

Nancy was already dashing up the steps. She crossed the terrace and tried the door. It was locked!

"Oh, I must get in!" Nancy thought desperately. She turned to Bess, who had followed her. "You stay here and watch. I'll run to the main entrance and see what I can find out."

She sped off and tried that door. It, too, was locked!

Desperate, Nancy banged on the door panels as hard as she could. In a few minutes a guard came out.

"The palace is closed for the day, mademoiselle," he said, annoyed.

"But listen!" Nancy pleaded. "A friend of mine was forced inside by somebody near the top of the L'Orangeri steps."

The guard looked at Nancy sceptically. She knew he was wondering if she had suddenly gone mad.

"This is serious," she said. "I'm not fooling. Please! My friend is in danger!"

Suddenly the guard seemed to sense that perhaps

Nancy was telling the truth. He admitted her, and together the two raced up a staircase and to the door in question. No one was in sight.

The guard gave Nancy a look of disgust. "I do not like people who play jokes," he said brusquely. "Now you had better leave. And quickly!"

Nancy was at her wit's end. How could she convince this man? Then her eyes lighted on a pale-blue button from George's blouse. She picked it up from the floor.

"Here's proof," she said to the guard, and explained where the button had come from.

"Then where is she?" he asked, now worried himself.

"We'll have to find out," Nancy replied.

She led the way, practically running from room to room. There was no sign of either George or her abductor.

"Maybe the fellow sneaked down one of the stairways and went out," the guard suggested.

As the two stood debating where to search next, they suddenly saw a man in uniform dash from one of the rooms and head for the main stairway.

The guard with Nancy muttered, "Very odd. I am supposed to be the only one left on duty."

Nancy cried out, "That man may be a fake! Come on!"

They dashed after the uniformed figure, but by the time they reached the top of the staircase he was out of sight. A door below slammed.

Out of breath, the guard said worriedly, "The fellow has probably escaped. I hope he did not steal anything."

"He must have left my friend behind. We'll have to keep searching!" Nancy gasped.

Nancy and the guard pressed on. Presently they reached Louis XIV's bedroom and stood still in amazement.

George Fayne lay on the ornate bed asleep!

At least Nancy hoped that George was *asleep*. Fearfully she went towards her friend. Just as she reached the bed, George opened her eyes. She looked around wildly, murmuring, "Where am I?"

"Oh, thank goodness you're all right!" Nancy cried out.

The guard's expression was one of utter disbelief. For a moment he could only stare at George as if she were an apparition.

"George, how do you feel?" Nancy asked solicitously.

"I—I guess I'm all right," George answered shakily. "When something hooked around my neck I blacked out." She started to sit up.

By now the guard was thoroughly alarmed. "No, no!" he insisted. "Do not move. I shall call a doctor. And I must also inform the police at once." He hurried off.

George protested, but Nancy agreed with the guard and insisted that George lie still. It seemed an endless time before the man returned with a physician and two police officers. After examining her, the doctor said that George was all right but should rest. Then he left.

Suddenly George burst out laughing. "This is so ridiculous! I can't believe it really happened!" Between gales of mirth, she said, "Imagine me sleeping in Louis XIV's bed!" Finally Nancy, the guard, and the policemen were also laughing.

George's eyes became so filled with tears of merriment that she had to wipe them away. As she pulled a handkerchief from the pocket of her blouse, a folded sheet of paper fluttered to the floor. Nancy picked it up and handed the paper back to George. When she opened it, a strange expression came over her face.

"What's the matter?" Nancy asked.

"Somebody put this note in my pocket! It's another warning!"

The two officers instantly became alert. "What do you mean?" one asked.

"First I'll read the note," she said. "Then my friend Nancy can tell you the rest." George read aloud the typed message:

> " *'You girls mind your own business or
> grave consequences will come to you!
> The Red King'* "

"The Red King?" the second officer repeated. "*Mais* —but who is he—this Red King?"

"That's a new name to us," Nancy answered the question. "Other warning notes have been signed Monsieur Neuf and the Green Lion."

She explained sketchily about Mrs Blair's mystery which had brought Nancy to France. The officers said that they had never heard any of the names.

"Earlier today we noticed that on the 99th step of the stairway from L'Orangerie someone had put M9 in black chalk," Nancy went on, and told the whole story of what had happened.

The officers and guard were impressed. All said that these pretty American girl detectives were brave indeed to undertake such risks.

Nancy inquired, "You are sure that none of you knows a man named Louis Aubert?"

The three shook their heads. One of the policemen asked, "Does he live round here?"

Nancy said she did not know his address. "We saw him in Paris twice—once he was dressed as an Arab. I suspect he's involved in this mystery, and that he's the man in a guard's uniform we saw running away from here a while ago."

"We will make an investigation," the officers assured the girls. One of them reached for the note. "And examine this for fingerprints. You will come to head-quarters if necessary?"

Nancy smiled. "Of course." She told where they were staying.

"*Très bien.* Very good!"

George insisted that she felt much better. "Let's get back to Bess. She's probably frantic."

The two girls hurried to rejoin their friend. Bess was relieved and delighted to see her cousin safe, but horri-fied to hear what had happened.

When the girls reached home, the Bardots were very much worried by the girls' adventure. "It is quite evident this Monsieur Neuf knows you three are on his trail. He is getting desperate," said Monsieur Bardot. "From now on you girls must take every precaution." They promised they would.

That night after dinner Nancy asked the Bardots where Josette Blair had lived as a child.

"Only a few miles from here," Madame Bardot replied. "Would you like to see the place? I'll take you there tomorrow morning after church."

"Oh, wonderful!" Nancy exclaimed.

The journey took them through rolling, verdant country. There was acre upon acre of green pasture and farmland filled with a profusion of growing vegetables and flowers in bloom. It was late morning when they reached another attractive, old château.

In the garden a man and a woman were busy snipping off full-grown roses. Madame Bardot turned into the drive and asked the couple if they were the present owners.

The woman replied pleasantly, "Yes, our name is Dupont. May we help you?"

The visitors alighted. After making introductions, Nancy explained that Mrs Blair, a very good friend of hers, had lived there as a little girl. At mention of the strange dream, the Duponts were greatly interested.

"Ah, *oui*," said Madame Dupont. "I do recall that Mrs Blair lived here when she was little, but we cannot explain the dream."

Nancy asked, "By any chance do you know her governess, who was Mademoiselle Manon?"

"We do not exactly know her," Monsieur Dupont answered, "but a woman did stop here about five years ago. She told us she had once lived here as governess to a little girl but had lost track of her."

"This is very exciting!" Bess spoke up. "Can you tell us where Mademoiselle Manon lives? Mrs Blair would like to know."

"I'm sorry, but we cannot help you," said Madame Dupont. "At the time of her call she wanted to get in touch with Mrs Blair but had no idea where she was. We could tell her only that Mrs Blair had gone to the United States."

Nancy wondered if the couple could give any kind of clue leading to Mademoiselle Manon's present address.

"Did she happen to mention where she was going?" Nancy inquired. "Or where she might have come from?"

"No," Monsieur Dupont replied. "But she did say she had married. Her name is Mrs Louis Aubert."

· 13 ·

Schoolmaster Suspect

WHILE Nancy and the other girls were mulling over the startling bit of information about the governess, the Duponts' maid came from the house.

"*Pardon*, madame. I could not help but overhear your conversation about a man named Aubert," she said. "Perhaps I can be of some help to the young ladies."

Everyone looked eagerly at her, and Mrs Dupont said, "Yes, Estelle?"

The maid, who was a little older than the girls, turned to Nancy. "I come from Orléans. I went to school there two years ago, and one of my masters was Monsieur Louis Aubert."

This statement excited Nancy still more. Was she on the verge of a really big discovery?

"Tell me about the man. Was he in his fifties?" she asked.

"Yes." Estelle described her schoolmaster in detail. He certainly could be the Louis Aubert for whom Nancy was looking!

"Can you give me his address?" she asked the maid.

"I am afraid not, except I am sure his home is in Orléans."

"Did you ever meet his wife?" Nancy inquired.

Estelle shook her head. "I do not even know her name."

Nancy thanked the girl, saying, "What you've told us might be of great help." She also expressed her appreciation to the Duponts, who said they were very happy to have met the Americans and wished them luck in their search.

During the drive home, the entire conversation revolved round Louis Aubert. Bess remarked, "Do you suppose he's leading a double life—one as a respectable schoolteacher, and the other as a crook?"

"It certainly looks that way," George said.

Nancy suggested, "How about going to Orléans and checking?"

Everyone thought this a good idea. After an early breakfast the next morning the three girls set off, prepared to stay overnight if necessary.

Madame Bardot kissed them goodbye, saying, "If your sleuthing in Orléans should take much time and you girls plan to stay, please phone me."

"I certainly will," said Nancy, "and let you know how we're getting along."

A short time later the girls' conversation turned to the city of Orléans and its place in history.

"From the time I was a child," said Bess, "Joan of Arc, the Maid of Orléans, was one of my favourite heroines."

George added, "The idea of a girl soldier appeals to me. What terrific courage she had! That much of her story I do remember well."

Nancy smiled. "I wish we had Joan on this trip with us. She was a pretty good detective, too."

"Imagine a young peasant girl saving her country!" Bess remarked.

"Yes," said Nancy. "Joan was only seventeen when she requested a horse, armour and an escort of men from a French commander to help fight the English invaders."

"I'll bet he laughed at her," George remarked.

"He did at first," Nancy continued, "but finally consented. Joan also wanted to help put Charles VII, the Dauphin, on the throne at Reims which was held by the English. Charles was a weak man and had little money."

"And still he wanted to be crowned king?" George asked.

"Yes. He didn't want the English to take over France," Nancy went on. "When Joan arrived at Charles's castle and offered to help, the Dauphin decided to test the peasant girl's ability."

"How did he do that?" George interrupted.

"By slipping in among his courtiers and asking one of the nobles to sit on the throne. But he couldn't fool her—she showed up the hoax at once."

Nancy smiled, brushing a strand of hair from her forehead. "Joan glanced at the man on the throne, then walked directly to Charles and curtseyed. Everyone was amazed, since she had never seen the Dauphin in person."

Bess put in excitedly, "Yes, and Joan claimed she had seen a vision of the Dauphin. That's how she knew him."

George wrinkled her brow. "Joan finally did succeed in getting the king to Reims, didn't she?"

"Oh, yes," said Nancy. "Charles gave her a sword and banner and troops. In 1429 she rode into Orléans and freed the city from the English. Then the king was crowned."

"Unfortunately," Bess added, "she was captured a short time later and burned at the stake for heresy!"

"And you know," Nancy concluded, "twenty-four years after Joan's death at Rouen she was declared innocent. Now she's a saint!"

The girls became silent, thinking about the brave peasant girl as they drove through the lovely countryside of the Loire valley. The soil was rich and the air sweet with mingled scents of fruit and flowers.

Later, as Nancy pulled into the city of Orléans, Bess requested that they go directly to the famous old square called La Place Ville Martroi, where stood a statue of Jeanne d'Arc on horseback. Nancy parked in a side street, and the girls went to gaze at the figure in armour high on a large pedestal.

At that moment the girls heard music. "That's a marching tune," said George. "Wonder what's up."

A crowd had begun to gather in the square. Speaking in French, Nancy asked the man standing beside her the reason for the music. He said a small parade was on its way. Soon the square was filled with onlookers.

Again Nancy spoke to the man. "*Pardon*, monsieur, but do you happen to know a schoolmaster in town named Louis Aubert? I should like to find him."

He nodded. "*Mais oui*, Monsieur Aubert is the band-leader in the parade."

Nancy and her friends could have jumped in excitement. In a few moments the schoolmaster suspect would appear!

As the music came closer, the girls strained their eyes to see the beginning of the parade. Suddenly a small boy standing near Nancy found he was too short to see the parade. He jumped over the flowers and onto a section of bench that surrounded the base of St. Joan's statue. Like a monkey he clambered up the pedestal.

"Oh, that's dangerous!" Bess cried out. "He'll fall!"

The boy was just pulling himself to the top of the pedestal when Nancy saw one of his hands slip. Instantly she jumped onto the bench. "Hold on!" she called to the boy.

The lad clawed wildly at the pedestal, but lost his grip. With a cry he dropped into Nancy's outstretched arms. The shock knocked the two into the flower bed. Neither was hurt.

"*Merci*, mademoiselle," the boy murmured, as they got to their feet.

By this time the crowd had begun to cheer. Nancy was embarrassed, particularly when the boy's mother rushed up and threw her arms round Nancy. In voluble French she expressed her thanks over and over again.

Nancy smiled, freed herself gently and made her way back to Bess and George.

"Great rescue, Nancy," said George. "But in all the excitement we missed seeing the beginning of the parade. The band has gone down another street."

Dismayed, Nancy's instinct was to run after the band and try to spot the leader. But that was impossible. Several policemen had appeared and refused to let the bystanders move about until the entire parade had passed.

"It's a shame!" George declared. "Maybe we can catch up with Louis Aubert somewhere else."

Nancy signed. "I hope so."

The man to whom Nancy had talked earlier turned

The shock knocked them into the flower bed

to her and said, "*Pardon*, mademoiselle, I see you have missed your friend. Would it help for you to speak to Madame Aubert?"

"Oh, yes!" Nancy replied.

"She is standing in that doorway across the square."

Nancy caught a glimpse of the woman as the marchers went by. But by the time the square was clear and the girls could cross, Madame Aubert had vanished.

"We've had so many disappointments today," Bess said wistfully, "something good is bound to happen soon."

Nancy urged that they try to catch up with the band. The trio ran after the parade, but by the time they reached the line of marchers, the band was breaking up. Nancy asked one of the drummers where she could find Monsieur Aubert.

"He has left, mademoiselle," was the answer.

"Can you tell me where he lives?"

The man readily gave the Auberts' address, but he added, "I know they will not be home until this evening, if you wish to see them."

Nancy thanked him, then turned to Bess and George. "Would you like to stay here overnight?"

"Oh, yes!" Bess's eyes danced. "Orléans is such an intriguing place. Let's have a long lunch hour, then do some more sightseeing."

"The place I'd like to see next," said Nancy, "is La Cathedral St. Croix, where there's another statue of Jeanne d'Arc. Shall we go there after lunch?"

The others agreed, and the three girls walked to a delightful little restaurant, where they ate a fish stew called *macelote*. It was served with a frothy white butter sauce to which had been added a dash of vinegar and shallots. For dessert they had plum tarts, which, on the menu, were listed as *tartes aux prunes*.

The stout friendly owner came to chat with the visitors. "Today people do not each much," he said. "Banquets in medieval times—ah, they were different. Once at the country wedding of a nobleman near here this is what was served." He pointed to a list on the back of the menu.

9 oxen	*120 other fowl*
8 sheep	*80 geese*
18 calves	*60 partridges*
80 suckling pigs	*70 woodcock*
100 kids	*200 other game*
150 capons	*3000 eggs*
200 chickens	

"Wow!" George exclaimed. Even food-loving Bess said the idea made her feel squeamish.

The restaurant owner was called away, and the girls left a few minutes later. They went back to the square to visit the cathedral. Though not considered so grand as Notre Dame, it was a beautiful edifice with spires and domes. What interested the girls most about it was the statue they had come to see.

The sculptor had pictured Joan of Arc more as a saint than soldier. She was not wearing a suit of armour as usual, but was dressed in a long simple white robe. Her hair was short and in her clasped hands was her sword.

"Isn't the expression on Jeanne's face marvellous?" Bess said.

Nancy nodded. "Serene and spiritual. The sculptor certainly caught the spirit of her life."

As the girls finished speaking, a voice behind them said, "*Bonjour*, Nancy. I thought I might find you here."

Nancy turned. "Henri!" she exclaimed. "*Bonjour!* Where did you come from?"

Henri Durant, grinning broadly, greeted Bess and George warmly. He said, "I phoned the Bardots and they said you three were coming here. I offered to do an errand in Orléans for my dad," the French boy added, "so he lent me his car. Nancy, I hope you and your friends aren't too busy to take a ride with me."

Bess and George graciously declined, but urged Nancy to go ahead.

"Are you sure you wouldn't like to come along?" she asked. The cousins said No, they would go at once to the hotel where they had decided to stay. Nancy handed her car keys to George and said she would meet them at the hotel later.

The group left the cathedral and Henri led Nancy to his car. "Have you found that Arab yet?" he asked. When she shook her head, Henri added, "I was in the post office here this morning and saw a man who looked like the one in the taxi."

"In disguise?" Nancy asked.

"No, in ordinary clothes. He was just leaving the stamp window."

"That's very interesting, Henri!" Nancy exclaimed, wondering if the man could be Louis Aubert, the schoolmaster. It certainly seemed plausible. "I'll find out tonight," she thought, then determined to enjoy the afternoon's outing.

Henri drove to an attractive reach of the river and rented a canoe at Collet's boat dock. Paddling in and out of various small coves, Nancy was enchanted by the landscape, some pastoral, some wooded.

Her companion proved to be humorous and told Nancy of his life as a student at the famous Sorbonne in Paris. "Some day I hope to be a lawyer." He grinned. "Then I shall give you some mysteries to solve." Henri said Madame Tremaine had told him confidentially that Nancy was an amateur sleuth.

"I can't wait for your first assignment," she said, her eyes twinkling.

Time passed quickly and only the sinking sun reminded Nancy that they should get back. As Henri pulled up to the dock, the owner said a telephone message had come for him. "You're Monsieur Henri Durant?" When the young man nodded, Collet told him he was to call his father the instant the couple landed. The man walked off.

Henri laughed. "My dad certainly guessed where I would be! Please wait here, Nancy. I will be right back."

Almost as soon as he had left, a rowing boat slid out from under the dock and bumped the canoe. Startled, Nancy turned to look squarely into the face of a heavily bearded man. Instinct told her to flee and she started to scramble to the dock.

"Oh no you don't!" the man said gruffly. "You are trying to solve a dream. Well, I will give you something to dream about!"

Nancy started to scream, but the stranger reached up and covered her mouth with one hand. With the other he slapped her face so hard that she fell, dazed, into the water!

· 14 ·

Amazing Number 9

THE cold water shocked Nancy back to semi-consciousness, so she automatically held her breath while plunging below the surface. Rising again, she tried to swim but had no strength to do so.

"I—I must turn over and float," Nancy thought hazily, and barely managed to flip over. A drowsiness was coming over her. "I mustn't let myself go to sleep," she thought desperately.

By this time Henri was on his way back. Seeing Nancy floating motionless in the water, he sprinted to the end of the dock and made a long shallow dive towards her.

"Nancy!" he cried.

"I'm all—right. Just weak," she murmured.

Henri cupped a hand under Nancy's chin and gently drew her to the shore. Here he put an arm under her shoulders and helped her to the boat owner's office. Monsieur Collet's eyes blinked unbelievingly, but he asked no questions. Instead, he poured a cup of strong coffee from a pot simmering on a gas plate.

Nancy drank the coffee and soon felt her strength returning. Finally, able to talk, she told her story. Monsieur Collet was shocked and called the police at once to report the bearded stranger.

Henri frowned. The incident, he told Nancy, seemed to tie in with his telephone message. His father had not called him. "Evidently this villain planned the whole thing to harm you, Nancy. I shouldn't have left you alone."

"Don't blame yourself," Nancy begged him. "And now, if you don't mind, I'd like to go to the hotel and get dried out. Henri, will you bring my handbag from the canoe—if it's still there."

Fortunately it was, and not long afterwards Henri dropped the bedraggled girl at her hotel. "I will telephone you tomorrow to see how you are," he said.

"Thanks a million for everything," Nancy said, "and I'll let you know if I find that Arab!"

When she reached the girls' room, George and Bess began to tease her about Henri having ducked her in the river. But they soon sobered as Nancy unfolded her story.

"How terrible!" said Bess.

"It does seem," George remarked, "as if you aren't safe anywhere, Nancy, and what did he mean about the dream?"

"I guess he found out somehow about Mrs Blair's dream," Nancy replied. "Who can he be? Everything happened so fast I didn't notice anything but his beard."

"I'll bet it was false!" George declared.

Nancy's spirits revived after she had showered and changed into fresh clothes. She insisted that they call on the Auberts directly after a light supper.

The girls had a little trouble finding the couple's house, but at last they pulled up in front of a small bungalow. As they alighted, the trio wondered if they were finally to face their enemy Monsieur Louis Aubert!

Nancy's ring was answered by a man who was definitely not the suspect. She politely asked if he were Monsieur Aubert.

"*Oui*, mademoiselle. You wish to see me?"

"Yes, if you can spare the time. And I would also like to talk with your wife."

"Please come in. I will call her."

He led the girls from a hallway to a neat, simply furnished living-room. Then he returned to the hall and went upstairs.

A few minutes later the girls heard two sets of footsteps descending. They tensed. Were they going to meet Mrs Blair's governess? Would she solve the mystery of the disturbing dream?

The schoolmaster and his wife entered the living-room and he introduced her to the girls. Madame Aubert, slender and dark-eyed, wore a puzzled expression. "You wish to see me?"

"Yes," Nancy replied. "We were directed here by a former pupil of Monsieur Aubert's. Please forgive our unannounced call."

The woman smiled. "As a matter of fact I am flattered that you have come to see me. Usually our callers ask for my husband."

Nancy explained how the Duponts' maid had overheard the girls say they were looking for Monsieur and Madame Louis Aubert. "Estelle directed us here. Mrs Aubert, by any chance, was your maiden name Manon?"

To the disappointment of Nancy and the cousins the woman shook her head. "No. May I inquire why you wish to know?"

Nancy explained about the Lucille Manon who had been Josette Blair's governess. "We are eager to find her so she can give us some information about Mrs Blair's childhood."

The schoolmaster and his wife were sympathetic and promised if they came across any lead to the other Madame Aubert they would let Nancy know.

George spoke up. "Monsieur Aubert, did you ever happen to run across another man with your name?"

"Yes. I have never met him personally, but letters for him have come here by mistake."

Nancy at once recalled Henri's statement about the man at the post office. "You mean his letters come to your house?"

The teacher smiled. "I am well known at the post office. When any letters for Monsieur Louis Aubert arrive in Orléans without a street address, they are naturally delivered to me."

Nancy asked eagerly, "Was there a return address?"

Aubert shook his head. "No. That is why I opened the envelopes. Of course, when I found out they were not intended for me, I returned the letters to the post office."

"How were they signed?"

"There was no signature—just the initial C."

The girls exchanged glances. "C" might stand for Claude—Louis's brother!

Excitedly Nancy asked, "Could you tell me what the contents of some of the letters were?"

Aubert replied, "Ordinarily I would not remember, but these letters were unusual. They were written almost entirely in symbols and numbers. The number 9 was especially prominent."

The three visitors were elated.

Bess spoke up. "Have you received any of these letters recently, Monsieur Aubert?"

"No. None have come in the past two weeks."

During the conversation that followed, it developed that as a hobby the schoolmaster had studied alchemy. At once Nancy told him that only recently she had learned a little of the subject and mentioned the Green Lion symbol in particular.

Her remark set off Monsieur Aubert on a lengthy but very interesting discussion of the medieval science. He brought a portable blackboard from another room and with a piece of chalk drew a circle with a dot inside it.

"That was the symbol for the sun," he said.

Next, he drew a half moon on the left and on the right of the blackboard drew what he said was the alchemist's sign for it. The symbol looked like a quotation mark, only a little larger.

"In olden times alchemists and astrologers worked hand in hand. The positions of planets on certain days were very important. Metals and chemicals were named after heavenly bodies. For instance, mercury—which we use in the laboratory today—was named after the planet Mercury."

He sketched the symbol and Bess began to giggle. "That's a funny-looking sign. It reminds me of a scarecrow wearing only a smashed-in hat!"

Everyone laughed, then the teacher continued, "I translated one of Aubert's letters to mean, 'Turn all gold to silver quickly with mercury.' Very odd to correspond in this manner. The writer must also be interested in alchemy."

Nancy herself had exactly the same idea. Not only

was Monsieur Neuf the mysterious chemist, but his brother might be one also! But how did this connect either brother—or both of them—with Monsieur Leblanc's secret? Was the financier buying up the rights to some important formula concocted by the Aubert twins?

As Nancy was speculating on this, the schoolmaster took up his chalk again. "The story regarding numbers is really quite fascinating," he said. "Take the 9, which appears so frequently in the other Louis Aubert's letters. The number was considered a sign of immortality."

On the board he wrote 9 = 9, and then the number 18. As if he were addressing students, the teacher went on, "The sum of digits in successive multiples of 9 are constant. For instance, if we take 18, which is twice 9, and add 1 plus 8, we get 9." He grinned. "Who can figure out the next multiple of 9?"

Jokingly George raised her hand. "I feel as though I were back in school," she said with a laugh. "The third multiple of 9 is 27. The 2 plus the 7 equals 9."

"*Trés bien*," the schoolmaster said. "And, Mademoiselle Marvin, how about you answering next?"

"I never was very good at arithmetic," Bess admitted, giggling. "But I do remember that 4 × 9 is 36. Add the 3 and the 6 and you get 9!"

"Exactly," said Monsieur Aubert. "This is true all the way to 90. After that, the sums become multiples of 9."

The girls were fascinated and would have loved to hear more, but Nancy said they had taken up enough of the Auberts' time.

"We've had a wonderful evening," she added, rising.

Twenty minutes later the girls were back in their hotel. While getting ready for bed, Bess remarked, "I still think Louis Aubert, alias Mr Nine, has cast some kind of spell over Monsieur Leblanc. All this alchemy business sounds like black magic."

George scoffed at the idea. "I think Monsieur Neuf is just a plain crook who's robbing Monsieur Leblanc unmercifully. All we have to do is prove it."

"A big order." Nancy knit her brow. "I feel what we must do now is find Lucille Manon Aubert. I have a hunch she is the key that will unlock at least one mystery."

The following morning the girls set out early for the Bardot château and two hours later pulled into the driveway. Madame Bardot herself opened the door. At once the girls detected a worried expression on her face and sensed that she had bad news for them.

"What is wrong, Madame Bardot?" Nancy asked quickly.

The Frenchwoman's voice quivered. "My darling poodle Fifi has disappeared!"

"Oh dear!" Bess exclaimed. "You mean she ran away?"

Madame Bardot shook her head. "Fifi was locked in our house and could not possibly have left it of her own accord. But somehow she has just vanished!"

· 15 ·

Missing Gold

"POOR Fifi!" cried Bess. "She must have been stolen!"

"But that seems impossible," said Madame Bardot. "Every window and door on the first floor was locked. If some thief did get in, he must have had a key. But where did he obtain it?"

"Do you mind if we make a thorough search of the house?" Nancy requested.

"Oh, please do. We must find Fifi!" Madame Bardot's eyes filled with tears.

The group divided up to hunt, but with no success. As time went on, Nancy became more and more convinced that some intruder had entered the house. On a hunch that the dog might have been hidden, she began a systematic search of all cupboards but did not find Fifi. Finally the only place left was the attic tower of the house. There was a door at the foot of a stairway leading up to it. Nancy opened the door and began to climb. At the top she looked round the small square room lighted on each side by a tiny window.

"Oh!" she cried.

In the centre of the floor on a faded rug lay Fifi!

Since the dog did not move at Nancy's approach, she was fearful the pet might not be alive. Then she realized Fifi was breathing, but unconscious. There was a strong medicinal smell about the animal and she guessed the dog had been drugged to keep it from barking the alarm.

Nancy was angry. Who would do such a mean thing? But there was no time to think about this at the moment.

Taking the steps two at a time, Nancy hurried to the second floor and called out loudly, "Come quickly! I've found Fifi in the tower!"

Madame Bardot rushed from a bedroom. "Is she all right?" the woman asked worriedly.

"I think so," said Nancy, "but a vet should see her as soon as possible. She's unconscious."

By this time Monsieur Bardot had appeared in the hallway. He offered to phone the vet and the police while the others hurried to the attic.

When the vet arrived, he examined Fifi and declared that the intruder had injected a powerful sleeping drug. "She will be all right, however," he assured Madame Bardot. "And I do not think she needs medication. Just let her sleep off the effects."

As the vet was leaving, two police officers drove up. They talked briefly with the vet, then began to question the Bardots.

"We have little to tell," Monsieur Bardot replied. "My wife and I heard no unusual noises last night." He introduced the American girls, singling out Nancy. "Mademoiselle Drew is here trying to solve a mystery. Perhaps she can be of some help to you."

Both policemen frowned, and Nancy felt sure that the suggestion was not a welcome one! Quickly she said to the officers, "I'm sure you won't miss any clues the intruder may have left. But if you don't mind, I'd like to do a little investigating myself."

The policemen nodded stiffly, then said they wanted to see where the dog had been found. The Bardots led them to the tower.

After they had gone, George whispered, "Nancy, I dare you to solve the mystery before those policemen do! Bess and I will help you find some clues before they get back downstairs!"

Nancy grinned. "All right. Let's start!"

While the girls were searching the first floor, Bess remarked, "Nancy, do you realize that several houses—or buildings—you've been in lately have been entered by an intruder?"

"That's right," said Nancy. "But in this case, I hardly think the person was out to find me or take anything valuable of mine."

"If he was," said George, "he certainly got nothing, because we were away and had our passports and money and jewellery with us!"

Nancy examined the outside kitchen door. It had a Yale lock, but when she tried the key, she discovered that it was hard to turn.

"This must be how the prowler got in," she concluded. "He tried various keys before he found the right one, and almost jammed the lock."

"He's just a common burglar then," George declared. "He probably stole things from the house."

By this time the police and the Bardots had reached the first floor.

George blurted out, "Nancy had discovered how the intruder got in!" She explained about the lock, then added, "The intruder put Fifi to sleep so that she wouldn't bark and awaken anyone. Then, to keep the Bardots from notifying the police right away if they found the dog unconscious, he carried her to the tower."

The two officers stared at the girls unbelievingly. Finally both grinned at Nancy and one said, "I must admit you do have a good detective instinct, Mademoiselle Drew, and your friend here too. Perhaps you three girls can give us some more help."

This time Bess spoke up. "Yes, we can. I believe Monsieur and Madame Bardot will probably find some things missing."

At once Monsieur Bardot went to the desk in his den. He pulled open the top drawer, then said, "Well, at least the burglar wasn't after money. The notes I had here in an envelope are intact."

Meanwhile, Madame Bardot had hurried upstairs to her room. In a moment the others heard her cry out, "They're gone!"

The policemen rushed up the stairs followed by the girls and Monsieur Bardot. They crowded into the bedroom.

"All my gold jewellery!" Madame Bardot gasped. "Some of it was very old and valuable—family heirlooms!"

This second shock was too much for Madame Bardot. She dropped into an armchair and began to weep. Her husband went to comfort her.

"There, there, dear, do not let this upset you," he said. "Fifi is going to be all right, and you rarely wear the old jewellery anyway."

His wife dried her eyes. By the time the police asked for a description of the missing pieces, she had regained her composure enough to give them a list.

Nancy asked if any other jewellery had been taken, and Madame Bardot shook her head. This set Nancy thinking. The intruder must have been only after gold! She inquired if there was anything else in the house made of the precious metal.

"Some demitasse spoons in the sideboard," Madame Bardot replied, "and a lovely collection of baby cups."

She rushed downstairs to the sideboard and opened the top drawer. "The spoons are gone!" Pulling the drawer out farther, the Frenchwoman cried out, "The baby cups too—all of them! I had one that once belonged to a queen. It is priceless!"

The Bardots opened every drawer and cupboard in the house to examine the contents. Nothing else had been taken. The police made no comment, but took notes.

Nancy herself was wondering if the intruder had a mania for gold. Suddenly she thought of the Green Lion, and Monsieur Neuf—Louis Aubert!

"Is he the housebreaker?" she asked herself.

Nancy was tempted to tell the police her suspicions about the man but decided that without any evidence she had better not. Instead, Nancy decided to consult her father about her theory.

After the police had left, she put in a call to Mr Drew and fortunately reached him at once. He listened closely to Nancy's account of her adventures and agreed with her that Louis Aubert was indeed a likely suspect for the château thefts. "He must have known Madame Bardot owned objects of pure gold. I hope they can be recovered," the lawyer said.

Nancy mentioned the strange letters which Monsieur Aubert the teacher had received in error. She asked her father if he thought the elusive Louis Aubert, assuming he was a chemist, wanted the gold to use in an experiment.

"Very probable," Mr Drew answered.

Nancy's father said he had news of his own. He had learned that Monsieur Leblanc had recently purchased a lot of uncut diamonds. "The reason is not clear," Mr Drew added. "It would not be feasible for him to have such a large quantity of stones cut for jewellery, and diamonds are certainly of no commercial value to him—they're not used in his factory work as sharp drilling tools."

Mr Drew went on to say that Leblanc had served notice that his factory was closing down in a month. "Of course his employees are in a dither."

"That's dreadful!" said Nancy. "Dad, what are you going to do?"

Mr Drew sighed. "I don't seem to be making much headway, but I have invited Monsieur Leblanc to luncheon today. I hope to find out something without his becoming suspicious."

"Please let me know what happens," Nancy requested, "and I'll keep you posted. I wish you luck, Dad. Goodbye."

A little later the Bardots and their guests sat down to luncheon. Suddenly Madame Bardot said, "In all the excitement I completely forgot! A letter came from Marie and Monique. They have some news of special interest to you, Nancy. Incidentally, everyone at your home is fine and our daughters are having a wonderful time. I'll get the letter."

Madame Bardot rose and went to the living-room. Presently she returned and handed the envelope to Nancy.

"Shall I read it aloud?" Nancy asked.

"Please do," Monsieur Bardot said.

The message for Nancy was near the end of the long letter. It said that the night police guard in charge of Claude Aubert understood French. The day before the sisters' letter was written he had heard the prisoner mumble in his sleep, "Hillside—woods—ruins—go Chamb—"

"Whatever does that mean?" George spoke up.

"It is only a guess on my part," said Monsieur Bardot, "but I think the "Chamb" could be Chambord. That is one of the loveliest châteaux in the Loire valley."

"I certainly will investigate," Nancy said eagerly. She recalled the reference in Mrs Blair's diary to the haunted ruins of a Château Loire. Perhaps the girls would have a chance to go there, also. Nancy now asked if there were any special stairs at Chambord.

Monsieur Bardot smiled. "If you are asking me about 99 steps, I cannot tell you. There is a double spiral staircase which is architecturally famous, and for that type, unusually wide and ornate."

As soon as the meal was over, Nancy suggested she and the cousins visit Chambord. Bess and George were enthusiastic and eager to go. In case of an unexpected overnight stay, the three took along suitcases.

They climbed into the rented car and Nancy started off down the drive. As she neared the street, Nancy noticed a car approaching and pressed the foot brake. To her dismay, it did not work. Her car moved on!

Quickly Nancy leaned over and pulled on the hand brake. This would not hold either! With a sinking heart she realized there was no way to stop her car. It rolled onto the road directly in the path of the oncoming vehicle!

· 16 ·

Followed!

THE three girls sat petrified. There was nothing Nancy could do to avoid a collision. The other car was too close!

But with a loud screech of brakes its driver swerved sharply and managed to avoid a collision by barely an inch. Nancy's car coasted across the road and stopped against an embankment. The shaken girls murmured a prayer of thanksgiving.

The man at the wheel of the other vehicle had stopped and now backed up. "Are you *crazy?*" he yelled at Nancy, his face red with anger. Then he went into a tirade in such rapid French that the girls could catch only part of what he was saying. They understood enough to learn he had had a dreadful scare also. "I ought to have you arrested!" he shouted.

Nancy started to apologize but did not get a chance to finish. The irate driver put his car into gear and sped off down the road.

Nancy turned shakily to the cousins. "Do you realize how lucky we were?" she said.

"Sure do," George replied fervently. "What went wrong anyhow?"

Nancy told her that neither of the brakes would work. "I'd better move and not block the road." She steered slowly back into the drive and stopped by rolling against the sloping edge.

The Bardots had seen the narrow escape from a window and now came rushing out. "Thank goodness you are all right!" cried Madame Bardot. "What happened."

Nancy told them quickly and at once Monsieur Bardot said, "Did you have any trouble with the car this morning?"

"None at all. It worked perfectly." She frowned. "I'm sure someone tampered with the brakes."

"But when?" Bess asked.

"Probably during our search in the house," Nancy replied. "I also think the person who did it was trying to keep me from investigating some ruin near Chambord, perhaps even the Château Loire."

"Whom do you suspect? Louis Aubert?" George put in.

"Yes," Nancy answered. "He probably came back here after the police left and eavesdropped on our conversation. When he heard what his brother had mumbled in his sleep and learned our plans, Louis decided he had better do something quick to stop us."

"He must be a good mechanic to know how to damage brakes," Bess commented.

Nancy reminded her that the man was supposed to be a scientist. If so, he probably had a technical knowledge of machinery. "A simple thing like letting air out of our car's tyres wouldn't have delayed us long enough, so he chose something more important."

Monsieur Bardot hurried indoors to telephone a service station. He returned with disappointing news. "They can send a man to pick up the car, but they cannot have it ready until tomorrow. If they tell me there was sabotage, I will report it to the police."

Nancy smiled wanly. She did not say how she felt at having to give up the trip but apparently the Bardots sensed this.

"You must take our car," their host offered.

"Oh, thanks, but I couldn't," Nancy said. "You might need it."

Madame Bardot smiled, saying they had many friends close by who would help them out in an emergency. "I think you girls are on the verge of making an important discovery," she added. "We want you to go to Chambord. Perhaps you will solve the mystery of my sister's strange dream."

Nancy finally agreed. The luggage was transferred to the Bardots' car, and once more the girls set off. Their recent harrowing experience was almost forgotten as the three gazed enchanted at the countryside on the way to Château Chambord. Due to a late spring, poppies still grew in profusion by the roadside and fields were dotted with marguerites and buttercups.

When they reached the town of Chambord, the girls soon realized why the main sightseeing attraction was the château. Nancy parked near it and the trio alighted, exclaiming in admiration.

The castle-like building stood in the centre of a park and was approached by a long walk. The main part of the building was three storeys high and there were many towers. A pinnacle in the middle, shaped like a gigantic lantern, stood as high again as the château itself.

On either side of its main entrance, and at each corner of the vast front of the château, was a huge rounded tower that rose well above the roof.

"I can't wait to see the interior!" Bess exclaimed.

But at the entrance, a guard told them, "Sorry, mesdemoiselles. The last tour of the day is just ending."

Nancy glanced at her wrist watch. It was later than she had realized. Nevertheless, smiling beguilingly, she said, "Please, until the tour group gets back here, couldn't we look round just a little?"

The guard softened. "I cannot let you go by yourselves," he said, "but I will show you a few things."

He let them in, locked the door, and led them straight ahead. When the girls saw the double spiral staircase of stone they gasped in wonder. The guard said with pride that the design was a unique one.

"You have to see it to believe it," said Bess. "What period does it belong to?"

"The Renaissance. This staircase, and in fact the entire château, is one of the finest examples of Renaissance architecture. It was built by King Frances I. He was fond of hunting and the woods here at that time were full of deer and wild boar. The monarch also loved art and brought it to a high degree of perfection in France."

The group climbed to the second floor and he showed them several rooms. The girls agreed with their guide—the décor, although ornate, was beautiful.

The man grinned. "You might be glad not to see everything here—this chateau has 440 rooms, 13 large staircases, and stalls for 1200 horses."

Bess exclaimed, "Think of all the servants and gardeners and grooms King Frances I must have had to take care of his castle!"

The guide laughed. "You are right, mademoiselle.

But in those days, a king was a king, and he had to have an extensive retinue!"

Regretfully the girls followed him back to the first floor. At the entrance Nancy thanked the man for the "special" tour, then asked if there were any ruins on the property.

"No," he answered. "You can see this place is very well kept. There are, however, a couple of ruins in the town—and, of course, some are scattered over the countryside."

The girls decided to walk through the streets of Chambord. They had not gone far before Bess complained, "I have the strangest feeling we're being watched. It makes me nervous."

Nancy had paid little attention. She was too busy absorbing the atmosphere of the château town. But presently she became aware that two young boys had come from one of the houses across the street and seemed to be trailing the girls. Whispering to her friends, Nancy suddenly did an about-face. Bess and George did the same, and the three girls started in the opposite direction. The two boys stopped, and after a momentary conference, they also turned and once more kept pace with the girls.

"I'll bet they're purse snatchers," Bess said fearfully. "Hold on to your bags."

Nancy did so, but her mind was suddenly running in another direction. Hunting for the ruins to which Claude Aubert had referred was like looking for a needle in a haystack. The young detective decided to concentrate first on learning if there were a chemist in the neighbourhood. If so, he might be Louis Aubert!

Excusing herself, Nancy hurried into a chemist's

shop. To her annoyance, the two boys followed her inside! In a low voice she put her question to a white-coated man who came forward.

But his answer could be heard by everyone in the place. "I do not know any chemist who lives around here. Why do you ask?"

Nancy thought quickly. She must think up an excuse!

"I am interested in chemistry," she said. "And I believe a brilliant chemist lives somewhere in this vicinity."

Out of the corner of her eye, Nancy could see that the two boys seemed to lose interest in the conversation.

"I am sorry. I cannot help you," the man said.

Nancy left the shop, but when she reached the pavement, the boys were standing halfway up the street, apparently debating whether or not to continue following the girls.

Seemingly they decided not to, for they turned in the opposite direction. For an instant Nancy was tempted to ask them what they were trying to find out. But she refrained. The boys might have been engaged as spies by some enemy of hers. "It would be better to leave well enough alone," she thought.

As the three walked back towards the main street, Nancy asked a passer-by if there were any interesting ruins outside town.

"*Oui*, mademoiselle," the friendly man replied. "Château Loire. I would advise the young ladies not to go there alone now. You had better take a strong male escort with you. The ruins are some distance from the road and the access is difficult. Besides, it is rumoured that tramps are living among them."

Bess spoke up promptly. "Definitely we're not going there. Nancy, I can't let you take such awful chances. Your father would never forgive me and George."

The man to whom they were talking smiled. "Ah! *Oui!* A most sensible decision."

Nancy thanked him for the information and words of caution. She and her friends walked on to their car. Just as Nancy started the engine, a white sports sedan roared down the main street. The girls were close enough to catch a glimpse of the driver.

"Monsieur Leblanc!" George cried out.

"It certainly is!" said Nancy, swinging the car into the road. "Let's follow him!"

·17·

Knight in Armour

IN moments Nancy and the cousins were racing after Monsieur Leblanc. But he was driving at such terrific speed that Nancy felt wary of trying to overtake him.

George did not seem worried. "Step on it!" she urged.

But Bess had other ideas. "If we have a blow-out, goodbye to us," she warned.

Fortunately the road ahead was straight and Nancy thought she could keep the financier's white car in sight for a time. George remarked that Monsieur Leblanc might suspect he was being followed.

"Yes," said Nancy. "And if he does, he certainly won't go where he plans to unless it's on legitimate business."

The sports car sped on for several miles. Then, a short distance ahead, Nancy noticed a sharp curve. Monsieur Leblanc did not slacken speed but roared around it.

"I mustn't risk that," Nancy told herself, and slowed down enough to take the curve safely.

As they reached the far side of the turn, George said in dismay, "He's gone!"

"But where?" said George. "To meet Louis Aubert perhaps?"

Nancy accelerated and drove for another few miles. Their quarry had vanished. "It's no use," she remarked. "We've lost him!"

She concluded that Monsieur Leblanc must have left the main road not long after passing the curve. "Let's go back and watch for any side roads." She drove slowly and presently the girls spotted a narrow dirt lane through the woods. There were tyre tracks on it.

"Better not go in there," Bess advised. "What would you do if you met somebody driving out?"

Nancy smiled grimly. "How right you are!"

She parked the car by the roadside, and the girls proceeded on foot down the rutted, stony path. The tyre tracks went on and on.

Presently Bess complained that her feet were hurting. "This must be a woodman's trail that nobody ever bothered to smooth out," she said. "Where do you suppose it leads?"

"I hope to a ruin," Nancy answered. "The one Claude Aubert talked about in his sleep. It could be the Château Loire."

A little farther on the girls stopped and stared. Before them was a tumbled-down mass of stone and mortar. It had evidently once been a small, handsome château. Little of the building was intact, but as Nancy and her friends approached, they saw one section which had not yet suffered the ravages of time and weather. The tyre tracks ended abruptly, yet there was no car in sight.

"I guess Monsieur Leblanc didn't come here," Bess murmured. She looked round nervously, recalling the warning about tramps.

Nancy did not reply. Her eyes were fixed ahead on a

series of stone steps leading below ground level. She assumed they had once led to a cellar or perhaps even a dungeon!

"Let's do some counting," she urged, and took out her pocket-size torch. Bess and George followed her to the steps. Would there be 99?

Nancy descended, counting, with the cousins close behind. When they reached thirty-five, Nancy stopped with a gasp. About ten steps below, at the foot of the stairs, stood a knight in full medieval armour. He was brandishing a sword!

George exclaimed sharply and Bess cried out in fright. But Nancy boldly took another step down. As she did, the armoured figure called in French in a high ghostly voice, "Halt! Or I will run you through!"

Bess turned and fled up the steps. Nancy and George stood their ground, waiting to see if the figure would come towards them. He did not, but again warned them not to advance. This time his voice seemed a bit unsteady.

At once Nancy became suspicious. To the surprise of the other girls, she spoke up calmly, "Come now, Sir Knight! Stop playing games!"

The figure dropped the arm which held the sword. He fidgeted first on one foot, then the other.

"Take off the helmet!" Nancy ordered, but her voice was kind.

The knight lifted the visor to reveal a boy of about twelve! Bess and George marvelled at Nancy's intuition.

Smiling, Nancy asked the boy, "What is your name?"

"Pierre, mam'selle. I was only pretending. Do not punish me. I did not mean seriously to threaten you."

"We're not going to punish you," Nancy assured

"Halt!" Or I'll run you through!" the Knight cried out

him. "Where in the world did you get that suit of armour?"

The boy said it belonged to his father who let him play with it. "I knew about this old ruined château and I thought it would be fun to come here and make believe I was a real knight."

Bess, looking somewhat sheepish, came back down the steps. "You had me fooled, young man!"

Nancy added with a chuckle, "I guess you didn't expect visitors to see your performance."

Pierre grinned and admitted he certainly had not. Now the girls asked him about the ruin and he told a little of its history. The place dated back to the fifteenth century and was not the Château Loire.

"Are there any other ruins near here?" Nancy asked.

The boy said there was one across the road, deep in the woods. "It is Loire. But do not go there," he advised. "Funny things happen."

"Like what?" George questioned.

"Oh, explosions and smoke coming out of the ruin and sometimes you can hear singing."

"Singing?" Bess repeated.

Pierre nodded. "It is a lady's voice. Everybody believes she is a ghost."

"Who's everybody?" Nancy asked.

"Oh, people who wander around there to explore. Some of my friends and I have gone as close as we dare to the ruin, but something strange always happens. We have not been near it for a long time because our parents forbid it."

Nancy was intrigued by this latest information. She asked for directions to the mysterious ruin.

"You go about a mile up the road towards Chambord. If you look really hard, you will see a narrow lane which leads to the place."

"Thank you, Pierre. Have fun." Nancy winked at the boy. "Don't let Sir Lancelot come and overpower you in a duel!"

The girls left Pierre laughing, and set off once more in the car. Nancy drove slowly and finally they spotted the entrace to the lane, well camouflaged by low-hanging branches.

Nancy pulled over and parked. Then the searchers trudged through the woods. Again the way was rugged and bumpy. Projecting underbrush kept catching the girls' clothes.

"If Monsieur Leblanc came this way," said George, "he sure scratched up his car."

"I doubt that he stopped here," Nancy replied. "No tracks." Suddenly she asked, "What's the date?"

George told her it was the 17th. "Why?"

"I'll bet," replied Nancy, "that tomorrow will be an important day here. It will be the 18th. One plus 8 makes 9, the magic number!"

Bess's eyes opened wide with fear. "Please! Let's get out of here fast! We can come back tomorrow and bring the police."

But Nancy and George wanted to proceed. Nancy said, "We'll need proof, Bess, if we expect police help. We don't know yet that this is Monsieur Neuf's hide-out. Are you willing to go on?"

Bess gulped hard and nodded. The three girls walked on.

A few minutes later Nancy stopped short. "Listen!"

The cousins obeyed. Somewhere ahead a woman was singing softly! Nancy whispered, "That's one of the madrigals Marie and Monique sang." An electrifying idea struck her. "Girls! The singer could be Lucille Manon Aubert, the governess we're trying to find! Her husband Louis might be here too!"

Excitedly Nancy started to run towards the singing sounds which seemed to be coming from the woods to her right. George and Bess hurriedly followed her.

"We're getting closer!" Nancy said, breathless with suspense.

· 18 ·

Dungeon Laboratory

THE singing ceased abruptly. Had their footsteps alerted the woman? A moment later the girls heard someone scrambling among the bushes ahead, but the underbrush was too dense for them to see anyone.

"Do you really think that was Lucille Aubert?" Bess whispered.

George answered, "If she had nothing to hide, why would she run away?"

"What puzzles me," said Nancy, " is if she is Mrs Blair's former governess, how did she get mixed up with a crook like Louis Aubert?"

The words were hardly out of her mouth when George caught her friend's arm. "Look over there!"

Some distance ahead in a clearing on a hillside the girls glimpsed the corner of a tumble-down château. A woman had darted from the woods towards the ruin. She was a tall, slender, greying blonde of about fifty-five.

"Do you think that's the governess?" Bess asked.

"She's about the right age," Nancy replied. "Come on!"

The three girls dashed forward up the hill, but when they reached the ruined château, there was no sign of the woman. Was she concealed nearby or had she gone on through another part of the woods?

Suddenly Nancy said, "Perhaps we shouldn't have

given ourselves away. The woman may have gone to warn somebody else that we're here. We'd better hide!"

"Oh yes, let's!" Bess begged. "I don't want to be caught off guard by that awful Louis Aubert."

The girls ducked behind a cluster of trees and waited for over ten minutes. There was not a sound except the chirping of birds. No one appeared. Finally Nancy said, "I guess it'll be all right to investigate now. Shall we see if we can track down a few ghosts?"

"I'm game," George answered, and Bess reluctantly agreed.

Nancy led the way in the direction the woman had taken. They did not see her, but Nancy was fascinated to discover a very steep flight of stone steps leading down into the basement of the château. Suddenly the girls became aware of a faint roaring sound coming from below.

Nancy was excited. Intuition told her she had found the right 99 steps! "I must go down there!" she exclaimed.

George grabbed her friend's arm. "Not alone!" she said with determination.

Bess did not want to participate in the venture. "I think you're taking a terrible chance, Nancy. You know what you promised your father. And frankly I'm scared."

George snorted. "Oh, Bess, don't be such a spoilsport. This could be Nancy's big chance to crack the mystery."

"Tell you what, Bess," said Nancy. "We really should leave somebody on guard here at the top of the steps. Suppose you stay. If anybody comes, give our secret bird whistle."

"All right, but don't go so far underground you can't hear me if I have to warn you."

Nancy descended the steps, counting as she went. George was at her heels. Farther down, the daylight grew dim. To the girls' amazement two lighted lanterns hung from the crumbling walls. Somebody *was* below!

When Nancy reached the bottom, she could hardly keep from shouting for joy! She had counted exactly 99 steps!

Ahead was a narrow corridor leading to a huge old-fashioned wooden door. In the upper part was a small square opening containing parallel iron bars.

"This must have been a dungeon!" the young sleuth thought. Cautiously she and George peered through the barred opening. Nancy gasped. A medieval lab! Maybe it once had been an alchemist's prison!

The laboratory was fully equipped with an open furnace in which a fire roared, and there were numerous shelves of heavy glass beakers, pottery vessels, assay balances, crucibles, flasks, pestles and mortars. At the rear were several long benches, one of which held bottles of assorted liquids.

What amazed the girls most, however, was a man in Arab garb standing sideways at one of the benches! Nancy and George glanced at each other. Was this Louis Aubert again in disguise? The light was too dim for them to be sure.

The girls watched the man intently. In his left hand he held something black which the girls guessed might be charcoal. In his other hand he had a knife with which he was gouging a hole in the charcoal.

Evidently deciding it was large enough, the Arab picked up a large nugget of gold from the bench and dropped it into the hole. Next, he opened a jar and with one forefinger scooped out a pasty black substance and filled the opening.

Immediately Nancy recalled the old alchemists' experiments with metals and wondered if the nugget were real gold. Watching closely she detected a look of satisfaction on what little she could see of the man's face. Now he set the charcoal on the bench, walked to the rear end of the laboratory and through a door. Before it closed, Nancy and George caught a glimpse of a corridor beyond.

The girls were wondering what their next move should be, when they heard Bess give the secret birdcall. The sound came loud and clear and was instantly repeated. The double call meant:

Someone is coming. Hide!

"Hide where?" George asked in a whisper.

Without hesitation, Nancy opened the laboratory door and motioned George to follow her. She tiptoed across the room to several large bins holding logs and charcoal. The girls ducked behind them.

They heard footsteps descending the stairway and a moment later Monsieur Leblanc strode in! Immediately he reached up above the barred door and pulled on a cord which rang a little bell. Within seconds the Arab walked in through the rear entrance. He bowed and said in a deep voice:

"Monsieur, you are welcome, but are you not a day early? Tomorrow is the magic number day. But it is well you came." Suddenly his manner changed. He added gruffly, "I cannot wait longer."

Monsieur Leblanc's face took on a frightened expression. "What do you mean?"

The robed chemist replied, "I have finished my last experiment! Now I can turn anything into gold!"

"Anything?" The financier grew pale.

"Yes. Surely you do not doubt my power. You have seen me change silver into gold before your very eyes."

Monsieur Leblanc stepped forward and grabbed the Arab's arm. "I beg you to wait before announcing your great discovery. I will be ruined. The gold standard of the world will tumble!"

"What does that matter?" the Arab's eyes glittered. "Gold! Gold! All is to be gold!" he cried out, rubbing his hands gleefully. "The Red King shall reign! And when everything is gold, the metal will no longer be rare and precious! The value of money will collapse." He laughed aloud.

Monsieur Leblanc seemed beside himself. "Give me a little time. I must sell everything and buy precious stones—they will never lose their intrinsic value."

The chemist walked up and down for several moments. Then he turned and said, "Monsieur Leblanc, your faith in me will be profitable. Watch while I show you my latest experiment."

He picked up a bottle filled with silvery liquid which Nancy guessed was mercury. He poured a quantity into a large crucible.

"Now I will heat this," the Arab said, and walked over to the open furnace on which lay a grate. He set the crucible on it.

The chemist waited. When the liquid was at the right temperature, he took the piece of charcoal from the bench and started it burning. Presently the man dropped the mass into the crucible.

Nancy and George never took their eyes from the

experiment. Once George leaned too far out beyond the bin and Nancy pulled her back.

Blue flame began to rise from the crucible. The Arab placed a pan on a bench near the furnace, then picked up the crucible with the tongs and dumped its contents into the container. The charcoal had disappeared and out of the mercury rolled the lump of gold!

Monsieur Leblanc cried out, "Gold!"

George looked disgusted, and Nancy said to herself, "That faker! He has Monsieur Leblanc completely bamboozled. Why doesn't he see through the trick?"

Both girls had a strong desire to jump up and expose the whole procedure. But Nancy was afraid the swindler would break away from them, and decided that it would be better for the police to arrest him.

Monsieur Leblanc seemed to be in a daze, but presently he pulled a large roll of franc notes from his pocket and handed them to the Arab. "Take these, but I beg of you, do not make your announcement yet. I will come at this same time tomorrow with more money."

"I will give you twenty-four hours," the Arab said loftily. "This time the price of my silence will be five thousand dollars."

The demand did not seem to astound the financier. As a matter of fact, he looked relieved. He said goodbye and left by the same way he had come. The Arab went out through the rear door.

The two girls arose from their cramped positions, hurried outside and up the 99 steps. Bess was waiting anxiously at the top.

"We must run," Nancy exclaimed, "and notify my father immediately that Monsieur Leblanc is being swindled!"

· 19 ·

Nancy's Strategy

I⊤ was bedtime when Nancy, Bess, and George burst in
upon the Bardots. Twice en route Nancy had tried
unsuccessfully to get her father on the telephone.

The couple could see from the girls' excited faces that
something unusual had happened. Nancy quickly
poured out the whole story, feeling that the time was
past when she had to keep her father's case a secret.

Monsieur and Madame Bardot were shocked. "You
think this Arab you saw in that laboratory is really
Louis Aubert?" Madame Bardot asked.

Nancy nodded. "Something should be done as soon
as possible. I don't want to call the police until I talk
to my father and ask his advice."

She telephoned Mr Drew, but found he was not in.
The switchboard clerk at the hotel, however, did have a
message for Nancy.

"Your father said to tell you if you should call that
he tried to reach you at Monsieur Bardot's but received
no answer. Mr Drew is an overnight guest of Monsieur
Leblanc."

"Thank you," said Nancy.

After she put down the receiver, the youg sleuth sat
staring into space. She was perplexed by this turn of
events. Nancy had so hoped to warn her father that

Monsieur Leblanc was being hoodwinked by an alchemist's trick! Had Mr Drew also learned this? Or had he come upon another lead in the mystery of the frightened financier?

"I'd better try contacting Dad at once," she told herself.

She called Leblanc's number. A servant answered and said that both men had gone out and would not be back until very late.

"Will you please ask Mr Drew to call his daughter at the Bardots' number," Nancy said.

"Yes, mademoiselle."

When Nancy reported this latest bit of news to her friends, the others looked puzzled. She herself was fearful that her father might be in danger—perhaps from attack by Louis Aubert! Resolutely she shook off her worry. Surely Carson Drew would not easily be caught off guard!

The three girls, after a late, light supper, tumbled wearily to bed. In the morning Mr Drew telephoned Nancy. She thought that his voice did not have its usual cheerful ring.

"I'm leaving here at once," he told his daughter glumly. "I will come directly to see you."

A sudden idea flashed into Nancy's mind. "Why don't you bring Monsieur Leblanc along? I have some exciting things to tell you which I am sure will interest him too."

Nancy did not dare say any more for fear some servant might be an accomplice of Aubert's and be listening in on the conversation.

"I'll ask Leblanc. Hold the line," The lawyer was gone for a minute, then returned to say that his host would be happy to see Nancy again. "He'll postpone going to his office until this afternoon."

When the two men arrived, Nancy greeted Monsieur Leblanc graciously. Then, excusing herself, she took her father aside. "Dad, tell me your story first."

The lawyer said he had tried diplomatically to impress Leblanc with rumours he had heard of the financier's transactions. "I told him that reports of his selling so many securities was having a bad effect on the market and that his employees were panicking at the prospect of his factory closing down."

Mr Drew said Monsieur Leblanc had been polite and listened attentively, but had been totally uncommunicative.

"I can understand why!" Nancy then gave a vivid account of the girls' experiences of the previous day.

When she finished, Mr Drew said he could hardly believe what he had just heard. "This Arab alchemist must be captured and his racket exposed, of course. The question is what would be the best way to do it without tipping him off? I certainly don't want Monsieur Leblanc to be harmed."

Nancy suggested that they tell the financier the whole story from beginning to end. "Then I think he should keep his date with the Arab this afternoon and turn the money over to him as planned.

"In the meantime, Bess, George, you, and I could go with a couple of police officers and hide near the 99 steps. Then, at the proper moment, we can pounce on Louis Aubert, or whoever this faker is."

Mr Drew smiled affectionately at his daughter and put an arm around her. "I like your idea very much,

Nancy. I promised you a present from Paris. Now I think I ought to give you half my fee!"

Nancy's eyes twinkled. "Only half?" she teased.

She and Mr Drew returned to the others and Nancy whispered to Madame Bardot, "Would it be possible for you to find errands for the servants outside the house so that nobody will overhear our plans?"

"Yes, indeed. I'll send them to town."

As soon as the servants had left, Mr Drew said, "Monsieur Leblanc, my daughter has an amazing story to tell you. It vitally affects your financial holdings and perhaps even your life."

The man's eyebrows raised. "This sounds ominous. Miss Drew is such a charming young lady I cannot think of her as having anything so sinister to tell me."

Bess burst out, "Nancy's wonderful and she's one of the best detectives in the world!"

Monsieur Leblanc clapped a hand to his head. "A detective!" he exclaimed. "Do you mean to say you have discovered why I am selling my securities?"

Nancy smiled sympathetically. "I believe I have."

Then, as Monsieur Leblanc listened in amazement, she related the story of Claude and Louis Aubert. She told about the many ways they had tried to keep the Drews from helping Monsieur Leblanc, and finally how she and George had seen the financier come into the secret laboratory at the foot of the 99 steps.

"You saw me!" he cried out. "But where were you girls?"

When Nancy told him they had hidden behind the bins, he knew she was not inventing the story. Leblanc sat silent for fully a minute, his head buried in his hands. Finally he spoke up. "To think I, of all persons, have been duped! Well, it is only fair I give you my story. In the first place, if this chemist is actually someone named Louis Aubert, I do not know it. To me, the man is Abdul Ramos. I never saw him in any other clothes than Arabian."

Monsieur Leblanc said that Abdul had come to his office one day a couple of months before and shown him several glowing letters from Frenchmen, as well as from Arabs, attesting to his marvellous experiments.

Nancy at once thought of Claude Aubert. He could very well have forged the letters!

The financier continued, "Abdul wanted financial backing for a great laboratory he planned to build. Because of the letters, and some experiments he later showed me, I was convinced he knew how to turn certain things into gold. Yesterday when I saw the solid gold emerge from the heated charcoal—" Monsieur Leblanc's voice trailed off and he shook his head gloomily. "How could I have been so foolish!"

After a pause the financier admitted what Nancy had already overheard—he had intended to sell all his holdings and put the money into precious stones. "Since gold is the standard of all currency in international trade, I really feared the economy of the world would be disastrously harmed when Abdul's ability to transform substances into gold became known."

Mr Drew remarked, "That explains the large quantity of uncut diamonds you bought recently."

The Frenchman looked surprised but did not comment.

Nancy spoke up. "Also, you figured that diamonds would replace gold as the world standard."

"Precisely. I realize now that my self-interest is

unforgivable. It was neither patriotic nor humanitarian. Instead I've been unforgivably greedy. Thank you for showing me up. This has been a great lesson to me and I shall certainly make amends for it.".

George asked, "Monsieur Leblanc, what about the number 9?"

He explained that Abdul Ramos knew a great deal about astrology and the magic of numbers. "He convinced me that on the 9th, 18th and 27th days of each month new secrets were revealed to him and he threatened to announce his discoveries to the world."

George next inquired if he had left money on the 99th step at Versailles where M9 had been chalked.

Monsieur Leblanc nodded. "I did not see Abdul that day, but left the money there exactly at the time he had told me—directly after lunch."

When Leblanc was told of George's experience, the Frenchman was shocked. "All I can say is I am very sorry. I was foolish to let that man control me and cause so much worry." He shook his head sadly.

Bess, too, had a question for him. "Is Abdul married?"

The financier shook his head. "I have never heard him speak about a wife."

Nancy had been mulling over Leblanc's remark that he had allowed himself to be controlled by Louis Aubert and would like to make amends. She described her plan for exposing the fake alchemist.

"I will be glad to cooperate in any way," said the Frenchman, and Mr Drew nodded approval. Soon afterwards, Monsieur Leblanc left for his office.

Late that day three cars converged on the château ruin in the woods near Chambord. One vehicle carried

Mr Drew and the three girls, another two police officers, Beaumont and Careau. In the third was Monsieur Leblanc. The first two cars were well concealed among the trees and the passengers proceeded cautiously on foot through the woods.

At the small clearing near the ruin, they paused until they were certain no one was around. Then they darted to the 99 steps. Again the lanterns were lighted. The group tiptoed down.

Nancy peered through the barred opening of the door. Everything inside the laboratory looked the same as on the day before, even to the glowing fire in the open furnace. The grating lay over it and she wondered if Abdul planned to show Leblanc another experiment.

Softly Nancy opened the door and one by one the watchers went inside and hid themselves behind the bins. Ten minutes passed, then Monsieur Leblanc strode in. He tinkled the bell and in a few seconds the Arab came through the rear door.

"Ah, I see you are on time, monsieur," he said smugly, with a little bow.

The financier reached into a pocket and brought out a roll of banknotes. He did not hand them over at once, however, saying, "Do you agree to a waiting period in return for this?"

"Have I not always kept my word?" Abdul said haughtily.

Leblanc laid the notes on a bench and immediately the Arab snatched up the money and tucked it into a pocket.

"How much more time do you wish before I reveal my great work to the world?" he asked.

"At least a week," Monsieur Leblanc replied. "I

have several big transactions I must complete first."

"A week?" Abdul repeated, and began to walk round the room.

Presently he paused at the door which led to the 99 steps. The hidden group could see him reach towards it and heard something click. Nancy wondered if he had used a secret latch to lock the door and why. Were they all in danger?

Suddenly apprehensive, she watched the Arab intently as he returned to the furnace. He gazed at the fire, then with a brisk movement picked up a small sack from a bench. He hastened to the rear door, opened it, and whirled about. His eyes held a menacing gleam.

"Leblanc," he cried out, "you have double-crossed me! I know you have spies hiding in this room because I followed you to the Bardots! But I shall not be caught. Everyone of you shall perish!"

Without warning, the Arab threw the sack into the furnace, then backed out, slammed the door and bolted it from the other side!

· 20 ·

Surprising Confession

IT took but the fraction of a second for Nancy and the others trapped in the laboratory to realize the danger they faced. The sack hurled into the furnace might explode at any moment!

Instantly Beaumont jumped from his hiding place and made a grab for the bag. Fortunately, it had not yet ignited. As a precaution, he dropped it into a pail of water which stood nearby.

By this time everyone else had jumped up. Nancy exclaimed, "We mustn't let that awful man Abdul get away!"

She started for the doorway through which the Arab had fled, but then remembered he had bolted it from the outside. Those in the room were prisoners!

Nancy collected her wits. First she thanked Beaumont for saving them all. He shrugged this off and said, "We will have to break down the door and go after that crazy fool!"

Suddenly Nancy stared across the room in horror. Monsieur Leblanc had collapsed and was lying on his back, apparently unable to get up. Bess had already noticed this and was searching in vain for fresh water to revive him. Frantically she dug into her dress pocket and pulled out a small phial of perfume. Bess held it under Leblanc's nostrils. He took a deep whiff and almost instantly sat up.

In the meantime, the two policemen and Mr Drew were heaving their bodies against the rear door. There was a loud splintering sound and finally the door began to give way.

The second it crashed down, the officers scrambled out and dashed up the corridor. Nancy started to follow, but her father held her back. "Let the police handle the job," he said. "Beaumont was right when he called the faker crazy. No telling what he'll do."

The young sleuth was impatient at the delay. But only ten minutes had elapsed when they heard footsteps and voices in the corridor. Everyone gazed out and in the dimly lighted area they could see the police officers returning.

With them were Louis Aubert and the greyish-blonde woman!

"She was the one who was singing the madrigals!" Nancy exclaimed.

Those in the laboratory could hear the woman saying, "My husband is a great scientist! He could not do anything wrong!"

"We'll see about that," said Beaumont. "Anybody who wears a disguise and cheats people by pretending he can turn almost anything into gold has a lot of questions to answer!"

Careau added, "To say nothing of threatening lives!" Madame Aubert said no more.

As the four entered the laboratory, Louis glared malevolently at Leblanc, Mr Drew, and the girls. At first he would answer no questions, but when confronted with accusations from the financier, Nancy, Bess and

George, the would-be scientist broke down and admitted to engineering the hold up of Monsieur Leblanc as well as practically all of the other charges against him.

Bess, proud of Nancy's sleuthing, said, "He has confessed to just about everything you suspected him of—even the canoe incident and to hiring two boys to follow us and get information."

Nancy, too, was elated—not only at the capture, but also because her father's mystery had been solved. There were still a few questions in her mind which she now put to the prisoner.

"Your brother Claude forged the letters of recommendation which you showed to Monsieur Leblanc, didn't he?"

"Yes."

Aubert also revealed that it was Claude who had written the letters about a helipad being built on the Drews' roof.

The young detective suggested that the various other happenings in River Heights had been Claude's work, while those in France were Louis's schemes.

"That's right. I suppose you'll get it out of me sooner or later how I knew about you Drews, so I might as well tell you. A servant at the Tremaines is a friend of mine. It was he who stole an invitation to the soirée for me. He used to eavesdrop on conversations and found out that Mr Drew had been retained secretly to investigate why Leblanc was selling his holdings.

"I did not want my scheme ruined, so I sent Claude to the United States. With his ability to forge all kinds of documents it wasn't hard for him to enter your country under another name. Unfortunately your father had left. But he did learn that you were coming and he did his best to frighten you into staying home."

"You used lots of names besides Abdul," George said to him. "Monsieur Neuf, the Green Lion, the Red King."

Aubert admitted this, adding that Claude, too, had used Neuf and the "Lion" on the warnings to the Drews. The prisoner bragged, "I know a lot about astrology and the practices of ancient alchemists. That's what gave me the idea about the gold and using alchemists' symbols." The M9 chalk mark had been left by Aubert at L'Orangerie to mark the place where Leblanc was to leave money, but he had rubbed it out upon spotting the girls there.

During the interrogation, his wife had been sitting on a bench, pale with shock. She kept dabbing her eyes with a handkerchief and murmuring, "I knew nothing about this."

Nancy went over and sat down beside the distraught woman. The young sleuth had not forgotten she had a mystery of her own to solve!

In a kind voice Nancy asked, "Were you Mlle. Lucille Manon?"

"W-why, yes!"

"I'm a friend of Mrs Josette Blair. You were her governess many years ago. She has a recurring dream that frightens her. We thought perhaps you could explain the meaning of it."

The woman looked puzzled. "I do not understand," she said. "I took care of Josette when she was only three years old."

"Her dream dates back to that time," Nancy explained, and told her about the nightmare.

As Nancy finished speaking, the woman began to

weep aloud. "Yes, yes, I can explain. In a way Louis was responsible for this. I suppose he has always mesmerized me—as he has Monsieur Leblanc. During the time I was taking care of Josette, he was a guest at a château where the little girl and I had been left for a short time while her parents were away."

"Louis and I fell in love, and as it was not considered proper for a guest and an employee to be friendly, we had to meet secretly."

Madame Aubert went on to say that Louis had already come upon the ruin with the underground alchemist's laboratory.

"It became our meeting place. One day I had to bring Josette along. He did not want her to recognize him or to see the laboratory for fear she would tell others about it. Louis wanted to keep the place a secret until he was ready to reveal a great scientific fact to the world."

The ex-governess went on, "I thought up the idea of playing blindman's buff. I took Josette to the woods and blindfolded her. After we had played the game a while, I led her there. When I told her she was going down steep steps, Josette became afraid. I said I would hold her hand and she should count. Of course she could not count very far, so I did the rest."

"And the total, of course, turned out to be 99," Nancy put in.

"That is right," Lucille Aubert answered. "Louis thinks the alchemist who built this place chose that number of steps because it's a multiple of 9, a magic number for alchemists. The château dates back to the fourteenth century."

The ex-governess continued, "After Louis and I had

looked at his laboratory, we three climbed up the steps. Josette was still blindfolded. Just as she reached the top, she lost her balance and started to fall. Louis caught her, but for a long time after that, poor little Josette used to cry out in her sleep."

"No wonder the 99 steps made such a deep impression on her," Bess remarked.

Madame Aubert hung her head. "Not long after the incident, Josette's mother discharged me. She suspected I was responsible for scaring her daughter. A short time later Louis and I were married."

Her husband spoke up. "When I found out the Bardot sisters were going to the Drews' house, I eavesdropped at the Bardots a good deal. One day I heard Madame Bardot read a letter from Mrs Blair about the dream and I decided to send the warning note to her. Claude carried on from there. My wife didn't know anything about it."

Nancy said she was sure that when Mrs Blair heard the story, her nightmares would cease. Nancy expressed her sympathy to Madame Aubert for her present predicament.

At that moment Beaumont walked over to them. "I'm sorry, madame," he said. "You must come with us for further questioning."

Tears rolling down her cheeks, the woman arose. But suddenly she turned and said to Nancy, "Remember me to Mrs Blair and tell her I loved her dearly."

Nancy blinked a few tears from her own eyes. "I'll be happy to," she replied.

Louis Aubert was made to release the secret lock on the door leading to the 99 steps. Before mounting them, Nancy suddenly remembered that one part of the mystery was still unsolved. She asked Beaumont, "Did you search the Arab costume?"

The officer admitted he had not. "Wait here!" he directed, and hurried back into the rear corridor. He returned holding the robe, turban, and false hair. Beaumont searched the various pockets the costume contained. As Nancy had suspected, Madame Bardot's missing gold pieces were hidden in several of them! After a search, the rest were found hidden about the laboratory.

Everyone looked at Nancy admiringly. The officers shook their heads and Beaumont commented, "Mademoiselle Drew, *vous êtes merveilleuse!*"

George grinned. "In other words, Nancy, you're the greatest!" Her words were to prove true again when Nancy met her next challenge in *Mystery at the Ski Jump*.

The Auberts were led away. Then Nancy beckoned the others to precede her from the laboratory. Smiling, they all exchanged knowing glances. The young sleuth wanted to be the one to close the door to the mystery of the 99 steps!